# On the Level

## Mark Wagstaff

LEAF BY LEAF

Published by Leaf by Leaf
an imprint of Cinnamon Press,
Office 49019, PO Box 15113, Birmingham, B2 2NJ
*www.cinnamonpress.com*

The right of Mark Wagstaff to be identified as author of this work has been asserted by him in accordance with the Copyright, Designs and Patent Act, 1988. © 2022, Mark Wagstaff.
Print Edition ISBN 978-1-78864-936-0
British Library Cataloguing in Publication Data. A CIP record for this book can be obtained from the British Library.

Designed and typeset in Adobe Caslon by Cinnamon Press.
Cover design by Cinnamon Press using picture elements:
St Paul's: 60459432 © Martinmates | Dreamstime.com
Nelson's Column: 88848728 © | Dreamstime.com
frame: 166330056 © Shepherdingtheflock | Dreamstime.com
rubble: 139748744 © MrIlkin | Dreamstime.com and 146151181 © Naropano | Dreamstime.com
Cinnamon Press is represented by Inpress.

Is this stuff on the level, or are you just making it up as you go along?

Groucho Marx, *Horse Feathers*

On the Level

# 1

Such a damn simple idea. In London for that conference. Worst horror show since the last meltdown. But Dad was tight with the guy sent to save us. The global loans guy. Same week as the bitchingest retrospective. Ten rooms of Rothko.

TV was my best *amiga* then, because most times I went outside I got beaten up. Sick and wretched one night, I caught this Rothko edutainment and those pictures, man, those pictures soothed my bones.

Such a damn ordinary idea. Me and Dad head to the city, mind our own business, him with his global power play, me with Rothko. Only my Mother could screw that into a family occasion. Only she could decide her and her kids tag along. If I talk about her, I'll need a truck of tequila.

Now Dad, he was with the band: big shot diplomat, he rated full security. Which means we all did. So we got stashed at this eight-star luxury prison—the London Royale Grange Plaza—directly across that Kensington street from the conference. Steep grey concrete, cops everywhere—not exactly Tahiti. But the rooms, man: my lounge with a big TV, those creamy low chairs only hotels have, shower, double bedroom—I had the whole Seven Year Itch going down. See myself, truly, living that way. When I brush the road from my hair.

So I said, a suite—lounge, bathroom, bedroom—exclusive to me. The lounge had these godawful pictures. Nasty non-art Rothko wouldn't use to mop his blood. I was trying to lever them off the wall when I noticed the room had this extra door for no obvious reason. So I opened it, as anyone would. There was another door behind. Though my folks bought me a tie for a very expensive school, truthfully that place had nothing to teach me. I got educated from heavy metal and *The Twilight Zone*, so to me the risk was wholly real that through that second door there'd be another, and another, and each successive door would slam behind me, and I'd be doomed to scratch my last against some freaking door. You can see how that might happen.

Pulling a painful stretch, I wedged the first door with my foot and gently opened this unexpected other door. Daylight. A room. Still certain I'd entered another dimension where people drove Zodiacs and would call me kiddio, I stepped into a lounge—picture this—the exact, absolute same as mine, reversed. I mean the furniture. The furniture was mine reversed. I'd scored a deuce. Two TVs, dual music, double sets of bathroom freebies. Thinking this pretty fine, I tried the bedroom—yeah, another king bed. So this was my backup suite—I could take half the week sleeping one way and half the other.

Just then, something interesting and ghastly happened. That chk-chk-chock of a keycard, the brusque release of a handle. Somebody walking into the lounge. Maybe I panicked, maybe what I did was dumb: I drop-rolled under the bed. I mean, I could have pretended I was some nosy kid. But if my parents found out they'd take my suites away and I'd have to bunk on some bouncy castle mattress in their lounge. And, yeah, I did think I was smart enough to slip away when whoever was busy. So I hit carpet.

Pretty fast I knew the maids were just taking the money: under that bed was dust and lint and this taste of hideous hairs. It was also tight and close and scary. I got footsteps from the lounge: loud, then stopped, then faded, then stopped. Then a door shutting, and another. Not that I unpacked anything personal, but whoever must have seen into my place and I felt pretty invaded. Those footsteps moved with purpose—lot of opening and closing cupboards and drawers. I got shoes—hard shoes—on the bathroom floor, then a clatter of toiletries. Whoever was checking the place.

Those shoes strolled into the bedroom. The wardrobe door snapped back, hangers chinged and clattered. A limited commotion—they were tapping the walls. Man, I got to tell you, I was rushing like I smoked a half soused with special sauce. The shoes, those damn shoes, started round the bed. Deliberate, firm, parking just east of my midriff. Damn nice shoes: kind Dad wore, though more polished and consequent-looking. And charcoal grey trousers, neat, perfect length, not laying over the shoes nor showing sock.

Staring into the sweet maple bedframe, I tried convincing myself that whoever would leave, just go.

Till I saw more and more those trouser legs scissoring-down, steady and sure—not one squeak of knee bone. Then the jacket swept across my view like poorly-hung scenery. Then a sideways face, staring into mine.

'Are you asthmatic? You breathe too loud. What you here for?'

Truly, I was that near to crying like a girl. 'I'm here for Rothko.'

'Get up.'

An awkward shuffle, and being laced with dust and crap made worse an already thorough disadvantage. Way taller than me—which is to say nothing—he was also taller than Dad and that was impressive. Devilish smart, that English-cut suit. To say his voice was cold is to say the Titanic had issues with frost.

'What you doing here?'

Channelling Lara Croft, I gave it every inch of teenage scorn. 'There's a door into here from my place. Thought this was my place too. I mean, wouldn't you hide, if you didn't know who was coming in? You could be crazy, all I know.'

The Man—forever I think of him as The Man— took one second to get to the root. 'Why you acting the kid?'

That persecution so did it. I gave him the dagger-look and made to walk—surprised and massively scared when he slapped my shoulder. Physically with his actual palm, the heritage invitation to take it outside. Now, I had plenty fights in school, beat down by girls in sweaters pumped on chicken grease. That was kids. I wasn't down with the etiquette of fronting a grown man. With my Dad's fine name and the fact I'd done nothing illegal, I needed foot-stomping anger. What I got was a real deep blush.

'You are a kid.'

'I'm new adult.'

'You're an idiot.'

'Huh?'

'You hide someplace with no exit.'

I never did get round to ask where he'd hide. I trailed him through his lounge, feeling weirdly cheated that he thought the matter settled.

He bust open the back-to-back door. 'You from the next room? Why you here?'

'I said: for the Rothko show.'

'Alone?'

'Yeah.'

And d'you know what that guy did? Only followed me into my room. My actual room. Course I asked did he think that was okay, course I showed him my middle finger. By then he was giving my place the care he gave his.

'You a cop? Cops need warrants.'

'So I'm not a cop.'

'I'm calling security.' Could have said I was calling Dad, not.

'Would you say you're popular?'

That messed with my head. What I heard: would I stay long under floorboards without getting missed. Strangely, though, some part of me thought, really, he was asking.

'You're what? Sixteen?'

So I looked older to him. Cool. 'Yeah.'

'It's twenty minutes since we got acquainted. You haven't taken a call.'

'My phone's to mute.'

'Why do that?'

'Chill time, y'know. For my soul.'

He moved slowly to the through-door, checking me with heavy distrust. 'Tell you what's going to happen. I'll close this now. Lock my side. You damn better lock yours. I find one ginger hair messing up my rug, you're hitting the bricks, get me?'

'Sure.'

'Damn sure.'

His shape still filled the air when the doors slammed behind him.

After my neighbour's invasion, I felt to lay low the rest of the night. Getting dragged to the restaurant by Mum at her worst so wasn't it. It's majorly obvious we were not what you'd call an eating together family. My memory's thankfully hazy, I think back then my sister only ate stuff cut pussycat-shapes. But because this was some fake holiday, and because Dad faked he liked it, and because we're damn good at faking, we faked a Waltons dinner.

Most any guidebook says you don't eat at the hotel. But it got late, and the horror of getting the little dweebs scrubbed and ready, and security—always security—meant Mum told Dad we'd do fine in that chandelier-crusted slum. These days I live places that melt when it rains, so naturally I hated the granite, the marble, starched linen, and starchier, up-themselves waitresses. Man, I could deal with them now.

Without TV, the kids had nothing but kick the chair legs. Worse, I wasn't allowed music—I had to listen to their voices. The food was these potty-scrapings adults eat. So was the conversation. Masochistically, I tried getting traction on Rothko. But they only knew him as cause of the holes specking my bedroom ceiling, where I pinned his greatest hits. Of course, Dad copped out a wholly-predictable fashion, taking messages and calls on matters of national importance. Different rules for him.

Starved for distraction, I checked for The Man. I could maybe have claimed him as an acquaintance—anything to get me away from the changelings finding stuff not to like about ice cream. I lost track the number of times I had to explain to my sister how vanilla is black.

Who I did see swanning around was the maître d'—the tight-dressed guy who stiffed Dad so completely over the room bookings, which caused the little kids to bawl and finished with me having sole use of a suite I sorely wanted to get back to. The maître d' was showing the restaurant—indeed, displaying it with a generous sweep of his arm—to a tall, surly woman busting a really neat sand-drab suit. Even at distance, the maître d' looked keen to reassure her, while she found everything a source of wrist-flicking annoyance. I couldn't think why she might look at me, just knew she did.

Not till I tried to leave did Mum ask if I was going

to 'that gallery' tomorrow. Well, yeah, what else did she think I'd do? Not feeling that answer, she squawked about family time right up till I left the room and—probably—after.

When I stepped from the lift to head back to my suite, a stressed suit and earwig patrolled the hallway. Got to say, as a lone female, I wasn't assured by his presence. He took an over-close interest—I mean, sure, I had the kit even then. But his trailing eyes suggested some other bad mischief. So much, when I shut the door, I searched that suite top to toe. Checked under my bed, every cupboard and drawer; smacked back the shower screen so hard one of the hinge bolts bust. I found nothing and wasn't content there was nothing to find.

A suburban kid, I had this sketch for big city nights. Flashing billboards, always cool—the room lit, then dark from neon, intermittent. Traffic below: cars pumping bass, chicks laughing, a clubby sense of night independent from drab day. Step to the window—hot, damp air makes everything dangerously slippy. Lit apartments across the way—a woman named Blanche or Adele or Nina or Joey getting changed beneath a harsh, bare bulb, getting made for midnight downtown. I'd be there, sipping something long with ice and limes, waiting the big deal to happen. So what happened? The air con buzzed, the night set still, and that's all.

Numbers beside me said 2:32am when I woke still dressed. Woke to something new about the dense silence. A phone ringing through the wall. I slid to the joining door, trying to hear past the squabbles in my head. That murmur: the low, low sound of a big man talking soft. I guess he was pacing—a restlessness leaking through the cement. I saw him walk, gesturing, shaking his head. That pointing move he pulled: I bet he was pointing, pacing with his phone. The Man next door, on some whole other business.

## 2

Through a ton of motels where I learned or didn't learn Spanish, when vanilla-scented *camareras* asked how the world was treating me, I thought they meant I looked as crap from lack of sleep as I did that morning. As daylight dirtied the blinds, the grey slab building across the street was busy. Barriers blocked the road, dodged-around by presented-looking women in serious suits. Everyone accessorised with slab laminates. Every guy a cop.

I checked the hall door was super-locked, dragged an armchair against the charm school entrance, and caught a shower. Like always with hotels, the shower ran high Arctic one second, uptown Zambesi the next. Jinking the knobs made zero difference, the whole thing tediously hateful.

Dumb as I am, I got very aware of my rawness, just tiles and plaster from the bathroom next door. Stupid, I felt shy. Through steam that softened the light into some gothic, misty morning, the water inside of the shower screen hung vivid as sunburnt ice. Those moments—regular to me—when I get overtaken by the massiveness of how things exist. When the way things exist gets under my skin and flays me. Sure gets distracting when I'm gunning my Harley down a wet highway. I get bewildered, I guess, by cracks across walls, how trees twist, the pathways of cuts in my skin. I get seasick from patterns of leaves. I get shipwrecked from Rothko.

Takes a while, after those moments, to come back level. When the shower burnt my flesh and cold from the air con hit, flung from fire to ice, I towelled and dressed, the neat cottons and linens I'd bought for the city stinging my skin.

Fixing my face, I got that sound again: his phone next door. I find this hard to put over without sounding hippy, but something to how his phone rang made me think these calls were more significant, somehow. I could no more imagine him take a courtesy call than watch game shows.

A different slab guy furnished the hall, though with the same troubled tailoring. Always, I'm uneasy with random heavies. The whole city muscled-up for the conference—I knew Dad's job, he rolled with the grownups. That didn't explain the guy stood watch in my hall. Behind his shades and waxy skin, seemed to me he was worked by wires. That made a brick of lead in my gut as I went downstairs.

From the lift I tumbled into a tide of linen and handheld devices. Everyone so perky and focused, I wanted outsider cool but just felt uninvited.

This goofball guarding the restaurant hassled me for ID. 'Name and room number.'

'What?'

He looked me down. 'To prove you're a guest.'

'I have a suite. Riz Montgomery.'

So he checks his rinky list. 'I have an Amelia Montgomery.'

Take a razor to my heart. 'That is so much a typo. I'd fire the arse of who did that.'

Weirdly, the oaf seemed puzzled. 'Are you waiting for your party, Miss Montgomery?'

'Yeah, sure, I want Mum and Dad and the twinklets of Satan to make my misery complete.'

I'd only just soiled the tablecloth with my midnight velvet nails when this sweet-chocolaty waitress tells me they cook eggs to order. I cannot begin the horror of any cooked breakfast. 'No, just coffee and toast and Wackios.' Tell you, Wackios make a fine meal, straight from the pack.

She gave me this practiced look. 'If you prefer cereal there's a serve-yourself counter.'

Bottling my fear of the bright, chattering crowd, I went to the counter but found just muesli and crap. The toast she brought was cold. By the feel of it, it was cold the day before too. A slug of coffee and I'm making to walk, when I clock the tall woman I'd seen before—wearing the same or another sandy suit—her hands describing shapes with agile anger to a crew of dodgeball-headed cops. These officers—meaty guys with years on the street, I guess—looked suitably thrilled to have a strong, ethnic woman bossing them round.

Now that woman did not have a laminate. She didn't need one. The starch of her shirt and razor creases gave her whole ID. She broke off talking to intercept me.

'Hello. Amelia, isn't it? I'm Detective Chief Inspector Salwa Abaid. I'm security command for the hotel.'

I was just trying to leave against the tide of starving delegates, I never thought I'd get recognised. How did she recognise me? 'Oh yes?' I said, like an idiot.

A flicker across her cheekbones hinted she made some decision about me. 'We won't inconvenience you.' A lie from any cop. 'Just the situation, you understand.'

Yeah, I mainlined rolling news. 'The loan fund guy? I heard he's not popular.'

'There are always challenges.' Her smile so many ways worse than her scowl. 'Be assured, though. We have security arrangements for immediate family members of vital staff.'

With the laminate crowd making whoopee around us, a tiny, fatal delay crept between what she said and me getting what she said. Already, she turned away, giving her men instructions.

'Excuse me.'

Her look said we were done.

'What does that mean, family members?'

At school I was used to nasty, dried up women telling me I should consider the words just said. Usually while girls around me were laughing. Detective Chief Inspector Salwa Abaid was no way dried up: very fine bones, fine skin, powerful—guess I'm meant to say a strong role model. Her date palm eyes had exactly the look I knew from school. 'We, the police, the security services, we understand it's not sufficient just to protect key personnel. For key personnel to function, they have to know their families are safe. We've got your back.'

I'd get a good laugh from the notion my family wanted me protected. What Abaid meant was wholly more disturbing. 'You have a file on me?'

She stroked down her jacket where she kept her gun. 'If you have concerns the liaison team are here to assist.'

By the time Mum messaged to say they started breakfast, I'd hit the street.

Grazed-looking guys in brown Harringtons, hoisting shoulder cameras, filmed gleaming women saying the same things over and over. You could only walk the hotel side of the street, single-file behind concrete barriers. Knightsbridge at the corner, that well-heeled, overplayed avenue ablaze with sunlight. You can't do crisis without retail. High end traffic jammed both ways, and blondes—a city stacked with blondes. Girls every colour, all blonde.

I already checked which Tube to get and once I made it onto that cramped cylinder of dirty metal, I had a whole city-girl thing going on. A clear shot of myself as a young woman riding the train, rushing beneath a landscape wholly high-rise. Some cool place I was part of: a chick with a mouthful of truth, intelligent eyes, the city mapped to her synapse. Not scared, not makeshift—the girl upstairs whose air con breaks, so she climbs in through your window.

Each station brought a compelling flow of Black girls, pumped little chicas among mad old fools stained from years of glum weather. Tidy Arab women in serious jackets, dudes busting baggies and skateboards, looking straight at me so I looked away. Families that weren't my problem, struggling luggage. A poised older woman, her guide dog comfortably sprawled against the seats. So naïve, I actually wondered how she got her makeup so perfect.

So I should have felt cool—the roach in the jelly being I couldn't enjoy it. For all I felt strong in my head right then, solo and independent, each time I saw someone a bit off someway, I thought how many friends Detective Abaid must have, the embrace of security freezing my spine. Would they follow me? Did they bug my clothes? I checked my pockets, scratched the seams. What if they bugged my lingerie? My secrets, all laid open. Maybe they'd always been watching, right since I was a kid. I slumped against the door, overwhelmed with anxiety and, at the next station, fell backwards off the train.

Walking up from Charing Cross, even I couldn't miss the National, tricked up with almighty banners of Purple Brown 1957, the colour-render on tent canvas not exactly authentic. Willy-waving by the curators, for getting the Rothko gig ahead of Tate Modern. Though really it was the sponsors—some US bank squeezing the culture nipple—that wanted iconic Trafalgar Square, not a steam shed south of the river.

None of which meant spit to the miniskirt leggings and tie-dye flowing up to the door: art school chicks, nursing cartridge pads my x-ray eyes confirmed as portfolio work for glamourous lives under construction.

Glad at least of strong lashes and talked-up cheeks, defiantly freckled, I lined for the paydesk with the amateur beards and gents of a single nature. At least the crowd wasn't touristy, none of that poor muscle tone you get with Monet or Renoir. I faced the elderly paydesk jockey.

'Do you pay student rate?'

'Er, yeah.'

Crabby old fingers pinched the air. 'Your student ID, please.'

That whole scene of ID remains, to this day, unexplored to me. Clearly I was a student, I got a tattoo—not that I planned on showing her that. So I played along, hunting my pockets till I got told to pony or leave. I would have wished her herpes, but her looks and attitude guaranteed immunity.

Next came examination by gruff types with the x-ray thing. 'I got to empty my pockets?'

'And unclip your belt.'

'My belt?'

This scrubbed-down, sensible-shoe type looked dumbfounded as I unwillingly popped it loose. 'A cat head buckle? Really.'

Stepping through the main hall was to stumble in space, the ceiling high behind banks of lights that churned through green and ochre. A cool vastness where people—even smart people—got kept to their proper size. Big sculptures, metal and stone, awesomely sifting light. I ran my hand along a gleaming bronze, its cool solidity questioning the clammy catch of my fingers. Everything beautiful the big way, the way a girl's unmade bed can be beautiful, when it carries the care and forgiveness of people who've needed her or been needed. Art is that or nothing. Ask Delacroix, man, ask Turner or Vincent or Marcus Rothkowitz.

The concept of Rothko might seem weird to folks with seedless-grape imaginations. But those pictures have been my endurance. A place like no other, where I can lay quiet and still. You love Rothko or you don't dance with me.

Beyond the rope, the light respectful and sombre, the walls a tone so neutral it was nothing. Black cubic sofa blocks where sketchbook girls could settle. Rothko everywhere. Wall upon wall, room upon room—I actually felt myself not breathe, utterly stilled. Faced with Yellow and Orange, with Untitled 1950, I knew clarity, fields of pure life. Voices around said Rothko got abstract—bullshit, he never got abstract. He got clear, precise, fried on hard liquor. Not abstract.

Man, I dissolved in those paintings. When you thought you'd seen the most tragedy and joy, you found more. People were crying, it's cool to cry with Rothko, you're better for it. He was Oppenheimer and Gagarin. He was Elvis and Willy Wonka.

Don't care it sounds dumb, I hit the floor in front of Black On Gray, feeling for every razor sting, while people flowed around me.

'Of course,' a woman said, above, 'he was the first to paint empty pictures.'

No way. Anger pulled me around. I drag-raced off my knees with the clamour of someone climbing from a hole. 'Bullshit.'

Humiliatingly, the woman didn't notice, so I had to say it again.

'Bullshit. You can't be more wrong.'

This large-breasted middle-ager, buttoned and smocky just like Mum's friends, looked me down with dog-ugly distaste.

'You can't be more wrong. They're not empty. They're full. They're filled with… with…'

'Hope.' Male, quiet—hard and sure. 'They're filled with hope.'

I never heard that before, but the absolute certainty how it was said, the woman's total disablement to answer, electrified my bones. I pivoted round. My neighbour, The Man, with the big snoot catalogue cradled open at Black On Gray. He read aloud, his voice the most violent calmness, "So much of Rothko remains—in a multiplicity of glowing presences, in a glory of transformations. Not all the world's corruption washes high colors away." In fact a quote, the eulogy Stanley Kunitz gave.

Still smarting, and wanting to be smart, I said, 'He didn't care for the haters.'

'He cared for his work. You can go anyplace from there.'

'To death.'

'Especially.' The Man gave a moment more to Black On Gray. Not just tidily dressed, perfect dressed. Not just the well-cut suit—starch white shirt, his classic tight-woven angle-stripe tie, his vintage, unflashy wristwatch: the type familiar from movies, an old Omega maybe. And cufflinks. Like blood stains, his cufflinks. Those stitched shoes I got such a view of under his bed. He didn't dress to own the joint. He dressed to eat whoever owned the joint.

You may ask what he was and I could say tall, a foot taller than me. Brown hair, left side-parted, short at the sides, first speck of snow at the temples. Skin showing a little experience round the eyes. Blue eyes, deep and direct. I could say all that. Tells you nothing about what he was.

Those eyes scanned me. 'We got off on the wrong foot yesterday. Reception didn't notify me of young women checking the carpet.'

Humour so heavy, my shoulders sagged. 'I shouldn't have been there.'

'You shouldn't have been so easy to find. Still, I was discourteous.'

What was his voice? Not American, not quite English. Some particular tone and diction, achieved through long scowling.

He didn't say come with me. He moved and I followed. Leaving the gallery, we passed biography stuff: photographs and letters, slideshow memories. Video loops of an overweight man who never missed a White Angel. Who, way down the line, got fat books written about him.

The Man swiped me a glance. 'Guess you want coffee.'

It felt okay to go off with him. I mean, he was my neighbour.

Nothing chainstore, he shipped me along Orange Street to this real Italian coffee place in a tiny hidden road. The waitresses had event-horizon hair no light could escape, and eyes to make you steal papa's hunting knife, kill a rival in some sweaty brawl, and take ship down the coast. The place served liquor.

We got seated by a beauty queen who flicked her hair, while catching a menu, while busting the meanest wiggle. I touched nothing on the table. I was scared to go near the table. I kept wholly still, pretending I looked happily young for my age. It was my parents' fault. If they'd brought me up right, I'd have finesse pre-loaded.

He batted the menu aside. 'Double-espresso. Ice water.' His very sharp eyes hit mine.

'Same. Please.' Damn, shouldn't say please. Shows weakness.

'*Due doppio espresso. Acqua con ghiaccio.*' Her voice a machine gun, her departure stiletto-sharp.

He manoeuvred the Rothko catalogue between oil jars that got stuff growing in them. 'That's yours.'

'You sure?'

'You don't want it?'

'I mean,' I fussed the cover. 'You bought it.'

'I read it. He dies in the end.' To underline the transaction was over, he checked his phone—a high-end job, not the type that comes free with a TV package.

I checked mine. Girls I knew then were real busy. I messaged that Rothko was great, said I'd post a review. Maybe some signal snafu stopped people responding. As he ignored me, I gently opened the catalogue, holding its edges two-fisted so it wouldn't crash and spill. Every picture sharp-rendered on weighty paper, skimmed around with weighty words about cyan and suicide. Shots of the Chapel, his studios, his kids, and some haters.

I learned early that I'm nothing. Not a textbook lesson, oh no. My school was keen for us paycheques to reach fruition, to claim our place in the sorority of good choices. We got told daily—me, more often—how each of us would blossom our own unique, predictable way. It was plain to me—reviewing my grades, discarding work too poor to complete—how I was the rich guy's kid who'd be nothing. Bumming around, never having to bother, when the end of each month daddy's cash would show in the bank. He'd never cut me off, not through any sense of love—he never had that—just because he was public and scrutinised and needy to do the right thing.

People I met since, in these years when I been kinda busy, seem to me to be mourning their younger selves. Checking old footage, trailing old friends, not grasping that you can't bottle a teenage crush. When I think about me sitting there with The Man, I feel no sense of chances wasted. Really, I lost nothing by what happened, for all that life's been a testy road trip.

At the waitress's scratchy, '*Scusi*,' I thumped the catalogue onto my knees while she fussed glasses and cups, arranging and rearranging. He slugged his coffee and signalled a refill. I took a lipstick pass at mine and damn near choked.

He stared, no doubt seeing me as embarrassing. 'How long you in town?'

'Couple days.' Like my voice just broke.

'That's what the water's for. You drink the water. You here alone?'

What I recall, this real acute fear that he'd out me as a child. To say that was worse than to say I look a bit brunette sometimes. 'Mostly by myself.'

'You're here with your folks.'

There wasn't a rising inflection so I didn't answer.

'More coffee?'

Part of me not so evolved as the rest wanted to try the cake. It's true, though, that cool kids eat only air—man, life on the road teaches you poverty chic—so I bulked with water and the heavy crude that place called espresso. A sleepless night, a day on my feet, Rothko—yet that coffee cleared my static quick as good speed. Coming alive, buzzing, I scattergunned words. 'Yeah, I see my folks. I mean, see them. We came here together. But really they're not in my face at all. They say Riz...'

'Riz?'

'Huh?'

'That your name?'

'Yeah. And you're...?'

'Staying all week.' He set his water glass between the fussy oil steeps. 'So I'll see you around.' His wallet so totally French leather, and the note he slung mythically large. 'You can owe me the change.'

Already halfway to the door, so I had to yell behind him, 'See ya,' like some scrape.

At the next table, a classy size zero sat alone—which you never saw in my town—sipping herb tea with an actual liqueur—which you never saw fifty miles of my town. I thought I'd score a liqueur, till the waitress scowled so nasty, I gave up and inched to the paydesk, displaying the kind of physical caution you see in a minefield. After I scooped the change into my pocket, her hiss made me haul it back out to leave a tip. She said something Italian, the gist of which I got from the spit off her teeth. Outside, boys were lean and girls were shining. I yanked my stomach tight and flowed into the city.

Trusting my shoes to Wardour Street, I headed into the knotty alleys of Soho, buildings pinched so tight they nudged each other to whisper, 'Who's that strange girl?' Windows gaped, spilling sounds of hunger, endurance, and love. A girl stripped to lingerie stretched from an attic window, laying her dress to dry on a neighbour's roof. I looked and looked away. My phone rang. I knew who it was. But turned back just the same.

Caffeine kept me alive for the ride, yet the second I left the Tube's fathomless echoes, the usual weight pressed my skull. Not improved by lines of cops and fenced off walkways that channelled me, inevitably, to bad news. Joy emptied from my squabbling head. It felt no surprise that Detective Abaid waited outside the hotel doors, pretending to check her phone. Ten thousand people saw me, any one could have tipped her the word.

'Hey, Amelia.'

I literally froze at that awful name.

'How's it going?'

Factually, I had no fight with her. She was doing a tough job, I guess, and as I was not-quite a civilian perhaps it was downtime for her to chew the fat. I thought she'd give up and talk to someone more important. But those clear, brown eyes kept at me. 'I suppose it's boring for you. All these men,' she grimaced, 'making speeches. Bores me too.'

I picked up that wasn't a confession. It was a lie to simulate friendship. There was nothing really wrong with her. She didn't wear a wedding ring.

'Still, at least you can go shopping. You been shopping? Sightseeing?'

'I been to Rothko.' As if just suddenly I remembered the half ton of paper filling my hand, I hoisted the catalogue, almost expecting some rooftop marksman to take it out for practice.

'Rothko?' She scanned her cultural references. 'The painter?'

'Kinda. There's a big show of his. Retrospective.'

'You like art?'

'Rothko.'

Really, I'm not sure what happened—I had the catalogue, I showed it her, and then the catalogue was in her hand. I think our hands did some dance while our eyes were busy.

She thumbed the slab of printed matter, making slight noise at its heft. 'It cost how much?'

'They're expensive. Catalogues. The ink I guess. And permissions. It's the permissions.'

If her laugh rang false it's because she wasn't born to laughter. A laugh that says, 'I'm trying to make this easy'.

'You must drive a hard deal with your pocket money.'

Which is to say, 'Your Dad's minted, and I'm on salary'. Truly, dumbo here, I could have shrugged it off. Said, 'yeah, I blew my cash for the year', or 'yeah, Dad buys me anything so I won't tell about that time in the shed'. You know, or just said nothing. Me and smart, we're not *amigas*. So I say to this charming, well-dressed, terrifying cop, 'I didn't buy it. It's a present.'

Click and blammo. Her eyes, a vivid gleam of detection. 'From your parents?'

She threw me that lifeline, knowing I wouldn't catch it. 'No, the guy next door.'

A tiny peek of her tongue. 'Your neighbour's into art?'

Still, still, I didn't bail, not with sweat running down my arms, not with my shirt stuck to my stomach. 'The guy here. I met him at the gallery. He'd done with the catalogue and gave it me.'

Sure there were helicopters overhead, cops joking each other, raw noise. Through that, a thread of fine silence. Salwa Abaid, sizing up what to do. 'You know,' her words rushed with sudden warmth, 'I really don't know Rothko. I'm not familiar with him at all. Would you mind if I borrow this? Just for tonight. I'm keen to know what I'm missing.'

Definitively, that catalogue The Man gave me came into her possession, carefully held by its edges, passed with equal care to an officer summoned by her look. The catalogue, gone from me. Maybe I could have said, 'Don't cops need a warrant?' So what if they do?

In that discreet, empowered busyness of the lobby was the place to find Mum lurking. She sharpened her lipstick specially. We could have done it upstairs, away from the hired help. But it was never her style to give me dignity.

'Where have you been?'

'Rothko.' Without the catalogue, spreading my hands just made me sorry-arsed.

'You've been gone the whole day. Did you switch off your phone?'

'Bad signal. Metal sculptures and stuff.' By then, the punch of getting waylaid morphed into sticky awareness that receptionist chicks, the maître d', the cops, all the badges were watching. And it was hours since I peed and that was distracting. 'I think we should…' I wanted to say, 'Go somewhere to smash your face', but she had the lines and leisure time to rehearse.

'You're fifteen. Do you know this city? Do you know what districts are safe? I've got to watch for you, remember.'

'No you don't.' Back in the affluent, nowhere town I lived then, I might just have let her rant—mortified, sure, but no one real would see. But in London, with bigtime people around. Maybe what I said wasn't precisely conciliatory. 'You don't have to watch for me. You don't care about me. You care about earrings. You care about neighbourhood meetings to swank your new hair. You care everyone gets to listen to you. What parts are safe? The parts you're not.' And most pleased at getting that down without flubbing a word, I moved forward to cuff her shoulder and swish upstairs. Would have been swell if it happened.

Shockingly, she grabbed my arm, for the whole lobby to see. Her silence held the heat of a life burned up with arrangements. That second, I knew she hated me good. 'Pack your things. Your Father's got your room.'

The one thing she had power to do: drag me back to her so-called family. Dad would get my towering suite. I'd bunk on the rug. Dad would get my city sky and The Man for his cheery neighbour. No way. How to explain it? No way. Couldn't reason with her—easier to reason with cops. All I had was all I hated: the sorrowful little girl from when I was too young to know better. 'You can't, Mum.' I called her Mum, Christ sake. 'Think about it: when we got here, how the kids were with Dad. They can't remember going places with him.' Because the waster was never home. 'They clung on his legs when we had to switch rooms. Right here, they made all that rumpus. They'll be in the lift all hours to see him.' And I hate the brats and they hate me. 'They'll be whiney. Just like at home.' I was whiney myself. In the real life of that family, only gross submission got play.

Through the heat of her hate for me, she understood how my punishment let Dad off the hook yet again. Those suites were palatial for one ginger girl; a tight fit with two antsy hellspawn. When Dad got back from the conference each night, he was trapped—that was the novelty. 'Maybe it's better,' her voice like nettles. 'This way I don't have to smell you.'

# 3

Without meaning to sound too meaningful, life is blood and texture. You learn that climbing walls and falling off motorbikes. I watched with the lights off till it got dark, seeing the sky damp down and city streets glimmer. Most women would say: call your friend, bitch it out. Get mileage on shared situations. I had friends, of course I did. Girls I smoked with. They were maybe too busy to call.

Listening hard at the wall I guessed The Man wasn't home. I have truthfully no idea how he filled his time. Sick and dirty, I wanted his stone-cold wisdom. He was bigger than routine. Blood and texture—I bet he knew.

The conference windows burned with evening meetings. Along the street, cops waved lazy guns. Round the clock, I could have watched it real time. But I packed for nights out. Mostly I wore jackets and jeans, never carried a bag and, yeah, I looked like a boy, which is a whole other subject. My hair wouldn't lay in a side-sweep, so I made the best of a centre-part, mussing the front to make depth. I got storm cherry lipstick that would've worked great, if my face wasn't a dustbowl. Yeah, I don't wear makeup now. It's an option I deleted.

What I'm saying, I dressed up to the extent I could.

Flung looks at the mirror, checked my angles. Said a bright good evening to the goon in the hall. His snitching on me must have been pure soap.

Trying to slink through the lobby, I got pulled by the maître d'. Now that guy was a tremendous swell, one of those guys way above the folks they serve. Sharp-dressed, a tad flowery, the master of agile gesture. He moved so tidily into my path, getting stopped was nearly a pleasure.

'Miss Montgomery.' He beamed fit to bust. 'I think your party is assembling for dinner.'

Damn, he made it fancy, like Mum got pearls and Dad was a diamond stud. 'Oh yes?' I picked up this habit of saying that.

'I believe the *Moules Provençale* is especially piquant tonight.' I'm sure he believed no such thing, just enjoyed saying it. 'May I escort you to the restaurant?'

His arm jacked out—perhaps I was meant to fold my elbow around it. I felt a twinge at leaving him hanging as, really, he treated me well. 'I'm going out for dinner.' Didn't sound compelling. 'I have friends in town.'

The maître d's steel-grey eyes could switch at a blink from genteel to severe. He brought his hand back to his side, waving its tension away. 'My mistake. I thought your friends were here.' I followed that gesture behind him, where guys in lounge suits stood looking keen and brutal. I knew, though, didn't I, that the cops had my back.

'Thank you,' I said, not sure why. 'I'll see you later.'

'We never close.' He graciously stepped aside. 'Like hospital or prison.'

Much as I hated that fenced-off street of bored, inquisitive cops, the city avenues, their evening crowds, got me more uneasy. Everyone taller than me, their looks more complete, engaged in phones, bubbling with purpose you could taste. I had a lot jumping off in my head, the mugginess and squalls.

I picked up the pace, like someone with real arrangements. My hair clammy against my face, my shirt pinching my shoulders and elsewhere. The local girls got that London swing. I tried pushing my body into those shapes. Opportunity everywhere. Just had to find it. Yeah, now I'd hit some biker bar, shake the dust from my hair, punch the counter. Back then was still the old country. Crowds got draggy, but London's good for thin alleys that keep out the tourists. A few uninformed lefts and rights, I felt miles away.

Looking for nothing specific, just everything, I tracked blocks of old houses cut into flats; dead-looking shops for brass band horns and herbal cures; the hidden, surprising offices of good causes nobody heard of. Heading through Chelsea, drawn on pheromone wires to the most backstreet of bars.

Cash was always the issue. They kept me poor, then got surprised I wandered. Denied credit by stupid rules, I had a few notes acquired from Mum at careless moments, and The Man's loose change from the cafe. Counted it out on the street like a tourist. The laughter inside that bar sounded expensive.

In turquoise light through rippled glass my hands shook, resistant to pushing that door. I'm no stranger to resistance. Once, a band I loved for years came to the next town over. Dad's plastic treated my ticket and I got dressed up for the bus. It was only an hour to the next town. I did my eyes so they really looked something. I was going to leave some music playing and slide out the back. Then it started to rain, then it rained a lot. I had a jacket—could have run for the bus with my jacket over my head. Right up to when the bus was due, I was ready. Then it got tight for the bus. Then I stayed home. Not the only time the size of my mouth exceeded the length of my stride. Forcing my hand to make contact, I pushed the door.

The place was wrapped with turquoise light, like sliding into a blue martini. Heads turned, which made me the girl that walked into a bar. Not just blue light: ultraviolet, and canned air vanillaed with dry ice. Black and white prints of random stuff—city streets, old video games, a horny pinup of Veronica Lake. Santa Veronica, patron of trouble. French and Spanish words I didn't know then—big, jumping letters: 'uprising', 'revolution', 'liberty'. Was there ever a more ridiculous word. Scratchy music to rile the blood. Sudden realisation that, really, I had to be older.

Tried to reach the bar, the floor sticky; though, factually, it was smooth and I was just scared. I thought of The Man, what he'd do. He'd swank right up, drop a note and stare them out like they were pond life. Difference was, he had cufflinks.

Things didn't improve at the bar, where a woman

39

built from beautiful tatts and intricate piercings poured shots with the grace of a priestess. To get my eyes off her landscape, I fixed on the mirror. Wrong move. Under ultraviolet, my face transformed to a cold moonscape of freckles, swarming, making me a sunken, craggy freak. My hair became pale, vapid straw, my eyes—my ginger eyes—the lead bolts of a corpse. I didn't look underage. I barely looked human.

'What you after?'

I was after what she had: a proper south London accent. Horrified at the bizarre vowels I got from school and my native attempts to squash them, I failed to smile—or look sane. 'I'll take a beer.' In the mirror, the words came from a mouth besieged by mauve eruptions.

'What beer?'

An empty St. Erhard on the bar, stubby and medical-looking. I may actually have pointed at it. I may actually have looked bewildered when she asked if I wanted a glass. Luckily, instinct answered: a real woman takes it by the neck.

That beer was hugely expensive. And fruity and chewy and blasted me to orbit. Vexed that I got elevated so fast. I worked keenly to build tolerance for drink, but where I lived was hard to get service. Shying from those shocking mirrors, I sank into soft blue light. Found a table for one, for necking fat beer and checking the scene.

The place was busy with complex hair. This one woman tied her hair two ways. Up top a pom-pom knot, the back a ponytail. Below her tied-up hair, shaved skin curved smooth and flawless.

Me, the five-four train wreck of freckles, I gawked at this stunning woman and her entourage. Kids in ripped jeans, raggy tees, chain saw fringes, metal and ink, all different skin tones, each lazy neighbourhood's nightmare. I knew what they were. Girls at school had older sisters and brothers who done that, dropped into college easy life, got tatts and a chic little worldview about sticking it to the system. They could afford it, their parents were minted. So were mine and I was uneasy with pre-pack rebellion. Still, that woman looked fresh. Warm and eager, I felt things develop around me.

Next thing, at the bar for a refill, odd how the light held my feet clear of the ground. Leaning to look at my feet, I collided with something warm, cigarette-smelling and velvety-hard. Baggy camos with thick, lumpy pockets, a midnight jacket in glossy sateen. And hair, tied two ways.

Taller, obviously, and I thought maybe central Asian. Dark eyes, interesting lips scrunched tight as the remains of her drink sloshed over her boots. She looked at me like I might have some explanation. 'Am I invisible?'

My jaw gaped. I tasted dry ice.

'You spilled my drink.' She raised the empty glass, fingers glistening. Long fingers, swagged with rings. 'It's pisco sour.'

'Yeah.' My voice a cartoon. 'Yeah.'

With that hair and those eyes that, right then, stripped my skull. 'You have a lot of freckles.'

'Yeah.'

'Bar's that way.'

Awkward, talking to the barmaid without looking up, scared what the mirrors made me. Actually, that went for talking at all.

'Same again?'

Some squeaky noise escaped my lowered head.

'Anything else?'

'Piss.'

'You want a piss?'

'Shower.'

'What?'

'Pisk hour.'

'You okay?' Like if I wasn't, it was a problem she wouldn't deal with.

Commanding the bar, the woman nudged me aside. 'Pisco sour.' That cigarette warmth took me down completely.

The barmaid must have pointed at me or something. 'She with you?'

The woman laughed. Didn't answer. Just laughed.

I scratched for cash—didn't have that many pockets and couldn't find it. Eventually, I located a note acquired in a raid on Mum's wallet. Sure didn't get much change.

'C'mon.' Those metalled fingers gestured me into the blue.

So why sit with kids that, a moment before, I despised? Because she said c'mon and that was enough.

Because obedience felt better. They had a big round table, everyone bunched and pally. More boys than girls, which was awkward. But a solid group sharing something specific, not huddled and coupling-up. Though the table was round, you knew she was its head.

No room for another body, so everyone had to shuffle and hunch while I got shoehorned in. Bewildered, the subtleties escaped me, but I sensed a lull in their talk while I disentangled my chair from its neighbour. That pause when everyone sniffs and ponders this thing that's arrived. Tattoos lit like Christmas. This one girl had a blacklight snake that twisted around and around her arm, hovering over the skin. This guy had a rose at his throat, petals edged blue that winged beyond his body. Some shave-head had an ink skull—guess it didn't show in normal light. Not one face staring at me had freckles.

'Hey. I'm Riz.'

Some chuckles. Some stinted hellos.

'You guys here for Rothko?'

Tumbleweed.

'Bitching retrospective.' I had trouble with 'retrospective'. 'Rothko's great, right? Yeah.' I thought maybe to say I liked someone's tattoo, break the ice a bit harder. But the woman who put me there swung it around.

'What brings you here Riz?'

'Well, I loved Rothko since I was a kid. I saw him on TV.'

'This place. What brings you here?'

I got that facts weren't the option. 'I got friends. I'm

seeing them later. Fancied a drink, you know, get started. Hotel bar's lame.'

'You staying round here?'

No way, *no hay manera*. Though I didn't say that. 'I'm at the London Royale Grange Plaza. Kensington, you know it? I got a suite—this actual apartment, truthfully, to myself.'

'The hotel where the summit's at?'

'It's pretty flat.'

'The global finance conference.'

'That? Oh yeah, across the street.' I did a double-blink when she asked exactly how across the street. I moved glasses around. 'Hotel's here, yeah? The conference place, this big nasty slab, is here. This,' I scuffed a finger between the glasses, 'is cops and cameras and stuff. They shut the road.'

Through UV fog, her features grew more absolutely enticing. I was young, okay? I had the apparatus but not the instructions. So lost in her, I jolted when a guy's voice said, 'How come you stay there?'

My head yelled for more beer. 'I'm with key personnel.'

Factually, the words made sense. But this kid with rivets for eyes gave me the dumb face. 'What?'

'I'm in the set-up.' Heat prickled my throat. 'I'm involved.'

'You a secretary or something?' One of the girls said that. Square-faced with a knot of black hair. I can't hardly express the pressure she drove on the word 'secretary'.

No, I wasn't sober and yeah, maybe a small voice said

stop gabbing. If it did, it was just a small voice. 'I'm a VIP.'

Now that was factual also. I had a goon with an earwig outside my door and a file with the police. I don't guess you got that paying with voucher codes. The woman who put me there tapped my arm. Nearly jumped out my splotchy skin. 'What sort of VIP, Riz?'

'I'm with Montgomery.'

'You his entourage?'

Now that was low. 'I'm his daughter.'

I never enjoyed those words, a lie only told with necessity. To define yourself by someone else—what's more tragic?

So then everyone looks at me very specific. *Mucho* breathing and shoulders. The handsome young woman with hair two ways rode the shock. 'Glad to have you along, Riz. You found the right spot.'

From what I recall, we washed into the night on a tide of real goodwill. Some party was on and I was invited. I mumbled about not catching her name. But I never got her name, she never told me. So I called her Mocha, because of her skin and the creamy severity that made her the head of the gang.

# 4

With no magic carpet, we got the Tube or Overground or something. I remember the beep of sliding doors. In a bright bubble of good-looking people, my phone going nuts, so let it. Obviously, it was no one with concern for me.

Warm-smelling streets and I picked up the beat from a warehouse. Big old place, strobing windows spilling bass and cigarette butts, tiny shooting stars, alight and gone. What a chance for me, after all the times I got turned back. The pit where big dancing happened, hands in the air, blacklight girls, flames across their bodies. Flames and angel wings. The floor in pools, the air fine rain. Smoke, burnt plastic and me.

Drowned in it all, I saw only Mocha. Hers were the eyes for me. What she said I didn't hear. She pointed up, touched my arm. It was okay.

Through a door onto metal stairs singing with the beat. Alone with her those few seconds, I had to say something. 'This your place?' My voice rough and clotted.

Walking ahead, her words didn't reach me. Just the clunk of her ponytail hitting her spine and the buzz from lights that streaked her shaved skin. Her walk like nothing I'd seen. Something terrific.

We rocked up to a lounge, I guess it was—a cement room with a bar and beaten chairs. Music shook the walls. She landed this glass of green stuff in my fist and sat me at a table scratched with white powder.

'Okay, Riz. Tell me about the hotel.'

That sticky green taste of crazy sweets. That whole stupendous clarity that follows. 'It's, like, these types, huh? Laminate necks. And I'm way high, penthouse nearly. I see in the building across the street. That's where it is. You should see those guys. They bring guns.'

'How come you scored the penthouse?'

'Conference got wider.'

'Wider?'

'Bigger menu. Then all the room bookings got switched around.'

'And you're up there alone?'

'Except The Man.' The green angel fluttered around me.

Mocha gave solid attention, dark eyes fully on me. No one gave me such attention. 'What man?'

'Don't know his name. Probably he doesn't have one. He rocks a mean suit.'

'What does he do?'

'Talks on the phone. He likes Rothko.'

While she got more drink, I needed to pee, that nasty ache stealing my insides. It was all my parents' fault. If they'd given me liquor I would have learned how to take it. So Mocha comes back with the medicine and I'm trying for cool, with a freight train of aniseed ripping me up.

'This man, a friend of your Dad?'

'A neighbour. It's not important.'

That calm look said everything was important. 'Okay, Riz. Your Dad, what's he working on?'

I wanted to talk about me. I thought that's why we were talking. 'Just goes to meetings and stuff. He travels.'

'Yeah, Riz. What's he working on at this conference?'

Maybe I looked extra dumb. My body cramping. 'It's not like I go there with him.'

'You could though. You could ask to look around. Get inside that building. Be awesome to know.' She nudged closer. 'You could do that tomorrow. Then we meet up tomorrow night, you tell me about it. I'd totally love that.'

Truthfully I had nothing for Dad's work. But this generous older girl wanted to know. Wanted to meet me, away from the others. Before I could enjoy that, a lightning bolt stung my gut. 'Can I use your loo?' I honestly sounded younger than my evil munchkin sister. 'Really,' I said, to make it worse.

'End of the hall, sharp left.'

Kinda hard to keep looking famous when you have to trot. This horrid fear I wouldn't make it mashed my guts the worse, and to top it off I was sweating acid.

I fell into this cupboard with no lights. I mean none—the room a stinking hole, just a metal rim toilet in the murmuring glow of the window. No lock on the door. For five unpleasant minutes I hovered and hoped.

Bass and shouting bust up the night but, through my heartbeat as it kicked and fluttered, a new sound revved up. Engines. Then the concrete room was raked by flashing blue lights.

I stretched to the jammed-open window. A contingent, maybe fifty cars and wagons. Doors slammed. Purposeful voices. I hustled to the bar, as folks downstairs realised they had company. Mocha stared at me. They all did.

'Well played.' Her voice stone cold. 'For a dumb bitch.'

Someone grabbed my shoulders. 'Sling her out the window.' I struggled, got dead-legged, the room shot past. Mocha pulled me back. 'Not worth it. Just not worth it.'

A blizzard of boots and a bottle smashed—the cops' signature greeting. Downed and drunk, all I knew were legs scuffling round me. Raggy ripped jeans, baggy shorts, and the hardshell knee pads and quarterboots of riot cops. I took a few kicks from those eight inch upsetters, too numb to feel shit. Then a pair of side-zipped cobras dragged me clear.

Detective Chief Inspector Salwa Abaid, flushed and breathless, quickly correcting her hair. A riot downstairs: the music canned, a whole lot of justice paid out. Salwa seemed bored. 'You can walk. You're not a baby.'

She hauled me up, wrenching my arm. 'Ow.'

'You're under arrest, stupid.' Her voice dirty gravel. 'These pricks'll kill you if I don't get you out.'

Some robocop had Mocha double arm-locked, elbows up her back. Stood tall in proud resistance while her soldiers chewed dirt. Downstairs was breakage and screaming.

This shave-head rocked up, body armour filled and chunky. His boots twelve glossy inches of premium damage. Helmet tucked under his arm like he just won it. 'What you reckon?' he asked the room. 'I bet there's warrants on these clowns.' A bit of low level abuse and a faceful of polyurethane. 'Eh?' He stuck his jaw near some guy eating concrete. 'What you reckon? There's warrants on you, mate.'

'Are we under arrest?' Mocha's voice had a battlefront edge. 'What's the charge? You have to tell us.'

'Don't worry, Tinkerbell. We got reasons for you.'

'Are you wearing body cameras? You have to wear body cameras.'

'Oh, we're wearing 'em.' He smiled, his head a split peach. 'Aren't we lads? Wearing 'em.'

'Ow.'

Detective Abaid gave my arm a foul twist. My eyes jerked up, then slumped back to her fashion boots. She didn't have riot gear, not even a hat.

My screeching got Pinhead's attention. He gave me a look I've seen often. 'What are you?'

Mocha struggled against restraint. 'We know what she is. Don't we, Montgomery's daughter.'

I'm slow, okay? I'm last to the joke. I got beaten

often, by sweater girls, random bullies—it was just body pain. What kicked me bad was the look in Mocha's velvet eyes, as the lie became truth in her heart.

'We know what she is. That bitch brought you here.'

'No.' Tried reaching her, but Abaid was strong. 'Let go. No I didn't.'

Baldy got more vexed. 'Get over here. We'll get the truth downtown.'

Abaid pulled me close, like a bargain swiped in the sales. 'It's my prisoner.'

'You see?' Some randoms, picking up Mocha's static. 'Special treatment. She's a grass'

'Am not.'

'She's getting special.'

'Yeah,' Mocha jeered, 'they'll let her go when they get outside.'

That got the mood more ugly. Kids struggled under cops who clawed them like angry crabs. One got loose, a lanky git in retro tee and dreads. He lunged at me, yellow teeth dripping spit. Then the gold commander or whatever he was primed his stick and the young bloke fell, a tree on a date with a chainsaw. His frozen scowl of hate broke apart on the concrete.

That set Mocha shouting about rights and process and cameras—always, the cameras: where are they? Who's watching the feed? The court will expect... Book-learned rebel stuff, pretty fresh and attractive, but where does it take you?

Boss guy prodded bone with his big man stick. Swaggered over where Abaid held me painfully rigid. 'Give her here. They'll rip her apart.'

'This is my prisoner.' Her hands sloppy with sweat.

'This is my operation, Detective,' like she was a dumb child. 'We'll get her hosed down and charged. You can see her in the interview room.'

As she moved in I got thrust aside, dangled at hard, spitting faces. 'My prisoner, Commander. Do I have to spell it out? Do I have to explain it to you?'

Swear, I felt lightning crack between them. Her thumb stroked the inside of my arm, on the ridge of bone popping with pressure.

The commander's voice dropped, like, ten thousand feet. 'You people make me sick.' Then back with the barnyard bellow, 'Okay, scumbags, we're going for a ride. But our guest will leave first.'

Abaid tensed, her hard breath resolved in my tangled hair. 'Come on.' She pushed me into the wall of jeers and spit. She wrenched my arm till I howled.

As we cleared the door, Mocha shouted, 'Tell Daddy. He'll buy you a pony.'

My first time getting pushed downstairs in an arm lock. Guess everyone has to start somewhere. The dance floor was the aftermath of a boots-to-the-ground operation. Everything busted, speaker stacks torn apart, their huge bull cones the mute mouths of a party murdered. The concrete carpeted with kids in bloody scraps. Girls were crying and I set my face hard. Some still tried to fight, but it was just showbiz.

Outside, bodies were packed into wagons. There were beatings and blood—what's to say? Fight the police, they do that. Next morning there'd be a story how some kid had a seizure, died, whatever. Some gorgeous epileptic who should have stayed home.

No wagon for me. I got slung in the back of a plainclothes car, driven by a pissed young man who, I sensed, would rather be breaking heads.

Abaid shoved me over with needless rigor. 'What the hell are you doing here? Do you know how much work you've caused? If you want to get wrecked, call room service.'

Excitement and pain and a shower of spit had muddied my senses till then. But her voice brought me back, drunk and queasy. No air in the car. Heat pressed my head, as fire ripped my guts. My shirt and jeans a clammy adhesion. There were things in my hair, crawling and biting. This detective wanted an answer. 'My Mum told room service I'm not meant to drink.'

'You're not meant to be here.' Abaid thumped the passenger seat. The driver gave me The Cop Look in the rearview.

'I just wanted to meet people.' So I was a scrape.

'And do you think you made a good choice?'

'Not really.' Though that was a lie because, actually, I liked Mocha. I liked her a lot. 'What will happen to them?'

She did this very adult thing, inhaling hard and straightening her cuffs. 'What's going on in London just now, Amelia?' That name imposed on me when I was a harmless baby.

'Riz.'

'What?'

'Riz. I call myself.'

'Why?'

'It means something good in a fly way.'

'Who to?'

'What?'

'Who does it mean that to?'

'Street kids.'

'On what street?'

So she had me there.

She said, 'In French it means rice.'

'Oh yes?'

'And in the Holy Qur'an, *Rizq* means all we are given, all we have to live.' She said something Arabic, a blessing maybe. 'And where I come from Riz is a boy name. So you want me to call you Riz?'

'I want to get out the car please.'

'No chance.'

'I'm going to be sick.'

We get to the cop shop and if the warehouse kids were there, I didn't see them. By then I was shaking—absinthe burns worse coming back. Sorry to say, I peed myself a little and got convinced everyone could smell it, which is why they looked at me how they did. When really, I guess, they looked because I was a damp, lumpy mess.

At first, getting parked in a room with a couch and TV was therapeutic. Though the TV was muted, I knew it was some show where people were laughing. Reassuring how ordinary night—the chat shows and sitcoms—went on whatever. I was thinking of calling for coffee when I got attacked.

Mum never looked good without sleep. And her ugly mood fit her just right. 'Where have you been?' She moved closer, raising her voice. 'I asked where have you been?'

What did she expect? I got busted. 'Really, let's not do this.'

'I have been calling you.' Anger flushed her cheeks. 'No one could find you. No one knew where you were. Your Father had to leave a meeting. A crucial meeting.'

'Oh why don't you just die?' Okay, I said the soft part loud. But it was feelgood, watching it land.

'What did you say?' She blocked any escape, her lithe form and cocktail stylings bringing to mind a green mamba whipping in. 'Have you seen yourself, you greasy slut? Stinking drunk. Vomit in your hair.'

'Most likely.'

'We'll stop this.' She sounded satisfied. 'I'll call Dr. Grover.'

'No.' Scared for real.

'Certainly. I'll tell him I don't want details. Just send you back when you're fixed.'

'And if I'm not fixed?'

'Then your brother can have your room.'

'Bitch.' I barged at her, glad my clammy hands stained her evening sweater.

She took a couple of pokes then shoved me down. I tripped, sprawling over the couch.

'Close your legs.'

Said so coldly, with such intent, tears I held back for hours burned through. There were girls at my school shared clothes with their mum. They did lunch.

She moved in, I guess to pound me. The door opened, we froze, caught in our guilty game.

Salwa Abaid had this thing of fixing her hair before intervening. She smoothed it back and snapped the clip. 'I need to speak with Miss Montgomery.'

'Go ahead, Detective.' Mum straightened her skirt and manners. 'Though you may find her a little incoherent right now.'

'Miss Montgomery.' She gestured get-up.

Mum stood beside me.

The detective scowled. 'If you don't mind, Mrs. Montgomery, I need to see your daughter alone.'

Mum did outrage cool and painful. 'I'm not sure I understand. She's fifteen. A child.'

'This is a formal interview. Miss Montgomery's legal representative may be present.'

'Those aren't the rules.' She'd read the same hymn sheet as Mocha. 'Her parent must be present. I'm her parent.'

'Miss Montgomery is not under arrest. She came here voluntarily to assist an inquiry. Any delay could mean serious crimes are committed. Miss Montgomery, this way please.'

Not that I'm petty or nothing, but it was neat how that door slammed on Mum's face.

So we go to this blue room: walls panelled with blue Velcro; a carpet of dusty, staticky stuff; the hardest chairs. There's audio kit on the table, there's cameras at each corner. There's a window up high. Outside is still dark.

Mum was right, that's not how it works. Unless

they're taking you to the dentist. 'At the party, you said I'm arrested.'

'I also called you stupid, so that's two lies.' She tweaked her cuffs. 'You don't have to say anything to me, but anything you do say could be used against you in court. If you don't mention something now and it comes up later, a court may wonder why you didn't say it sooner. Is this making sense? You are not under arrest. However, if you don't cooperate that could be awkward. This interview is not being recorded, but it's me the court will believe. Okay so far?'

'Where are the others?'

'Others?'

'The party kids. That girl. With the hair.' I did some pantomime of hair-tying, fingers itchy from a racing heart.

'Not here. You care about them?'

'I didn't grass them up. It wasn't me led you to them.' I felt sick again. My fingers pulled long, sweaty streaks from the table. 'Do we have to talk now? I want to go to bed.'

Guess cops feel helpless sometimes, faced with people's dumb choices. The striplights cased in frosted plastic—dirty inside, how it always is—shaped her as someone ready to take harsh action. There was nothing wasted with Salwa Abaid, no excess, no emotional spillage. She squared her hands into two low walls. 'No, you didn't inform on those kids. We had them under surveillance. Your Dad's little conference has drawn a crowd.'

'He's not that famous.'

'Trouble-starters like your friends are well-briefed. They can't get at senior assets, though they try. Then you come along, a back door to the system. We would have picked them up anyway. You were added incentive.'

'They spat on me.'

'Welcome to my world.' She leaned forward, quiet, coaxing. 'Why were you there?'

'Do I have to tell the truth?'

'It's usual.'

'Mum was mean to me so I went out. To find some friends.'

'Are you lonely?'

'That a police question?'

'One stranger to another.'

An actual puddle of sweat formed under my fingers. 'Next time I'll stay home, slit my wrists.'

She checked the soundbox was off. Glanced at the cameras. Each camera, corner to corner to corner to corner. When she turned to the cameras behind, her hair licked her collar. She met my bleary gaze, an odd weight in her eyes. 'When I was seven years old I had two friends, two girls I played with. Asma and Nasreen. I don't mean we were three friends. I mean they were friends and I was friends with them. They saw each other without me. I always wanted to mean something to them, to get thought of first, to be a special friend. You know how that feels?'

I was amazed she thought I might.

'Our town had a forest, a river. We were outdoor girls, tough. One day I went with Nasreen, the two of us, to the forest. We found an old freezer dumped by a stream. We climbed into this big white box, pretending it was a boat and the lid a sail. We were sailing away, looking for princes or something.'

I could think of no sane response to any of this.

'Time comes we get bored. I climbed out. The sides were slippy. As I climbed out, I kicked the lid and it fell. Nasreen was inside. I tried to open the lid but it was heavy, stuck tight. She tried to push it up from inside. She wasn't strong enough. So I shouted to her that I'd get help, I'd find Asma. I started running, then I got lost and fell and when I got to Asma's house she was out, visiting her aunties.'

'Uh-huh.'

'Maybe I thought it was okay, that Nasreen would get out by herself. She couldn't, of course. The more you struggle, the more air you burn, the more $CO_2$ you pump out. Those unavoidable rules. By the time someone asked if I'd seen Nasreen, two hours had gone by. So I said I hadn't seen her.'

'Jesus Christ.' All the wet gone from my throat.

'I thought afterwards Asma would be my special friend. Just us two, that we'd be close. But those unavoidable rules.'

'What happened?'

'Nightmares, Riz. Night after night. A frozen ghost coming at me. For years, I didn't sleep. Failed my exams. Missed college. Took years to get turned around. Till I joined the police. Found loyalty, purpose, honour. I still have nightmares.'

In some mad, female-bonding world I would have held her hands, said strong, nurturing words. Mixed a few more tears into the world's supply. Wholly beyond me. Just sat with my bone dry lips, my garbage can hair. While the terrifying tranquillity of her brown eyes probed my machinery.

'Tell me about your hotel room.'

'Uh?'

'Is there anything interesting about it?'

'Those kids thought so. It's right across from the conference place.'

'I know, Riz. I work there.'

Bone-weary, dead-feeling—what could I say?

'Your room, Riz. Is it like other rooms you've stayed in? Is it different?'

'You're talking at me like I'm Special Needs.'

'I'm sure your needs aren't special.' She pointed at the furry walls. 'This is a high security facility. The tourist bus does not come down this street. We can hold you for ninety-six hours, the judge won't say no. We can hold you for fourteen days if we think you're a terrorist. Or charge you with something—then, who knows? Tell me about your room, Riz.'

'It's a suite, okay? Bedroom, lounge, bathroom. A minibar with no booze and a TV full of crap.'

'Anything else?'

'Nasty pictures. A door that links to my neighbour.'

'The neighbour who gave you the catalogue?'

'That guy.'

'You have a door to his room?'

'Connecting door. Locks both sides. I guess for families and stuff. Can I go now?' I got whiney. 'I really need to lay down.'

'How well do you know this man next door?'

'I just met him. At Rothko. We stay at the same hotel.'

'This door, you know it leads into his room? It's not a cupboard or something?'

This massive weight pounding my head. 'I told you, it locks both sides. I opened it.'

'Why?'

'To see it wasn't a cupboard. You run security. You know how the rooms are laid out.' She did, though. It didn't fully land with me then that she would have to know. 'It was unlocked when I got there.'

'What do you think will happen to that girl?' She mimed tying a top-knot.

'Is she here?'

'The regular police have her.' She paused. 'Of course...'

'What?'

She flexed her long, fine fingers. 'There are ways to make things easy. For her. For her friends. It's a busy week and you know the police—we never like paperwork.'

'I don't understand what you're talking about. I want to sleep. I want to pee.'

She leaned in, her delicate mint and lime scent noxious on my bubbling guts. 'The kids you tried so brilliantly to make friends with have a problem. Problems can be solved.'

'Was she really locked in the freezer?'

'What?'

'Your friend. You left her there?'

'Shall we empty your pockets, Riz? Find some drugs.'

Even I wasn't so dumb to come back on that. Probably, I looked helpless.

'Your neighbour, you get along with him?'

'He thinks I'm annoying.'

'So do I. Do you and he get along?'

'Okay. Well enough.'

'I want you to do better. I want you to talk with him, ask questions. Sensible questions. I want whatever he says to come back to me.'

'You want me to ask what he's doing here?'

'Ask what he's doing next.'

'What?'

'I'm always around the hotel. The officers know where I am. Tread careful, Riz, keep your neighbour talking. Say yes, I'll make some problems go away.'

'Oh yes?'

'I'll get a car to take you back.'

'Really, though? The freezer?'

I got ladled into a plainclothes car, Mum beside me and I'm licking the metal, faking sleep so we don't talk. I mean, she talked, always. Talked a bunch of puke. Moist concern and phoney upset, for the benefit of the driver, who couldn't care.

At the hotel I got scooted so fast through the lobby, only just recall telling her, 'yeah that's fine, I will have a shower.' Though it's four in the freakin morning. Another new goon on patrol, so she couldn't beat me down in the hallway. She said we'd talk, which meant she'd beat me down first chance she got.

I fell inside and bang! I'm wide awake and quaking. That righteous terror: someone searched my room. Not turned over, not trashed, my unexciting lingerie wasn't rowdy on the rug. But I felt, as they say down Mexico, *un escalofrío de invasión*. Someone had very much done my room. The surfaces were wrong. Creases I made in the sheet got shifted sideways. How the window blinds hung, minutely skewed and the dust, the thin dust of the top-most slat, dislodged onto the carpet. One steel clasp on my luggage felt clouded from a touch not mine. The upturned glass I used to listen at the wall sat a quarter inch off. That's how I knew it wasn't The Man. He wouldn't make those mistakes.

Forgetting I smelled like crap, the time and everything, I gave my fist a workout on the connecting door. I had to speak with him—who else knew anything real?

He didn't surprise, nor disappoint. A pressed white shirt, a repp striped tie, razor creases, his jacket casual-laid across a chair back. With the table lamps gleaming in his eyes, he looked set to grip any problem and make it sorry. 'What's the time, Peaches?'

'Um, I dunno.'

'It's a phrase. It means what do you want?'

'Do you have a minute, please?'

'I ain't sleepy.'

Through my matted hair, I got a breeze from the open window. The windows were sealed, triple-glaze. A glass box with a sheet of glass inside. In each room, one window was hinged, I guess for maintenance. Somehow, he got it open to the early morning air. An ashtray and hard pack on the ledge, with this spiffy old gold lighter. He caught me staring and flicked a few sparks. 'Clark Firefly. There's not two of these in the city.' He offered a smoke. It seemed wrong to refuse. I held back my hair from the flame and his look said he understood what he saw. 'What's eating you?'

'Someone searched my room.'

'That's something. You sure you not just forgetful?'

'I left my Rothko ticket on the minibar like that.' I made a rectangle with my hands. 'And when I got back it's like this.'

'You notice that?'

'Yeah.'

'What else?'

'Door handle's smudgy. And there's dust from the blinds on the carpet. You believe me?'

'I'm starting to. Sure it's not just the maids getting sloppy?'

'Maids don't clean at night. Anyway, the mirror's still gunked with makeup.'

'So you been spun. Who you think did it?'

'I'm in trouble with the police.'

He looked at me a solid way, blue eyes keen as drills. 'Do you want to say more about that?'

So I told him—in a way that made me seem heroic—about the kids and the warehouse party, and getting hauled by sharp-dressed Salwa. He poured me a generous slug of scotch and stared at the conference building—part-lit, quietly humming with pre-dawn business. I didn't say about Mocha. It felt better not.

'Look at those guys with guns on the roof,' he said, matter-of-fact.

I freaked and jumped sideways, my voice at helium pitch. 'What if they shoot you?'

'That would be unfortunate. What else she say, this detective?'

'She wants us to be friends.'

'How delightful.' He studied the guys with guns.

'She wants me to ask you questions and tell her the answers.'

'A double-cross? You're a riot.'

'What?'

'So whatever I tell you goes back to the lobby detective?'

'No. I'm not like that.'

'What she offer you?'

'Nothing. Except those kids get out of jail.'

'The kids who think you ratted them out? You want them free to come find you?' He raised his glass to the conference building.

'She took the catalogue as well.'

He couldn't, I guess, show amusement. His skin didn't give. But those shoulders wrenched around, an over-large show of indifference. 'You really had a busy day. You let her take it?'

I felt stupid under his calm, blank eyes. 'Does it matter?'

'It's unsporting. But not the end of the world.'

'Why does she want the catalogue?' My head buzzing. Searchlights came at me.

He ran his thumb around the ashtray, scrunched it with persuasive pressure onto the back of my hand.

His sooty thumbprint, its dizzying swirls, gleamed as I flexed my fingers. Some ungodly tattoo with moves of its own. 'I'm sorry, I mean, you in trouble now?'

'Here's what you gonna do, Riz.' That voice, charged with unavoidable authority. 'You play nice with Detective Abaid. You don't want her to think you're a flake.'

'You think I'm a flake?'

'What I think about you comes higher up the dictionary. Now, scram. I got work to do. Hey, Riz.'

I turned at the door, deadbeat and shoddy.

'You might think about taking a shower.'

# 5

I woke not merely dead, but really most sincerely dead. It was, like, 7:30, two hours' sleep, the pillow damp where I crashed with wet hair. Through triple-glaze, engines revved. A helicopter hung on the sky.

Terrifyingly sick, I rolled onto the floor, dragged myself to the can for a therapeutic hurl. Can't remember drinking what I brought up. Sweating, my body rivered with booze. Collapsed against the bathroom wall to focus on breathing. My heart all kinds of noise, my head yelling I was in trouble. Cold, though the sun was screaming. That bone-deep cold, solved only by arms around you.

Spewing again, I was hungry. Couldn't face the restaurant so I checked the brochure, my sweaty hands stripping the glaze. Room service didn't seem pleased nor interested to serve me. They'd see what they could do.

Nothing on my phone. No one asking was I okay. Couldn't remember if I gave Mocha my number, but thinking of her wasn't great. I crumpled. The carpet smelled chemical. I smelled dumb. Troubled by notions that, outside the room, people expected things of me, I wanted done with it all. But it was just starting.

A very sharp knock at the door had me grappling furniture, trying to haul myself up. I staggered to unclip the chain and this sharp, belligerent whiteness knocked me backwards. *Lo que blancura.* This woman pushing the trolley, this incredible white waitress. Thick snowy hair, ice-white eyes, teeth from a dentist's wet dream. Skin like cocaine. Whitest woman I ever saw. In a waitress suit. In my room.

'You order continental breakfast?' Her voice Baltic, deep and cold.

'I order croissant.'

'Yes.'

'Yes?'

She pulled the cloth from this manifest banquet of toast, fruit salad, juice, pastries and a tower of pancakes dripping gunk. A tall pot of coffee flashed with the sun. 'I put here.' She bustled through the room, a white streak across my eyeballs.

'That's great, uh…'

'I am Lilija. I have feedback form.'

'What?'

She brandished a slip of card from her pocket. 'You fill form. I put in contest. You can win free stay at hotel. I can win new phone. You fill form.'

'You have a pen?'

'No, we use blood.'

This godawful pause while we gawked at each other, me hungover and dirty-sick, her some slice of the arctic. Then she laughed, sharp enough to crack ice. 'Your face, yes? Of course I have pen. You say there, your waitress is Lilija.'

When she left I was sweating so hard I had to change my shirt. I ate the toast, drank the coffee, threw up again, and went out.

Couldn't tell if the guy patrolling the hall was new or just differently tailored. He watched me the way they all did, irritated by every move. Mocha said body cameras. Maybe the hallway goons had body cameras. To betray me in real time to Mum, to Abaid. All in it together.

But, still, I went to see Mum. Because I was a brat with a fix on self-preservation. I couldn't let horror fester. No doubt an official report got written about me. No doubt they had every detail. I had to pass for contrite.

Mum and the children of Satan had long finished breakfast. Damn early birds, she already took a treatment and looked more lethal than ever. TV played. They were horribly happy together.

Little sister deigned to look up from her cartoons. 'She looks more horrid than ever.'

Kid brother—a fifty-year old fronting as a little boy—studied me with his signature condescension. 'Your breath smells, you know. It smells of pizza.'

On a good day, I'd cheerfully sling them through the window. Right then I couldn't even speak.

Doing nothing, but with great vigour, Mum paused long enough to check I was still wasted. Still, in fact, the daughter she couldn't stand. 'I won't ask that you watch for your brother and sister. I doubt you're capable.' She listed—as I knew she would—the names of other mums' daughters who were, factually, capable of minding their snot-face siblings. Who got good grades and showered often and didn't have a secret stash of black bras. Girls who didn't get hauled by police and wouldn't, as a matter of decency, wind up in slut-prison doing favours for soap. She didn't actually say that last bit, but it was there.

By then, I was thoroughly baffled why I'd gone to see her. I threw one last attempt to shift the mood. 'How's Dad? I mean, how's it going?'

She gave me her top-of-the-mountain glare. 'I'm not sure we should speak about your Father's work. Not with the company you keep.'

'Is she going now?' This time, little sister didn't even look at me.

'I just asked how he is. I mean, he's busy?'

'Of course he's busy. The high-value dignitaries arrive today. The global loan fund president is, I believe, at the airport now. The police are being most helpful.' Then, brisk as a newsflash, 'The city is filling with the most vile scum. As you well know.'

My cheek stung and she hadn't hit me yet.

'Your Father works very hard for you. He pays your keep and covers your messes. You need to start being grateful. I'm keeping a log of your antics for Dr. Grover.'

'You're spying on me?'

'Of course not. You can't spy on your own children, foolish. I'm your parent, I have a right to know where you are.'

'You know,' kid brother waylaid me at the door, 'you should try to be liked. You'd be happier if you were liked.'

Could have laid low, watched TV. That, or more aimless mooching. Down in the lobby the maître d' laid a gracious veneer on the hubbub of pointless bigwigs checking in. Each had an entourage of lean young men, shades welded to their eyes. Picking a path round the VIP mob, I saw it again: that wall between me and the rest. They had skin in the game. I was nowhere, locked behind glass. Sometimes I thought I could cheat it, scrape next to popular girls with their uptalk and shine. But, always, they stayed remote from me. Behind glass.

Tried not to get seen, but the maître d' saw everything. Excusing himself with polite condescension, he glided across the lobby to where I stood, indecisive at the door. 'Miss Montgomery.' His bowling cheeriness knocked me down. 'You're going for a walk? Marvellous. The forecast this morning is especially fine. I must say, we've got the weather. London is angelic in June, don't you think?'

I had no playbook for any of that. I just gawked, cracking like static.

'There's so much to see. A trip on the river, tea at Fortnum's, the Palace of course. I have the most splendid itinerary for you. Please.' He did that thing, sweeping his arm behind my back, propelling me without contact, his authority the more fearsome for being so graceful. Security guys out front so wanted to cuss and jeer me. But they had to zip it, in the maître d's terrific presence.

'There's so much you have to see.' He herded me into Knightsbridge, switching abruptly to a close, rapid tone, barely audible against the sound of Russian girls spending fast money. 'Someone called for you early this morning, Miss Montgomery. A very angry young woman. The police at the checkpoint turned her away. Fortunately, I was outside and asked what she wanted.'

'Oh yes?'

'She wouldn't tell me her name or leave a number. She wants to see you, Miss Montgomery. At the Rothko exhibition, at eleven o'clock.' He checked his watch. 'I suggest you go now.'

It was bewildering—this grown man, earnestly mumbling at me. 'What if I don't?'

'You should, Miss Montgomery. She was very angry and very clear she wants to see you. If she comes back and tries to make trouble, our friends here will get irritable. That may be worse for you.'

'For me?'

'I run this place,' he said surprisingly harshly. 'These are not usual police. They're not here to care for lost children.'

On the Tube I checked my clothes, fretting every notch and seam. When they searched my room they could have done any mischief. Bugs smaller than a pinkie nail. They could stealth a bug in an earring, a button, a label. They can stealth a bug in your head. I was their cyborg, their sight and hearing. Not just cops. Mum had spies. Pressed against cold metal, I scanned the train. All around me, watching, recording, building my file for Grover. Dr. Grover, this evil psychiatrist, his place in the hills a bajillion miles from a signal or navigable roads. Kids with problems go there and come back good citizens. The dirtiest kids come back sweet like honey. I did two summers. Eight miserable weeks apiece. I was ten and thirteen. Got pally with kids who were Satanists on Monday—come Sunday, they're babbling Jesus. Girls who opened their hearts to me, one dose of the doctor's mixture they didn't know my name. All cured and happy, primed for glittering futures. Not me. He fried my brain and that hurt a lot. But I stayed as I am. Third time with Grover, I wouldn't be back.

So with that stuff riding my mind, and cops all around, all I could cling to was Mocha. Even if she hated me, we could be friends. When it gets that I have to see someone bad, that itch becomes my blood. I don't have choice, I can't resist. So it didn't matter I spent my cash, till I hit the paydesk. 'I have to get in. It's important.'

That same old cow reprised the same look as before. 'Of course it's important. It's a paid-for exhibition.'

'Important for me.'

She did this pantomime, leaning, squinting, checking the line. 'And the twenty-two people behind you.'

'There's someone I need to see.' By then, I was scratching my sleeves.

'Me too.' This dumb voice behind. 'Rothko. I need to see Rothko.'

So I trudged away, scratching my sleeves, getting stared at. She'd be pissed if I didn't show. Most likely, she was still pissed at getting arrested. But the police didn't hold her more than four hours. The maître d'said early and for him that meant properly early. None of which got me into the National Gallery.

In the dusty sunlight of Trafalgar Square, between jugglers and dickwad mimes painted gold, a school outing was getting its fix those weeks before summer. The boys, blazered and neat, squinted respectfully at that monstrous Victorian frontage with its not-right Purple Brown banners. The girls, summer-shirted, fun little clips in their hair, plaid skirts dead on the knee, except the basic rebels who hitch it high for the fans. I felt years older than them and perhaps didn't look my best, by the way some glared and sniffed me. As they filed up the steps to the massive porch I tagged behind, rigging my alibi as some classroom helper, a friendly figure the ADHDs could relate to. Some kids namechecked what to see—I never heard boys talk Rothko before. A girl said she might cry and I was working on getting beside her, because I'm a comforting presence, oh yeah, when this meaty body blocked my light.

Naturally, everyone turned to watch this make-believe uniform cut me from the group and insist to know where I was going.

'To Rothko.' My voice too small.

The security guard chewed his face around. 'Weren't you just turned away from the ticket line?'

'No.'

He looked mournful. 'Yes you were. Just then. You were turned away for not paying.'

'I'm with these people.'

Teachers shoving kids at the door, to quarantine them from the crazy.

'So sad,' a girl's voice said.

'Oh,' said another, 'you see a lot of them in the city.'

'You might want to step outside, miss,' said the guard.

I itched poisonously. 'I've got to get in.'

He gently stroked his goatee, flexing its bristles. 'Then buy a ticket.'

# 6

The National Gallery in Trafalgar Square, London, covers around 150,000 square feet in a group of interlocked buildings with a service yard behind, accessed from Orange Street. By the time I found that yard I was sweating bad, a whole body itch stripping my skin, as voices screamed that I failed Mocha. Sure, as I trespassed into the yard, there were cameras on the high walls. London, factually, has more cameras than Pyongyang. But if you try to hide, a camera's more likely to find you. Guys who watch cameras are poorly paid, bored, frequent sociopaths. Excite them, they get excited. Stroll like it's regular business, they don't twitch from their zombie shows. A warm day and the loading bay shutters hitched-up, leaking attractive shadow. It's no crime if it's no effort. And I had an appointment.

I climbed the ramp and ducked under the shutter, a story about a job interview coalescing across my truth zone. The dark inside that concrete cathedral stopped me dead. This horrible moment of snakes, strung from rows of rubies. Big viper heads, jaws primed. Didn't scream, I was too scared.

By little, my eyes got tuned to the dark, milky from that slash of sun beneath the shutter. The snakes retreated to nylon ropes, steel hooks one end, and the other high among pulleys lined on a track. A steady red light on each crank where it was electric. So here was where art arrived, in transit from truck to wall. The paintings I loved and cried for. Still waiting for someone to stop me, I pushed through a door and lights came up—yeah, I jumped. Just motion lights. A room rammed with wooden A-frame boxes, stuffed with foam, labelled: Guggenheim, MoMA, Houston—the Chapel. I could hitch a ride to the Chapel. They'd know me. The crates that brought those pictures together again, for just those days. Somewhere a voice, older, New York-sounding, inflected with back home. His voice said to me, "It's a risky business to send a picture out into the world. How often it must be impaired by the eyes of the unfeeling and the cruelty of the impotent."

And I said, 'Same for a daughter.'

And then I got busted.

This young guy in coveralls filled the doorway—shaved sideburns and those dumb black earrings like bathplugs. He looked me over the usual way: angry and confused. 'What are you doing here?'

My cover dissolved under pressure. 'I got lost off the tour.'

'This is a restricted area. These materials can't be tampered with.'

'They're boxes. I haven't touched them.'

'You'll have to come with me.' He spoke so soft and looked so mad, I saw another long night with the special police. He chivvied me into this passageway—wipe-clean walls gleaming hard under striplights.

'Where you taking me?'

'Security.'

That figured. I'm a magnet for uniforms. At the intersection of one industrial corridor with another, a guy in jeans and a dude shirt stood goldbricking with his phone. He froze at our approach, eyes on me. A skinny young dude with a devil of charm.

Coverall guy took the high ground. 'Jake. Another one snuck through the discount entrance. Shutter wide open. Again.'

Jake nodded, vague and wary. 'I'll, er, get onto it.'

'I'll do it. You take her to security.'

Jake stared. Christ knows what he thought he saw. 'Come with me, er, Miss. We'll get you where you need to be.' Of course he couldn't touch, but did some hand jive encompassing me and the corridor. 'I'm, er, Jake.'

A twist of nausea told me where this was going. 'I'm late.'

'Crept in for Rothko, yeah? He's something. I mean, he had it.'

Maybe he really thought that. It's not an uncommon opinion. I was itching fit to scream. 'Yeah, I seen the show.'

'Makes you cry, yeah? Makes me cry.'

That was when I decided I needed a gun. For guys who say they cry. 'Look, is this far?'

'Security? It's near the Impressionists.'

'I need to be somewhere else.'

We reached an electric door. He stroked the keypad.

Other side, old Germans in long shorts were psyched for the Romantics.

I tried for some voice that was clear and not aggressive. 'Hey. About me breaking in and stuff. I know it spoils it for the rest. Tell you, though, I most actually need to be somewhere. I won't tell.' Icky taste of conspiracy. 'So I just cut along, yeah?'

Guys don't get it. They go faster to get nowhere. 'Haven't told me your name.'

'I literally don't have one.'

'You're cool, you know. I finish at six.'

What in hell? How ill did I look? 'I'm on curfew. I got a tag. Cops watch me. Look there.' I ran, shaking him off among stinky veterans.

There's art and there's art, and that place had plenty of both. The business is a butcher shop. The art world recognises nothing until it's dead. No living art comes to market. I barrelled through tragic sculptures and those video rooms where a guy drops a brick on an egg. Through the halls, down marble stairs, sweatily fugitive. No doubt messages flashed between radios: 'Suspect speeding through the Pre-Raphaelites. Head them off in Dada'.

Way past eleven, I hit that edge of desperation, my clothes scratching me up, sweat fouling my trainers. I sweat acid; my sweat is, like, three and a half pH. That's why I get rashes. Right then I was raw.

Mocha was where I knew she'd be, by the line for Rothko. She must have remembered I said about that. Remembered some good thing about me. She had her hair tied two ways, top-knot and tail, this grungy dress and trouser combo, black dress over skinny check pants. A denim jacket. A denim jacket is the finest thing a woman can wear.

I approached gingerly, trying to get cool in five seconds straight.

Her dark, mid-Asian eyes picked me up and held me—she had the most heart-stopping stare. I smiled—we were friends, right?—across the uncaring crowd.

She showed teeth. 'Let's talk.'

'In the Warhols. No one'll find us there.'

So I had her to myself, and there was no smile, no acknowledgment we'd been through stuff together. 'Sorry, I didn't get your name.'

'I didn't tell you my name. I'm not safe anywhere near you.'

That seemed odd, where she was so cool and together. 'I'm really okay. It's just my head. I'm not a risk to people.'

'You got me and my friends arrested. You got us beaten up.'

'I think we got off on the wrong foot.'

'Tell me something.'

Five for ten, she wasn't asking my number.

'Why am I here?'

'It doesn't matter here. We can't talk in the Rothkos.'

Those burnt sienna eyes had me. 'Why am I here today?'

Strong, beautiful, so much older than me. 'I'm sorry. I don't follow.'

'Me and my friends got arrested last night. Thanks

to you. We got slung round the walls. I got sexist and racist abuse.'

'Racist?'

'Then we got let go. Shoved out the door. Can you explain that?'

'Maybe you did nothing wrong?'

'And where were you? With the Syrian detective.'

'Syrian?'

'So I'm told. She took you away. We got kicked and let go.' She blocked the light. 'That interests me.'

I had the story, I'd set things straight. 'Shall I tell you a secret?'

'What will it cost?'

'I'm working for the police.'

Really, I didn't expect she'd say that's awesome. I thought maybe I'd have to explain, before she was cool with it. What I didn't expect was she'd move so close, her elegant, tawny face near mine. I felt her spit when she said, 'Tell me something I don't know.'

Which is when I got fatally distracted by some monstrous acrylic Elizabeth Taylor. Worst crap I'd seen.

Mocha's deep voice punched words at me. 'You are a filthy grass.'

All I could do was gape at the walls, at these horrible items.

'You stitched us up.'

'Not factually, not me.'

'What?'

'Police had you under surveillance. Lucky I was there, huh?'

'Is that some new type of lucky?'

'They were going to bust you anyway. If I hadn't been there, you'd still be inside.'

'You stupid little scrape.'

Why was she so horrid when I liked her? I really liked her. 'It's not you they're interested in. They want to know about my neighbour.'

'What about your neighbour?' Her voice climbing to bewildered rage.

'The guy next door. I said yes to spying on him, which got you out of jail. Win-win, huh?'

'How old are you? Twelve? Don't you know anything?'

I wanted to see her. I looked forward to it. I took chances to get there. I was glad she waited for me. My little heart made noise in her direction. But all I got were scowling lips, shouting at me. Watched by multiple prints of a jerk in a wig. 'No, it's okay. I got it figured.'

Why was she shouting? Why the confusion? 'What are you talking about?'

'I'm not spying on the guy next door. I told him about it. So now he knows the cops are watching him. Pretty neat, huh?'

Surely she had to crack, give me that smile, call me a heat-seeking missile. As if she'd been showered with glass, every point of her gleamed.

'And I could do the same for you. Be your agent, y'know? Feed the cops a line and tell you their moves. Next time they rock up, you're gone like smoke. Real ninja, huh?'

She grabbed hold—a firm, awkward hold—of my

jacket and shirt. Six inches close, screeching at me. 'You're mad, do you know that? You want me to trust you when you betray everyone you meet? First time I see you, I get busted. I don't know this "guy next door" but you betray him. You were up for betraying your Father last night. You betray the police. There's nothing about you that's any use. You don't even smell right. You're a stupid, noisy, clueless little kid.'

Now it wasn't wholly true there was no one in the Warhols. There were slackers, gonking at soup cans and Lennons and whatnot. And more and more eyes came into that space the louder Mocha screamed at me. Someone took a selfie with us, doing the peace sign thing. And all of it on camera. So security came to find us.

Two big guys, flanking this kitten-killing woman, barged through the art-challenged gawkers, glad at something to do.

'What's the problem?' That woman's teeth, I swear, were sharpened.

Mocha dug her fingers into my chest bone to push me aside. Felt kinda good. 'Who wants to know?'

'I'm the duty security manager. You're causing a disturbance.'

Looking round that room was disturbing. 'Have you actually seen these pictures?'

'Many of our visitors are students. Some have travelled a long way to study the collection. They have a right to do so without cat fights.'

Mocha fixed up. 'I'll give you cat fight.'

Need propelled me to her side. 'Yeah, you and who's army?'

One of the lunks scratched his goatee. 'That one. She didn't pay. I slung her out an hour ago.'

The other guy pointed a bandaged finger at me. 'I saw her walk round the back. She went under the shutter.'

Mocha glanced sideways. 'Real crime wave, aren't you?'

Did she mean that? Was it good?

'Leave now, both of you.'

That rebel woman, she wouldn't give. 'What have I done? There was a dispute, now it's over.'

'It is? Cool.'

'The gallery reserves the right to refuse admission.'

'But you didn't.' Mocha folded her arms. 'You took my money.'

'She's been refused.' Both lunks looked at me.

'Terms and conditions are at the desk. Any refusal to comply can lead to removal.'

'Show me that written down.'

'Take them outside.'

By then, a lot of cameras were going off, the woman shouting at tourists how photography was forbidden, while these two amateur bruisers tried without touching to shift us. Quite a crowd gathered. Even folks blind from Pollock felt the static. This milling mass of people, expanding through the galleries, watching us get slung.

The whole time, Mocha did that voice—smart,

brittle, full of each clause and subclause of her rights. Intelligent, confident, courageous I guess.

I so wanted things to be okay when we landed outside. Even if she kept shouting at me, that was okay. What I needed was her to listen to what I was saying. Once she did, things would be fine.

By the front doors we got into this comedy scuffle, the guards trying to move us against a crowd trying to come in. Mocha loved it: a big audience had her shouting about injustice, how there was no freedom, no place for truth. Sort of stuff gets everyone feisty. People looked at her and looked at me. I slandered a few modern artists—I felt ripped and full, thoroughly present with this raging woman.

The guards flanked us down the steps, me dazzled by de Chirico sunlight, Mocha, perhaps, imagining some crowd the size of a city, electrified to inventive destruction by her words. A fly Marinetti. Then the guards were gone, and ordinary daytime closed around us, and some old lady's dog was yapping its balls off.

'That was awesome.' I just wanted to be relevant to her. 'I loved that.'

'Stay away.' Her fierceness burned. 'Don't you hear anything? Stay away.'

A black cab idled on St Martin's Lane. Mocha took two strides to the kerb, yanked the door. I sprinted over. She slammed the door quick. 'Get some help. You need it,' she yelled as the cab pulled away.

Desperate, I scouted another cab cruising up from Whitehall. I flagged it down, waving both arms.

The driver looked concerned. 'Where to?'

'Follow that cab.'

'Piss off.' He drove away and, I'm sorry to say, I stood there, waving my arms far longer than a sane person would.

If I need somewhere and don't know the way, I don't think about it, just walk. I waded through the knotty swamp of drunk twelve year olds making Leicester Square their own suburban heaven and burrowed back towards Haymarket, avoiding each sprightly window where, reflected, I looked crap. By then, my head was screaming. I did everything to show Mocha I was for real, yet she made me stupid and small. I sprung them from jail. They'd've still been there if I hadn't played nice with Abaid. That's the thanks you get for caring.

I found the Italian cafe again, though it gave me no pleasure. Its pavement tables scattered with crumbs looked abandoned, bare as a break-up song. Varnish on the door seemed just to cover the scratches. The specials board with its pink and white chalk scuffed from careless coats. I wanted to take Mocha there, snug at a tight little table, explain how I wasn't so bad, not bad like she thought. This is how a cheerful, friendly young woman gets crushed. Still burns me thinking about it. About what happened next.

So I trudge inside and this different waitress—dark and fresh as they all were—lands me at this bare little table for one. None of the lunch menu made sense and I had no cash anyway. The hunger chewing my gut wasn't regular hunger. Around me, lives in progress, the other side of the glass wall.

The waitress expected something, so I said, 'Double-espresso and ice water, please.' She looked at me before gliding away. My phone caught another of Mum's abusive messages. She felt obliged to send them so I'd know nothing had changed. I messaged a girl I knew back when. Guess she was busy.

The waitress brought my sad little order, holding the tray shoulder-high how a man would. She swung it around and hitched down the drinks, so close to me her midnight hair brushed my cheek with the grace and indifference of a cat. Her scent so fine, I could taste those groves and hills and the quiet at dusk. 'I still go to my favourite place, bella, thinking he might return some day.' And she actually smoothed down my hair. The sweetest, loneliest touch.

Two seconds later I'm crying. That thing girls do, when they fan their eyes and the tears go away—I can't do that. With the tears, I started to whine. More I cried, more I whined, shaking like from a bad tab. Couldn't see my coffee, never mind drink it. Couldn't hear anything outside the noise of my chest. Not till the next table was shouting.

'Shut up.'

By then I was slapping my arms.

'Cut it out, Jesus Christ.'

Scraping a sleeve across my eyes revealed these monstrous men. Biblically ugly: two of them, necking beer, glaring at me.

'Quiet down, we're drinking here.'

Grief and snot balled my throat. I started choking.

'Jesus. What's wrong with you? Shut up.'

Enough was a feast. 'Make me.'

These ham-heads gawked.

'Make me shut up.'

The one with the wider vocabulary said, 'You be quiet, little girl. We're busy.'

My sinews tingled. 'You want a fight?'

'You what?'

'I'll give you cat fight.'

He nudged the other man's arm. They stood and my bowels made ready to drop. But they slung cash at the table and left, jogging elbows.

Tried drinking my coffee but my arms were rubber.

Then a cuss and someone scraped a chair. A summer-weight jacket swished by, growling at me, 'Way to go, you muppet,' as he jogged to the door.

I looked around for the waitress. Guess she finished her shift.

# 7

Shocked it wasn't even three o'clock when I got back. I headed for the hotel restaurant to score a late lunch. After ten minutes, I felt the truth of what Malcolm said: Sitting at the table doesn't make you a diner. I had to ask, 'Is the maître d' around?' before the waiters even gave me salad-space.

By then so hungry, so tired, so done with the day, I wasn't even fazed by the laminate people. If I worked at it, I could claim acquaintance of maybe a half dozen of 'em, at least for the smallest of small talk. I had no interest in Dad's work, but it so pervaded my time at home, with Mum always swagging how she was tight with those wasters. Which is not to say anyone said 'Hi' or sent a pint of scotch to my table. Too busy, too crucial to check the fried redhead who kept turning up everyplace.

For once, I managed to eat something before Abaid showed up. By now she didn't bother with small talk before getting angry.

'Where were you this morning?'

Borrowing from Mum's playbook, I sighed and sipped my juice. 'At the National Gallery. I had a fine time there. How are you, Detective?'

Without asking, she colonised my table. Any which way, she was neat: that tight, unmarked skin, those rich, unyielding eyes. Disappointed, vexed with me. 'I'll be better when this circus leaves town. After your lovely morning chewing culture, did you happen to go to a cafe? Did Mr. Rothko perhaps upset you?'

Shocked at this blasphemy, I choked on coleslaw. It blew back down my nose, left me croaking. 'I maybe went for coffee.'

'What I heard, there was more wailing than Jews at the Wall.'

'What?'

'What I heard, some young female made such a racket, grown men walked out.'

'They threatened me.'

'They're suspects, stupid. One of my team had to tail them down to Herne Hill. Where he lost them. We don't do this for fun.'

'I got upset.'

'Are you nothing but hormones and screwing up?' Where people sit, waiters pounce. Everyone's a tip jar. She snarled at this bloke splashing shadow across her. 'Yes?'

'Are you eating, madam?'

'Obviously not.'

'Can I get you a drink?'

'Mint tea.'

I thought, be a pal. 'Yeah, I'll have that.'

'Do you want…'

'Go.'

I watched his retreating bumfreezer. 'That was harsh.'

'Riz.' When she zoned, she zoned tight. 'Remember last night? We have an agreement. I make problems less problematic, you stay friendly with your neighbour. Remember?'

Looking deep into me. 'Yes, detective.'

'And some problems went away. For now.'

'Yes, detective.'

'So where's your neighbour, Riz? Where is he? This minute.'

'I don't know, detective.'

This blinding freshness muscled through. Making a goddam thing of it, the waiter installed two silver teapots, ripe with essence of spring. 'Mint tea, Madam, Miss. The mint is sourced from our exclusive supplier in Hampshire.'

Detective Abaid's shoulders crackled. 'Well, tell your exclusive supplier he's doing a stand-up job.'

The guy moved away fast, security goons smirking at him.

'So you don't know where he is? Your friendly neighbour. You don't have a clue? That girl last night, if we pick her up again, might that make you pay more attention?'

'Really, I don't care.' What's one more lie?

Her eyes gleamed, the blackest pools. 'Are you capable of cogent action?'

People asked me stuff I couldn't process. Stuff that fed scratchy nits under my skin. Against their clamour, that bright-smelling tea tasted of getting younger.

'I pulled your file.' So matter-of-fact I didn't get where she was going. 'Impressive range of interventions.'

Dragged back from some field of stinking mint, I lapsed into lame protest. 'You pulled my medical record? It's confidential.'

'You don't make a secret of it.'

'The stuff with the doctors.' Horrible, frightening.

'I read the case notes.'

'They're private.'

'Yes,' she said gently. 'And I'm the police.' Shovelling aside cups and plates to lean into my face. 'I need a win, Riz. I need it now. I can't go back empty-handed.'

Old timers and shamans tell you they feel, right before, in their bones, a change to the weather. I felt it, the heat of the dining room dropping away, an icy-cool chill swirling through. A frosty rebuke to fear and its petty agents. The Man was there, a plastic bag clamped under his arm. There beside me, sharper than ever, constructed of swellness and style. 'Miss Montgomery.' He dropped this neat little formal bow. 'And this is? Some friend? An older relative?'

'Detective Chief Inspector Salwa Abaid.'

'House detective?'

'Police detective.'

'Thank you for your service. I have something for you, Miss Montgomery.' With extraordinary delicacy, The Man unfurled the plastic bag, eased out a shrink-wrapped Rothko catalogue, daintily gripped by his fingertips. 'Don't want sticky prints.' He pressed the bag on a passing waiter—'Burn that for me, will you.'—

then gently slipped the shiny slab down beside my tea. 'I've been to Rothko,' he said, grandly. 'Inspiring, uplifting. Wasn't even a wait line. The security lad told me there'd been some kerfuffle. People fighting over Warhol. It's a different world. You wanted a catalogue, Miss Montgomery? Take this, I won't read it. Have you been, Detective? You should. They have Chapman Brothers.'

What made it awesome was the straightness of how he did it. A minute ago he wasn't there. Now he was the whole room.

Salwa had her share of fronting up, more than her share. Yet southern blood, her stew of place and culture, made her run hot: she hadn't his ice. Yeah, she was impressive; she had no feel for how it was a game. 'I don't think we've been introduced.'

He manufactured a dopey shrug. 'Just a traveller. Passing through.'

'You know Miss Montgomery well?'

'Hotels throw people together.'

As her hair shook back, her neck showed its hard tension, sinews solid as banyan roots. 'You remind me of someone. Tom Eliot. If that's his name.'

'Detective.' His stony voice couldn't have held more charm. 'If I see the unfortunate Mr. Eliot, I'll break the news of our resemblance gently.'

'You want tea?' Okay, I squawked too loud—I was enjoying the show.

'That's kind, however I need to call my Mother. I always call this time of day. Smells good, though, what you're drinking. Smells of England. Maybe later, Miss

Montgomery?' He gripped Salwa's hand, though she hadn't offered. 'A pleasure, Detective. Hope it works out for you.'

As he stalked the dining room, he slapped a few backs, waiters and diners, the sleekest pal at the club.

Salwa got peppery. 'If you knew half about Tom Eliot, you wouldn't be laughing.'

'He's not Tom Eliot, though. He said so.'

Mum was shopping and Dad, for sure, screwing a juicy deal, so I crashed without getting hijacked. More at home than at home, I washed my face then choked my guts. The TV. Sudden. Loud. Pumping cartoons. I hadn't switched on the TV. Yet insistent, little kid yackety-yacking came blaring through the lounge.

Flung around, I crashed against some solid body, lurched into the shower screen, banged my head, bounced back and these hands—strong, determined hands—wrapped around my face. Massive weight doubled me down. This nicotine finger probed my lips. Opened my teeth to bite it and, no lie, those damn fingers got hold of my tongue, yanked it forward. 'Nnnnnnn nnnnnnn nnnnnn nnnnnn.' I paddled behind with my fists. But he had me tight.

'Can it, Riz. It's me.'

'Nnnnnnn nnnnnnn nnnnnn nnnnnn.'

'It's so I don't hold you anywhere more controversial. Listen. Your room is bugged, so you need to be more fly. There are agents at the conference building watching this place with lenses that could find a pimple on Rita Hayworth's ghost. So act like you know. I am not offended you're working for the cops. Seems to me you're more a hindrance to them. But I have work to do, Riz. I have as much patience as Karen Carpenter had dinners. If you want to be useful, stay prepped and don't mess up. Now I'm going to loose your tongue because frankly it doesn't feel nice. When I do you will not shriek nor cry. You will remember the police, this minute, are listening to whatever crap is coming from that TV. And when you talk to yourself late at night they are listening still. Letting go now.'

I fell forward, grabbed the sink. Couldn't face him with teary eyes. 'You really hurt my head.'

'There's nothing in it.'

'Why don't you just smack me up? I'm fifteen, I should go down easy.'

That did it—I knew it would. 'I'm sorry Riz. I had to stop you talking. I didn't plan you'd hit your head.' Those vibrant arms turned me around. He brushed back my hair. 'It shouldn't bruise. It's the shock that hurts, not the dose.'

'Yeah, I know about that.'

He stepped back, his remarkable, expressionless face unyielding. 'Sure you do. You know about shocks to the head. What you think of psychiatrists, Riz?'

'Pushers of lithium cola.'

'What you think of lithium?'

'Someone else's idea of okay.'

He rubbed his thumb across his chin—the strong guy looking thoughtful. 'You're very attached to being crazy aren't you?'

'I'm not crazy.'

That rare glint of amusement. 'You're something.'

'My room's bugged?'

'Yes.'

'Is yours?'

'Oh yes. They stick these things the most obvious places.'

The cartoon din was scratching my nerves. 'So how come I hear you take calls, if you know you're bugged?'

'Because orderliness is everything. I'm not supposed to know, because I'm not a person of interest. I can't trash bugs I'm not meant to know are there. How could I do that? I'm a regular guy.'

He was bugging me with his swerves and evasions. 'So what's your business?'

'Regular business.'

'And you want me to be useful with that?'

'I'd like nothing better.'

'Okay, Mr. Regular, what you want?'

'I think it would be lovely for you to spend a day with your folks. Together. Maybe go to Hyde Park.'

'With Mum?' It was horrid.

'And Daddy.'

'He's working.'

Now the ice set in, now the voice froze. 'You get him unworking.'

I never, my whole life, told the great diplomat to let up. 'How I do that? It's a freaking presidential summit.'

'A girl always knows daddy's weak spot.'

'And what do I get?'

He opened the door. This ghastly kindergarten comedy came bouncing through. 'Now you're thinking.'

'Hey.'

'Why don't you open your mouth a little wider when you speak.'

'You don't like how my tongue feels?'

'And you're not crazy.'

'I don't like your finger taste. Why they so foul?'

'Copper solvent.'

Such a weird thing to say, so seriously said, and my mouth tasted of nail varnish remover. I know how that tastes. 'Copper solvent? What for?'

'For guys who handle loose change.'

It was soothing to know my room was bugged. Where I had doubt and pressure, now I was sure. That vacated space for a stark, new worry: how to do the most out of character thing my neighbour told me to do. Pitching to Mum for a family day seemed a fast track to more time with Grover.

Dad had this Exec Assistant. She was crazy not the least good way. I saw her when she stopped by the house to prep him for some big shebang. Rose Ducati, a name you might expect on pay TV, though no way glitzy. Real serious, real pissed at Dad for a boss. Mum hated her. But because Rosie wasn't young nor restful on the eye, Mum synthesised complex reasons to hate her. I mean, I'd just say she got loaded off lens fluid, something easy. Mum said Rosie had methodology incompatible with delivery, her thoughts unstructured and anyway, who wore slingbacks that shade? All because Rosie worked a tough job, while Mum got paid to stick around.

On Brompton Road the evening masses were shopping after work. I chose a clothes store for the call, figuring the jump-up music spilling from every corner added urgent authenticity to my message. Still working what that message was when she answered the phone.

'Good evening, can I help you?'

Helter-skelter I leapt to it. 'Is that Ms. Rose Ducati?'

'Who is this? How did you get this number?'

Off a wanted ad. A dog meat tin. A toilet wall in Mezcal City. 'I was asked to call you. This is the hotel nursery. For the kids.'

'Who are you?'

'I'm the nurse.'

'You have a name?'

Nurse Alex. Nurse Betty. 'Nurse Ratched.'

An over-long breath sapped my nerve a little. 'What can I do for you… Nurse?'

Surrounded by twinks breathless at cut-rate merchandise, I closed my eyes and let loose. 'Mr. Montgomery asked me to call. You know how it is. Such a busy guy. He was saying to me: "Elvira, I've been doing this vitally important work a lot of years now and this is the first time I've been away with my family together. It troubles me, to my soul, how the children have grown and I hardly saw it occurring. How they've blossomed. The small ones, I mean. Not the big one, obviously. You hear such terrible things these days," he says, "Kids drift, get restless. All for the lack of a parent's caring eye. I don't want my kids disenchanted and fall through the net. The small ones, I mean."'

The receiver clattered, then a muffled voice. She was speaking with someone across her shoulder. How slack.

'So Mr. Montgomery, he sees the setup we have here. The ball pool and Gymboree, our breakout pound where we fish for alphabet letters. Our Columbascope where kids match the outlines of places to the dates the white folks got there and he says to me, you know what he says?'

A weird, throaty sound. 'I really cannot wait for you to tell me.'

'He says it's good. Excellent even. He gives us a heap of cash so the tank fish don't die. He says: "I can see that my kids are cared for. Included and cherished and not left to cry with paintings. But you can't outsource everything, Elvira. You can't outsource a day with your kids at the park. Bright eyes. Simple joys. You can't buy that. So that's what I'm doing tomorrow. I'm having a playdate with my kids." So he asks me to call you, Ms. Ducati, because tomorrow, Mr. Montgomery, that fine man, he's taking a day with his family.'

There was quite the dilatory silence.

'So that's settled, huh?'

'I'm not sure I follow you... Nurse.'

'He's got a date tomorrow. With his kids. A playdate. So he's not coming in, okay?' The firmness I tried playing into that got muddied by me getting bumped aside by blonde princesses who only walk straight lines. I showed them the finger. They didn't turn to see it.

Some restless crackle fuzzed the connection. 'How do you mean he's not coming in? We're halfway through.'

Some puke-green halter-neck stood on my foot. I spat into the phone, 'Look, lady, we're more than halfway through.' Rosie's breath was giving me nettle rash. 'Mr. Montgomery loves his kids. He wants a day with them, okay?'

She sighed and pulled an obvious move. So obvious I hadn't seen it. 'Why didn't he tell me? He was just here.'

The dynamite charge faded from my head. I went lame. 'He forgot. He was going to call. There's an issue with his phone. His eldest chewed it. She's problematic.'

'Yes, he says that often.'

I had no strength to come back. 'Got to go,' I whispered. 'There's a fat kid face down in the ball pool.' When I killed the call my phone was hot and slippy, misty white from contact with my acid skin.

Bright colours around me, skirts and tees, rock star brands, fake music. Chrome walls framing females my age holding tops and jeans against clothes that looked just the same; arguing fit and colour; uploading shots of friends dicking round with shades and hats. Packing memories to solid bonds with women whose friendship would see them through adolescence, through college, into their bright wedding days and divorces to come. The jobs and promotions, hard work and successes, the houses and babies and lingering, wistful affairs. I had no clue where I was.

Some crop top girl's pierced navel caught the light: nice little hanging sapphire. Her belly so tight, the chain knocked as she walked. Just nice looking.

'What you staring at, you scabby cow?'

I was the freakshow, always.

Then a deep, serious voice—a security guy, who likely watched me the whole time. 'If you're not buying, move to the door.'

'I'm buying.'

'Move to the door.'

Second time that day getting slung. But with a hundred young women streaming their fans, as the guy steered me through tempting heaps of junk. Then blinding whiteness punched my eyes to the back of my skull.

Lilija's dress, so white it burned, showed a solid length of icy legs that ended in white ballet flats. Her face and body and clothes so without colour, I broke a cold sweat.

She marched over, the security guy hesitating to cross her spectral tail. 'Hotel girl, ha! You have breakfast. Remember, I am Lilija.' She swept close, the security guy melting. 'You buy clothes? You need clothes. I am here for raincoat.'

I shaded my eyes from her dazzle, relieved as suburban twinklets stared in terror. 'Raincoat?'

'Will not be summer forever. Now is good time to buy.'

'I'm just leaving.'

She gauged the security guard. 'He thinks you are thief,' that same cheerful, unsurprised way. 'Your eyes, perhaps.'

'My eyes?'

'He thinks you are strange. I walk you to hotel.'

'Aren't you getting a raincoat?'

'I walk you now.'

Couldn't look at her—swear, she glowed. Only 8pm and I was preoccupied with horrible things. Family dinner, getting Dad to take a day off, going with him on his bloody day off. It would have been preferable if The Man took a swing at me and I say that as someone slapped by blondes with puffball hair.

As we walked, this most extreme blonde seemed happy throwing off arbitrary statements—'The traffic, yes? This air is soiled. Those shoes. She will die a cripple.'—while I scouted for anyone relevant-looking. A person of interest who might know where to find a coffee-toned woman with complex hair.

The service road behind the hotel was guarded by bored police. An alleyway branched off to the storage yard. 'We take shortcut.'

Because I wasn't listening, she yanked my arm with Baltic vigour. I didn't protest. I was numb. Dad talked about me to Ducati. He talked about me more than he talked to me. Sure, I was dumb to be surprised.

She dragged me to a service door, the step pegged with coffee cups, cigarette ends dissolving to black sludge. Lilija stroked the pin pad. 'Trouble now. More trouble soon.'

'You what?'

'You hear many voices. Not all tell truth.'

'What you saying?'

The door rumbled open. 'For snack, for drink, call room service.'

Even the strip lit corridor, with its hospital paint and

signs about safety and service, couldn't dim her shine. Tried to ask what she meant, but those corridors were the noise of a vast machine at full gallop. She pointed at a door marked Front of House. 'Through there.'

'Excuse me?'

'I go. Get raincoat.'

Other side of the door those laminate people, busy guests, watchful police, and the maître d', owning it all.

# 8

Sweating so fierce, the cops heard every drop ooze into my waistband. They saw when I picked at my skin, when I walked figures of eight. I hadn't wanted any of it. I just wanted Rothko and someone nice to talk to.

When I'm on the down swing, I shower in boiling water. It hurts. It's soothing. I don't tell people. They get the wrong idea. With the voices and not understanding stuff, and the showers and crying and awkward things, people think I'm someone they don't want to know. Which isn't nice, because really I make a good friend.

To fake the right mood for my prying audience, I found the least objectionable music—soft non-rock—towelled and blowdried, brushed my hair soft and respectable. Cleansed my face, never pleasant, made discreet repairs to the startled freckle-scape. Dressed so orderly, I could have passed through an Amish village. Messaged Mum about dinner. Felt sick and held it down.

Stepped onto thin ice in the restaurant, trying to walk like I was keen for what was to come. An uplifting day, getting slung from places and attacked. Not even Mum with a spat-on Kleenex could scrub my smile. I slid beside the sprites of damnation, Mum and Dad waiting for me to barf at the walls. To this day, I have no clue what else they expected.

Kid sister, reliably pissy, pulled her chair away from mine. 'Why's she here?'

'To have dinner,' said my pleasant mouth.

Kid brother gave me his look of the scientist aghast at developments in the jars. 'You washed your face.'

'I do.' I kept cranking that smile. 'I wash every day.'

'No you don't'

'I do.'

He chortled—that damn kid could chortle. 'You go days without washing.'

'She makes stinky marks where she sits down,' said the miniature female, confusing herself with me.

Dad didn't need to say anything. How his fingers gripped the table said it all. Mum picked up the signal, 'We are here to have dinner together. To enjoy some time with your Father, who finished work especially early to be here.'

Dad looked modestly proud of something that goldbrickers do every day.

'I not seen him on TV.' Kid sister and her coven worshipped the pixels.

Dad gave his wasp-chewing smile. 'That's because I'm not on the cartoon channel.'

So confounded bizarre for Dad to crack one, the fact it was wholly unfunny got lost in the baffled malaise. We dutifully cackled, except sister who didn't get it. Through his days of meeting guys with rare earth metals and intricate banking arrangements, I guess Dad could bust the odd quip to seal a deal. After three sets of translators tongue-tossed it around, the table would smile and our most corroded leaders could breathe again. Basically, his job was greasing, and he was aces at what he did.

As one of the maître d's finest served greenish soup-like liquid, I began the grind of putting my plan into orbit. Sadly, it needed kid sister. Young and dumb, bemused at steep surroundings and multiple tables of linen, kidlet got entranced at laminates worn as eveningwear. A stretch from her usual pleasures of pussy cat toys, watching TV, and slipping off to the bathroom to play with her poop—as I happen to know she did because I happened to hide in the closet.

Anything subtle was lost, so I pinched her leg.

'Yoww.' She fetched up her little fist. 'Why she do that for?'

'Because you're deaf. Listen.' My nervy peripheral glance caught Dad's suspicion and disgust. Between that and baby sister's over-sharp eyes, I had to work fast. 'Ask Dad where we're going tomorrow.'

Shrewd, that kid, with a meanness to break planets apart. The grownups slurped their soupy slick, pretending it tasted okay. Brother watched his ill-matched sisters, a Zen master of gnarly smugness. She narrowed her baby blues. 'She can ask.'

Back came the waiter, swagging his à la carte, claiming to have things worth eating. I'd got a salad habit, to distinguish me from less-evolved eaters of hot food. And because even that kitchen couldn't screw salad. And because—shamefully, yes—I'd seen thin London girls and was feeling sturdy.

Mum had this rule where phones, games and music were banned from table. Not at home, for sure, with Dad never there and Mum not caring. But at the hotel we dumped on the aghast eyeline of important people. Important because Dad knew them. We had to front as a functional family, the sweet-arse family that sits to eat with civilised conversation. Every so often some cheeser would stop by the table, pat Dad's shoulder, say a quiet word. How business was done: bajillions in hard currency, moving on the nod. People told me that was the real world and inside my head was fake.

I was skull-cracking bored, waiting for their horrible, meat-heavy food to arrive. Sister was bored, lost without her plush pussies and the bratty princesses she called friends. Brother was okay, I guess. He treated the family as an experiment.

Brain-starved, even Detective Abaid swinging a warrant would have been a distraction. Or The Man—never knew when he ate. Dad took another call. At table. Where there was a rule. He was allowed. He was the dog and we owed him.

I nudged sister's arm as she tried to negotiate the kids' menu mac and cheese, god help us. Under orders to eat human-style, she was sludging her fork through the cheesy cement when I hefted her elbow, catapulting peas at the table. 'She did that. Not me. She.' Those horrid blue eyes sliced me wicked. 'She is not wanted. She should go home.'

'I told you to ask where we're going tomorrow.'

She flung back her callous blonde hair. 'Daddy, where we going tomorrow?'

From experience, I can swear that had the impact of setting an incendiary load freestyling downhill. Dad wasn't over-patient. He employed Mum to deal. Though with his youngest he took a 'strong-man-good-with-his-kids' approach, as one would with a peachy blonde muffin. That we were visible to his pals also bothered him. 'What do you mean, honey?' His tone the sound of a dessert one might feed to mental patients.

'She says. Are we going somewhere?'

Mum fixed me an awesome glare. 'You shouldn't mislead your sister. You are always doing these things. Telling lies, causing confusion.'

'I didn't tell her lies.'

Sister started bouncing. 'Are we? Are we going somewhere?'

Took a breath deep into my lungs. It hurt. I had to deliver. 'It would be kinda nice,' totally wrong voice: defensive, fissured, too girly to hold weight. 'You know, spend time together. Quality time. Doing stuff.'

Brother stepped into the blistering silence. 'What does "stuff", as in "doing stuff", properly mean?'

I knew from TV a kid could shuck off the wreckage, go feral, find a life that isn't an endless lousy day at the zoo. It was no help, sitting at that table. My head buzzed bad. No amount of Grover's candy would clear it. 'Doing stuff outside.' I sounded close to tears. 'A day at the park. That would be nice.'

Right then, Dad's phone rang. To avoid our hate and confusion, he thumbed the screen, stood without excuse and stepped into the greenery.

Mum laid me a look ten thousand percent worse than I thought possible. To her, I was an outcome no input could straighten. 'You know how important this conference is. You know how your Father's work matters. Not just to keep you at that school and to keep a good home. It matters for everyone, do you understand? It matters globally. Does that even catch hold in your head? You're all about your stupid, dismal wants. You've embarrassed your Father, you know that? I suppose you're proud of the hurt you cause.'

'Is she leaving?' Sister sounded so smug, I nearly put my fork through her head.

Nothing to do but fling oil at the flames. 'No, honey, Dad's leaving. He has to go. He's packing right now.'

Even dislocated from her pussy-cat quilt and the predatory munchkins she called friends, her junior cockiness blazed with extraordinary vigour. She didn't bother to process what I said, just attacked me. 'I don't like her. She's mad.'

'I am not mad.'

Mum weighed down on that. 'Amelia.' The next table half turned, saw it was us and went back to grinding through dinner. 'That is enough. We don't have those conversations.'

Brother, with his creepy cool, snaffled kid sister's soda.

'Hey.' She slapped him.

Commendably, he slapped her back.

'That's enough.' Mum's total incomprehension, faced with these animals. What was she even thinking, having kids?

Dad bust back, mightily pissed. Little Miss Evil's showy tears way out of line with a lost soda and genial crunch on the arm. Mum's attempts to shush her met with that foot-stompy, 'Shan't,' which pretty much was her playbook. Brother mooched off to some other family, boosting onto a chair to join them, enviably at ease with any social situation.

Lousy with anger, Dad waved his phone, part testimony, part weapon. 'Do you know who that was?' His voice that guy wearing tight pants on long-haul.

He was looking at me. 'Uh?'

'Ms. Ducati.'

'Uh?'

'She had a call from the hotel nursery. The nursery that this hotel does not have. A nurse, who does not exist, told her I'm off work tomorrow. Apparently, I have a playdate.'

Kid sister, that devious bitch, quietened her sobs.

'This is major. We have five days to agree long-run commitments. The global fund president arrives tomorrow. And someone thinks it's funny to make prank calls. I do not have time for this.' That professional freeze, man he had it. But he should have checked the thinness of that ice.

'What do you mean?' Mum's poise and obsessions made a hellraising combo. 'You mean you're too busy for dinner with us? Is that what you mean?'

'He's always busy.' Sister, muffled in Mum's well-scaffolded chest, hit the right blackmail notes. Just as if I got her head wired up, like I tried to when she was a baby, when the paramedics were shouting at me.

'You see?' Mum stopped blinking. 'You hear what the child says? How many birthdays have you webcammed? How many shows have you got tickets for and I've had to take them alone? The children need a Father, not a colonial presence.'

You can hate someone six ways to Saturday and still be glad they did what they did.

Cutting to the source of our disarray, Dad zeroed on me. 'Why did you call Ms. Ducati?'

'I just said we could go to the park.'

'The park.' That took kid sister unerringly from Mum's arms to collide with Dad's legs. 'Can we go park? She doesn't have to come.'

'We're all going.' Mum got there before my jaw started flapping. 'We're having a day together.'

'Oh, come on,' he breezed, his superior diplomat skills useless against her frustration.

'No. We're having a day together. We're having a bloody picnic.'

Among faces who knew him only as a sharp operator, Dad had no call but to fold. His eyes cut me raw, a plain look of disgust and repulsion.

Across the room, my brother was snarfing another kid's soda.

Such a strange, out-the-blue evening, me and Mum on the same side, couldn't end with easy sleep. So I snuck back to the lobby.

Just as the guys standing watch were a specified type, the young women who worked the front desk had a slim demographic. Long blonde hair with a swipe, or dark and swagged in a bun. Brimfull of starch and smiling—never at me. The young Polish miss working counter that night seemed disturbed I should even be in the lobby.

'Hey.' I tried to stay sisterly with them. It didn't help. 'You have a paper and pen, please?'

Her look said she got born sometime in the future, where such things were unknown outside the museum of the twisted mind. 'Paper and pen?'

Lost for how else to explain it. 'Please. Paper and pen.' We eyeballed each other. 'To write someone a note.'

Antsy, she rustled around for a hotel notepad and corporate pen, staring the whole laborious minute it took me to frame a message.

'It's 10:15,' I wrote, 'and I'm around by the big clothes store. Meet me please if you're here. I'll wait 15,' scribbled over that, 'I'll wait 20.'

'Hey.'

That pulled her eyelids right back.

'Can I get this delivered, please? I've written the room number here.'

'Delivered?'

'To this number. Like, now?'

I cannot express, not straight nor dirty Spanglish, how puzzled she looked. *Desconcierto total.*

'*Przepraszam?*'

'What?'

'You want what?'

'This piece of paper. To this room. I'll pay.'

She called some lanky jerk whose face of shredded

burrito registered doleful resentment when he realised she didn't need him and I did. I gave this boy an absurd piece of money to do something I could have done, if I wasn't under such heavy surveillance.

Stumbled through the front door, the earwig jockeys trading unpleasantries about me. I got pulled at the roadblock.

'Are you leaving the building, Miss?'

I already learned, with armed police, it's so not the point to say we're already outside the damn building. 'Meeting a friend, officer,' I volunteered, swift as a snitch.

'It's late, Miss. Does this friend have a name?'

But I hadn't learned not to freestyle. 'Why? Are they wanted for something?'

He gave me that put-upon look that goes with fronting other people's obsessions. 'DCI Abaid's particular orders.'

'Particular?'

'Who are you meeting, Miss?'

'Rose Ducati. She's cool. There's kids love her more than their stuffies.'

'I'll tell DCI Abaid.'

I grinned some cheese-grating way and managed to get round the corner before my spine turned to mush.

The big clothes store had not long shut, the last customers trailing sacks of must-haves, the staff clearing up, horsing around, music pumped after-work loud. The window display had these mini dresses, black and red and gold. I wore a dress once, the time I got let loose at a family occasion. Never forget that sense of feeling hobbled. My legs only get seen by the smart and stubborn.

I had nearly no experience waiting for someone. I got my phone and threw a pose to look busy and indifferent. No missed calls. My friends had hectic lives. Catching the store's free wi-fi, I checked the news—amazed how much paranoia existed outside me. Lot of trouble coming to town. Activists, hackers, attackers, angels of anarchy come to make hay. Tree huggers, real mothers demanding an end to '-isms'. Slogans and bogus celebrities resetting the protest key. War against floggers, tax dodgers, and toxic bloggers. Autistic achievers and Guy Fawkes believers. The raw and the awesome and not one thing they said meant shit to me.

And yet, a woman with byzantine eyes and hair tied two ways. I'd join her army whatever the war. Call me Ishmael.

That fedora suited him swell. A real man in a real man's hat. His fingers shooting the pavement. Guess he was handsome. Women's faces maybe said so. I don't know. I don't have that equipment. I felt his electricity though. The pulse that warned the serious to go careful.

He was angry. 'I got your note. Do not write stuff, ever. I burned it.'

So flattering, that I sent him a note, that he took the trouble to burn.

I didn't say go anyplace. He walked and I walked and we walked together. He walked on the outside, facing the traffic. Hadn't felt so protected all week. Still, that unfinished business. 'You shouldn't have hit me.'

'I said sorry about your head.'

'There was no need. You can trust me.'

He flipped back his jacket, easing his hands in his trouser pockets. 'Yeah, and you so pally with cops.'

'I'm not. I had to spring someone from jail.'

'And is someone happy you did that?'

'Not really.' Wilfully, I shifted away from those thoughts. 'You can trust me. I did what you asked. Dad's taking a day out tomorrow.'

'And that's true because?'

'Ask his Exec Assistant. I got her number.'

'You still have room for improvement.'

Strolling the big streets, plate glass, white lights, high altitude. Along Sloane Street, we stopped at a yacht place—yachts for the lavish city. That store had extraordinary models, four feet long, three decks, sixteen portholes, a damn swimming pool with miniature loungers and cushions. Like, not just a pool on a yacht—a pool on a model of a yacht. Drenched colour pictures—interiors Mum would literally kill for. Emperor beds and chrome kitchens. Floor lamps with gleaming jet hoods. Staircases, eight seat couches. Rugs thick and hairy as a dead bear. On a yacht.

The Man noticed my hungry breath. 'Mostly it's guys drive these things. Mostly, they don't own them. You have your people call up the broker and say, "I'm taking six Russians and twelve beauty queens to Polynesia," and these guys'll have something waiting at the end of your private flight. Privacy and control. That's where these happen. You get the right people onboard and it's privacy and control.'

'You been there?'

'Sure. And it's as glittering as you'd expect for a fistful of Euros. Not for me, though. I'm a regular guy.'

Real night came down: neon, hallucinogenic. Happy couples, arms locked, picking their perfect futures from store windows. Drunk girls, aimed at whatever. Some of the protest crowd, off-duty, young and dazzled like everyone. I took his silence for encouragement. 'You know, I have a horrible life. This week's not making it better.'

'You have a fine family and a prize role as a stoolpigeon.'

'I never wanted that. Either of that. They're not fine. He's never home. She fronts as a princess when she's his bitch. And those other two stains are so not my business.'

'That why you so tight with the lady detective?'

'I told you. She offered a deal. If I keep tabs on you.' Felt weird, me keeping tabs on this confident figure. 'And that's not even the worst. I'm going back to Grover.'

'Doesn't sound like going back to Cali.'

'California?'

'Columbia. Who's Grover?'

'Just the most evil bastard that ever put electrons through a kid's brain.'

'I'd bet there's stiff competition for that.' At Sloane Square, he watched the sluggish traffic. 'Riz, don't ask my advice. I'll only tell you one thing. You don't like the situation, you change the situation.'

'What's your situation, mister?'

'Sometimes the king, sometimes the jack. As we

cross this street I'll tell you something and you will not turn around.'

'My life's so toxic.'

'Focus, Riz.'

'Bloodsuckers, wanting a piece of me.'

'Riz, back to the concrete streets, okay? As we cross to the fashionable King's Road, we are being followed. Don't turn around. We are being followed by two officers, tricked out as young dudes. They think they do not draw attention with their summertime beanies and camo shorts. They are mistaken in that.'

'They're following me?'

'They're following me.'

That seemed harsh. 'I'm following you. I'm keeping tabs. Don't they trust me?'

'Shall we ask them?'

'Following you? So where you going?'

For a second, the freeze swirled off him. How he clenched, how his breath became ice. 'You're something, you know that? We got power here, you get it?'

'We got power?'

'We make their evening as lively or dull as we choose. What we do, they do. Like regular puppets.'

The situation bugged me, though. 'Aren't you bothered you're being followed?'

'We're being followed.'

'They're police. Don't you care?'

'Focus, Riz.'

Straight then, his phone gave up its solid, manly ringtone. He gestured me to stay quiet. 'Yeah. I been here the whole time. Someone say different? Well, of course there's interest.' Said this real arched-eyebrows way. 'If god's not at that conference, the heavenly choir slipped round the back. No it doesn't please me. Where? Oh that usual place. Say it loud for the guys on the wire.' He killed the call without warning, the acme of cool. 'I got to be somewhere.'

Not for the first, nor thousandth, time it struck me how other people had things to do. *Las reuniones de negocio*, or something near that. I had a fierce day and wasn't sleepy. 'So where we going?'

He dead-stopped. Gawkers and idlers swerved around him. 'There a plural here?'

No one wanted me with them. 'I'm okay, I'm no trouble.'

'You want to come with me?'

'I'm kinda free tonight.' It sounded goofier than I expected. I tried the failsafe freckly smile.

'Look, Riz.'

'This is rubbish. How do I keep tabs on you if I never know where you are?'

His lips hung wary. 'You're concerned that the police will think you an inferior snitch?'

'I said that?'

'And we don't want them to think that you're an inferior snitch. We want them to think you're a fine snitch. Don't we?'

'We do?'

'Come on,' he growled, walking fast. 'We ain't got all night.'

# 9

When he told me we needed transport, I thought he meant hail a cab. He didn't mean that. Off the King's Road, we brisked into Royal Avenue, power walking, which was okay for his legs, but for me meant an ungainly jog that worsened the awkward clamminess sticking my skin to my clothes. Guess the cops kept close behind. I don't know. He said he'd ditch me if I turned round.

In plain sight of this swanky horseshoe of ten and twelve million pound houses, he said, 'Looky there.'

'What?'

'Look with your eyes.'

'There's nothing.'

'There's a lamppost. See the lamppost? What's beside it?'

Some motor scooter, one-twenty-five cc four-stroke, though I didn't know engines then.

'Not some motor scooter,' he scolded. 'A Vespa.'

'Yeah.'

'And it's not chained up.' He was kicking the tyres, folding the stand. Easing himself aboard. 'Get on.'

'What?'

He kicked the thing into life. 'Put your dainty arse on the shelf. Riz, we ain't got all night.'

My palms, face, whole body sweating, that mild night a steam room. 'I'll fall off and get smooshed by traffic.'

'Well, no you won't.'

Shaking, scared. 'I got an echo in my head.'

He razzed the engine. 'You got nothing in your head.'

'This is bad. Very bad. When I get an echo, it means an episode coming.'

'I feel there should be punctuation between these words.'

'When I get an episode and there's an echo, a voice says do this, a voice says do that, and it's really bad because I don't know what to do and it's like I'm little and the world's all giants and I don't like giants.'

'There some dope you can take?'

'I got rights. I live unmedicated.'

So he gets off the scooter. 'You want to recreate a classic movie scene?'

'I don't follow what you're saying.'

'You seen *Vacanze romane*?'

See what he did? You can't kid a kidder. 'No, I hate Hepburn.'

'You surprise me.'

'She wrecked Holly Golightly. If you know the book, you know she puked on Holly Golightly.'

'Okay, Riz. You don't like Hepburn. She ain't fond of you. Get on the scooter.'

'I'm actually having an episode.'

'Yeah, you're psychotic as hell. You waved *adios* to reality. Get on the scooter.'

The handgrips were nice leather. The stitching came loose under my fearsome sweat. Put my feet to the plate, they were dancing with terror. First time I felt an engine shaking through me. Felt kinda neat. Then I felt something worse. 'Eek eek eek.' Lightning fast, I shot my hands down my sides, batting his fingers from my waist. 'Eek eek eek.'

'Stop it. Stop making that noise.'

'You put your hands on my body.'

'I'm holding you. It's how you ride these things.'

I felt horrible. Scuzzed. 'I'm not used to being touched.'

'By a man?'

'At all.' Burning tears slipped down my cheek.

'Okay,' he sounded angry. 'Let's do this, Riz. You have tidy hips. Indeed womanly, for your age. Now this is a Vespa and there's nothing else to hold onto and this is how people ride these damn things.' Then he reached around me, gave it the gas and everything came flying in.

I stopped screaming when he pinched my waist meanly. 'Shouldn't we be wearing crash hats?' My croaky voice got whipped apart.

'Turn.'

'What?'

'Now.'

Into traffic, squeaking our arse between cars, every

damn second a turn or lights or something. He leaned through me—pretty much through me—to capture the steering, bellowing every second to speed up or brake or something. The whole while, heat blazed through my head. Yeah, I felt scared and astonished—though busting 45 through traffic I maybe had grounding for it. I was seeing things, like, faces up close, with his voice yelling at me and voices yelling back, faces everywhere yelling, these coloured lines of burning metal flying into my eyes. Eating me, chewing me down. Stains, trains, photo frames of lighted towers, whipping skies dazzling me, blending me into this speedball of bones getting thrown at the distance. As controlled and unknowing as a shot from a gun.

His grip slacked and I pumped the gas. We blasted through street after street, till his fingers slammed over mine, controlling. I felt something though. I felt maybe this was something I could do.

Tearing up the riverside, the gracious reach of Chelsea Embankment, streetlights slung between trees, mystic globes stained yellow from leaves, laying ochre over my skin. Risked a glance at the water, dark and inviting, stretched out reflections of lights heading down depths, the pale columns of some drowned city. Spectral lights, shockingly close as The Man lunged by me to veer hard left onto Albert Bridge, a strange glinting web of chilly pixels. Terrifying view of water below and we're barrelling south by the dank emptiness of Battersea Park.

Took a while to understand the streets were changing. Lights faded behind, traffic thinned and expired. We were racing against a big box landscape, big, low, smooth, metal boxes—warehouses, closed and cold after dark.

He bellowed turn left and I managed it quite respectably. He bellowed stop.

'What?'

He mashed my hands into the levers, bringing on a heavy front brake.

He was off, lighting a cigarette. I sat at the kerb staring at my hands. They were blood red.

'I'll smoke this. And another. Then we go somewhere.' He glanced at the empty service road. 'Put the scooter round back. We don't know how far behind they are. Just push it. Walk it round back of the block.'

'Don't shout at me.'

'Stop squawking.'

'You can be quite unpleasant you know.'

True to his word, he dogged his smoke and lit another. 'I didn't mean to shout. I had a nerve-racking journey.'

Some small inspiration got into my head. 'You don't like that I was driving, do you? You don't like not being in control.'

He blew smoke across my eyeline. 'What a horribly perceptive young woman you are.'

So I lug the scooter round the side of this dark, blocky building. Grass and weeds grown pretty high, black, damp-feeling. Catch my breath, taste the silence. Body soaked with sweat, stinking. Quarrelling voices dialled down—a vague rumpus deep within. Feeling my breath, feeling the night. Reaching for Riz, the good way.

An expected—almost wholesome—shadow took out what light remains. 'We got to be somewhere.'

Just closed-up factories, empty roads, concrete silence. Even he gets it—his voice pinched small by stillness strung from power lines like scenery around us. 'We're going someplace,' he tells me. 'We're meeting people. I will say things, some of which you will not understand. Do not react. Do not squawk. You be less than a shadow at night time.'

'They dangerous, these people?' Kinda floating outside of myself.

'If you piss on their shoes.'

'That what you're doing?'

'What we're doing.' At a metal door, noise inside, heavy, serious noise, he gave me the nod.

'What is it?'

'They're speaking Russian.'

'You understand?'

'Only the parts that annoy me. Any last words?'

'What?'

'You have to shut up from here.'

So I flung a few cuss words at nothing and he slammed his fist at the door.

Silence. He slammed again. This little panel opened, this square of face, leather skin, dark eyes, hint of a moustache. The face spoke some harsh language.

The Man replied, the face vanished. We stood waiting.

'He's telling them I got luggage. They're arguing what to do.'

By then, it sunk in what a hole I got into. Not the detail, I didn't know then, just that the place was dark, quiet, the exact middle of Black-Form No 1, 1964. You think it's solid black, it ain't solid black. There's multiple layers of textured horror inside it.

The metal doors of the warehouse shook, clanking with someone unwinding a chain. This wicket door swung open, The Man made a gesture at me that said 'be cool'. He had to duck his head to clear the metal. I only just remembered not to trip over the step.

So, a warehouse, like millions the world over. Metal racks stacked with brown boxes, plastic-wrap stamped with export labels. A few oil drums, some hefty sacks. The place rigged with bare bulb lights slung from yellow power lines under the roof struts. Scuffling rats in the walls.

Ahead, a plasterboard table, cracked garden chairs. Five men. The leathered, hairy face that answered the door, two shadows back against a corner, and two others sat with uncomfortable ease at the table. Even I could tell the rest were muscle and these other two, the science. One had side-part hair and a sprinkle of stubble. He wore a suit, much more day-to-day than The Man's. The other had a greyed-out military frizz and cropped lumber shirt to show his tattoos: an exploding grenade, bullets, a big red star. Expecting The Man, they couldn't stop looking at me.

The geek suit said something Russian.

'English, please, gentlemen.' The Man's tough voice bounced off the racks. 'A little respect for our guest.'

The side-part frowned. 'What is this?'

'Let's do housekeeping first.' The Man turned to the muscle goon, who was damn near sat on his shoulder. 'Little room, okay, big fella?'

The goon got eye contact with his masters and stepped back.

'I'm troubled,' The Man declared. 'I don't expect to get called over the public airwaves, know what I mean? Spies everywhere, huh?'

Now geek guy looked troubled. 'You were followed?'

'Oh, I expect so, don't you?'

'You say we are careless?' He sounded vexed.

'I'm saying let's not get hung for the small stuff.'

'You have still not explained,' the suited guy stood, pretty solid, 'What is this?'

The old tattoos broke silence with what even I knew was cussing.

'English, please. And manners. He thinks,' The Man turned to me, 'you are some juvenile good time along for the ride. Very far from the truth.'

The older guy cussed again, smacking the table which shook impressively, being pretty much cardboard.

Then these two big figures—the other two guys—slumped from the shadows and my bowels made to drop because they were the monster-men from the cafe. Wearing the same clothes and ugly mood. One called me by a specific sexual cuss I don't much care for. 'What's she doing here? Her, we told you.' He appealed

126

on the Russians. 'She wrecked the downtown meet. We weren't lying.'

The Man considered these nutjobs. 'She did you a favour, fugly. That cafe was crawling with cops. If she hadn't made fuss, you'd be playing harmonica with the fat guy.'

They started chest-beating, till the old solider stopped them with a mad-dog bark.

Meantime, the young Russian dude stepped up. His eyebrows surfed their prominent ridges, his ears looked chewed, his cheekbones airbrush sharp and chin muscling through stubble. With a fat plaid tie and cufflink shirt, some celebrity brand cologne, he fronted as the brains. 'So,' he said, not polite. 'Tell us. What is this?'

'May I have the pleasure,' the Man tugged me forward. I didn't squawk. 'Of introducing Miss Riz Montgomery. Shake hands.'

The guy's hand felt actual plastic. Mr. Macho at the table threw a dismissive wave.

'So,' said the shirt and tie. 'This is social?'

'No, *tovarich*. Business.'

I totally had these five men looking at me. I mean, the wired guy—I felt how he was wired—stood behind and I knew he was looking at me. Drooling, I bet, some dirty-minded way. The two lard balls had my name now, sure bet they wouldn't forget it. The brainer guy looked bemused and trying to hide it. As for the military dude, who knew what he thought?

The Man busted the awkward pause. 'Miss Montgomery is helpful to you.'

127

'She's a child.'

The Man knew I wouldn't have that. He got loud, ahead of my breathing. 'She is blessed with youthful freshness. Compared to some round here. I assure you, she's very much deep with the set-up.'

I guess these particular guys had seen some life and believed things were possible. Plus, The Man's voice didn't allow contradiction.

To cover his soreness at getting wrong-footed, cufflink dude took a stroke at his stubble. 'Montgomery? Where do I know that name?'

The Man pulled me from the sweat-zone of the guy behind. 'Now you're getting it. Her Dad's the cubicle bunny running lengths for the global fund. When the president shows, he'll be as close to him as your friend there is to a gun.'

Cubicle bunny? I'd laugh if I wasn't dropping with fright.

'Don't tell me.' A cufflinked arm made a stop sign. 'While the Father oils the system, the little girl wants change. She has ideals. Pretty dreams.'

'She knows the arrangements. Timetables, room layouts, the logistic essentials. She's sealing the deal on the fund president's moves.'

'Oh, she's a cat burglar. Opens locks with a nail file.' Then he damn repeated it in Russian, though I guess with extra cussing. The military man had begun a slow wind to his feet, barging his way through the heavies.

'She got a date with her daddy tomorrow. Away from the office and out of my hair.'

'This interests us how?'

I had wondered if the old guy spoke English. Moving around the table, stiff as a tough guy hiding a metal leg.

'This pow-wow is your business. Not ours.'

Lot of breathing, The Man psyching up to be the biggest dog. 'I'll tell you what interests you, big fella. Getting this shit off your hands. How much you got? Enough logistics to put a hole through London. Enough hydrogen cyanide to wet-shave Iraq. Not getting caught—that interest you?'

The swell brainer fixed up a scoffing smile, weirdly resembling my brother. 'No? You say this little girl help with that too? She is a regular Joan of Arc.' He chuckled this gross way.

The Man affably bumped his fist against the guy's shoulder. 'Funny. No, she wouldn't know how to lose this stuff. Her friend does, though. The Syrian detective.'

My clothes sweat-solid, my head rattling. Words I wanted to say log-jammed under my jaw. Looking one to the other at glistening, dangerous men. They bunched tight, crowding us together. The two English heavies took up positions of close, keen hate.

The Russian's cologne like being dunked in Jason Statham's charisma. 'She is here? Is a small world.'

The grenade tattoo flexed as this grinding, spit-speckled sound came from him. A tobacco-black finger lunged at me—I flinched back onto the toes of the man with the moustache. He jabbed my spine gleefully. I didn't squawk.

'He says...'

'I heard what he says.'

The suit looked affronted. 'You heard, my friend. But I think your Miss Montgomery may have neglected her *Russkiy yazyk*. I enlighten her. My colleague says perhaps you bring the Syrian detective. Perhaps you are bait and betray us.'

If I say I was panicking, and couldn't hold my breathing, and swallowed snot, and was horribly conscious how far I was from the hotel, that's just a pin-prick of what I felt. Then business happened with pockets and something prodded my back.

Among it all, The Man said, 'Oh, please. You numbskulls jump if a lightbulb blows.'

'You tough guy.' The tattoos heaved up. 'How tough you in your grave?'

'Tougher than you, comrade.'

'Be careful, my friend.' The swell had a gun. An actual, up-close gun in his plastic hand.

'You plan to start shooting with the stuff you got here? You be careful.' The Man made a big, exhaling gesture to steal space. 'I'm not here to screw up your war. You're welcome to all that desert. Our interests happen to coincide on the guy who runs global loans. What I'm saying to you *borscht* heads is someone's here to pour sour cream on those little fires you're starting. It's okay, though, we can help with that. If you show some manners. Miss Montgomery got her Dad out the way. She can get "al-Sham five-o" out the scenery too.' Damn, he was having fun with a gun in his gut.

'You understand,' the Russian nudged the gun harder, 'our interests coincide, yes. But we are businessmen. We have product. Our buyers find it hard enough to move unnoticed.'

'They should maybe dress down a little.'

'Maybe you tell them that. If disruptive forces can be deterred, that is helpful. We and our buyers may remember your help, when your little deal is accomplished.'

'I want nothing from those crazies.'

'You have a conscience?' The Russian let loose this disgusting laugh. 'I shall tweet that. It will go viral.'

Tattoo man was growling again—growling and pointing and, without warning, smacked his palm into my shoulder. I flinched. I made no noise.

The death adder has the fastest strike. But the saw-scaled viper strikes to bite every time. The Man's grip bit the soldier's arm—his clean, limber fingers caught gnarled, painted skin.

'You understand,' the gun said. 'We are serious.'

'Sure.' The Man released the older guy's arm. 'You got talk. I got her.'

'What, precisely, is her?' This glassy female voice detonated clean as a Los Alamos bottle rocket. She was older than Mum, chiselled from rocks that saw too many hard winters. A soldier, from how she wore her sand-coloured shirt and grey trousers, from how she looked at these men with oblivious hardness. To be beautiful that way takes a lifetime. She sliced through the bad air. 'You are waiting for something?'

The Man raised his hat. 'Not anymore.'

This woman, fifty-five maybe. Tight, beige-yellow

hair, sinews built from wire. 'I heard you were here. I presume business?'

'With a little pleasure mixed in. May I present,' again, he dragged me forward, 'Miss Montgomery. She's the inside track.'

This awesome woman offered her hand. 'I am Dersima. I do not imagine these men have been so polite.'

Dersima's hand was scarred and cold, coldest flesh I ever felt. Burned my fingers. That cold, still there to this day. Told to keep quiet, I nodded like, yeah, I'm the inside track.

'Is it agreed or are you just arguing?' Her voice said she knew.

The younger Russian pulled some sickly charm. 'Our friend here was explaining the value of this... young woman. She has information. Her Father is lackey for the loan fund contingent.'

'He's a tool.' Okay, I was told not to speak—I hadn't, not for a long time. I physically couldn't hold tight anymore.

'Exactly,' the Russian looked put out. 'He's an instrument of the loan fund.'

'She didn't say that,' The Man groaned. 'She said he's a tool.'

A slight, confused silence. Dersima growled, 'Continue.'

The Russian glared like I actually pissed on his shoes. 'There is a complication. Abaid is here.'

'You know her?' It seemed okay to ask.

The woman's look schooled me. 'Your Father will tell

you, Miss Montgomery, of Mukhabarat, secret police. They are a monster even their masters cannot trust. So their masters keep someone to spy on the spies.'

'But Salwa's in our police.'

A shuffling of shoes and The Man said, 'Okay, show's over.'

'No.' Dersima cut in. 'She does not understand. She cannot be useful if she does not understand. Salwa, you call her, takes any guise she chooses. She has the trust of murderers with money to spend. She is mobile, as unconcerned for borders as a ghost. These conferences your Father works so diligently for, they are not just about the talk in meeting rooms. They are about this. All this around us. Justice and merchandise. The trades we make to win freedom. You think this is funny?'

The young Russian swallowed his smirk.

'We buy from whoever is selling and make friends among those who fear something worse. We,' she pointed at the Russians. 'We stand between you and something worse. We will not run away as you did from Afghanistan.'

That got the old solider cranking his chops, making muscular, vowel-heavy noise.

Dersima laughed, said something in Russian. The old guy tried grabbing the gun from his comrade. The meat-faced heavies barged them apart. Moustache-boy was growling.

'I am busy.' Dersima's voice split the room. 'Does this girl have information?'

The Man raised his palms. 'In her head.'

'It's no use there.'

'She's taking a day with her Daddy tomorrow. She'll get the blow on the president's moves. And while they enjoy family time, I'll pay her Dad's office a visit. You'll have what you need to get this stuff to Baghdad.'

'Tehran.'

'What?'

She gave a grim smile. 'You get a better kebab on Fayazi Boulevard.'

'Locals might be a tad awkward.'

'Shall we say goodbye, in case?'

Two men in camos appeared from whatever went down elsewhere in the building. Without saying or doing much, they showed us the door.

The Man raised his hat to Dersima again. 'Take it easy in those hot streets. Hug the shade when you can.'

Dersima had a glorious, wrinkled smile. 'I'll come to your funeral before you come to mine.'

'Most likely.'

'Me,' the old solider bellowed. 'I spit in you grave.'

The Man nodded cheerfully. 'Happy holidays.'

The rest just glared. Gun-chewing, violent men, glaring at me.

When we got outside and the door clanged, its echoes lost in the hollow night, I thought I might get a well-done, a good-girl, something canine. The Man ignored me, though, checking his phone.

From being numb—hysterically numb—my legs were bandy jelly. Palms burning, my armpits a swamp. A few drops of pee sneaked out. Swear, I don't make it a habit. 'They could have killed us.'

So he didn't answer.

'They could have killed us.'

That look he gave me, so often, like I wasn't right in the head. 'A guy driving an all-electric kiddie-car could kill you. You should overcome this delusion you'll live forever. I'll call a cab, take you to the hotel.'

'Take me?'

'I got somewhere else needs attention. Move, before they invite us back for shortcake.' He stalked up the barely-lit road.

I shook with his presumption that I'd follow. 'Hey.'

He didn't turn. 'What now?'

'The scooter.'

'The scooter?'

I had guns at my belly. That hardens a girl. 'Someone might be missing it. They might need it to get to work or the maternity hospital.'

'They'll claim insurance, get something better—why we even discussing this?' Again, he walked away.

'I'm taking it back.'

By then space opened between us. Guess he didn't want to shout, concerned we were still in the vicinity of people who hated his guts. And mine. Hated my guts more than his. He strode back, sick-looking in yellow-tinged dark. 'There's a cab at the road. You will take that cab.'

'I'm taking the scooter back.'

'You don't even remember where we got it.'

'Don't talk to me like I'm stupid. Of course I remember. My Dad's got six credit cards. I know the long numbers, expiry dates, and security codes. Of

135

course I remember the street where you stole that scooter.'

'I stole? It's your prints on the handles.'

'Arse biscuits.'

Took a second to retrieve his cool. 'I never heard that cuss before.'

'Are you helping me start this scooter?'

'Riz, I'm trying to get you back where you belong.'

'Mister, I have insects in my skin. I feel them. They are real. I will take back this scooter, okay?'

'I'm not babysitting.' He walked away.

No light at the back of the warehouse. Just the feel of tall, wet grass and that sense of how night moves, how dark has its own motivations. People inside with death as their business, while I faced this task alone. Paranoid, psychotic, yeah, but no slouch, I set into it a sensible way. I rolled the scooter onto the road, tried doing what he showed me to make it start. Maybe I hadn't paid full attention. So I got my phone, searched YouTube for how to start a scooter.

Punching and scrolling through no end of teenage kids ripping up car parks, pulling the handles head-high like wrestling a goat. Searched again and hit the wrong link—got videos of real hogs: chunky men showing off sport bikes and cruisers, BMWs, TMs, Kawasakis—what is it so cool about the word Kawasaki? Anger flexing my body, I stamped the kicker. It bit back. Vexed, I gave an almighty thunk with my heel and the engine got chuckling beneath me.

Pretty cocky at cracking that part of the deal, I strummed the handles. How hard could it be? I got us there didn't I? Went to ease my phone into my pocket and heard, behind me, the warehouse door crank open. A spasm of fear and my fingers hit up a biker video. The soundtrack kicked loud—Creedence: Sweet Hitchhiker. I banged the handles and the thing took off about fifty miles an hour, dragging me as Fogerty's highway vocals gave a somewhat misleading impression of where I was at.

Through terror, I managed the empty roads of the industrial section, throwing my weight and cacking my pants at generous curves built for trucks. Hit the junction as Fogerty bellowed 'Sweet hitch-a-hiker, we could make music at the Greasy King' or whatever the eff he says. Moving fast, shooting the dark, stood up on that little Vespa, screeching my face off. Traffic ahead and traffic behind, and above the noise and screaming, the squall of a siren.

Don't know what I'm thinking, I risk a look back—cops in a freakin Audi coming at me, lights blazing. By when I tear back around against the wind I'm five miles down the road. Ahead, brake lights pop for a circle of neon. With no clue how to slow down, I closed on those lights like Evel Knievel slamming in for a big one.

My magic beans was to slide through the cars, sling the turnoff and get back to town. Maybe lose the cops, if I dragged the right gaps between traffic. They were well-close by then, siren squalling, lights slashing me blue. Obedient drivers shuffled aside. I hit the curve at an engine-shredding sixty. Then up came the road and kissed my arse goodnight.

# 10

Blue sky above, tropic blue. Little spits of cloud like the Antilles strung around on a high breeze. Taste of grass, hot sun through my skin. Emerald trees and fields, ripe and heavy. Think I'm laughing. Kinda laughing. Maybe I cracked a gag or she did. Maybe we're just happy and laughing. Stretched flat in the meadow, Mocha propped on one arm, looking at me. Both laughing. So natural and easy to say, 'Come to mine.'

Quicktime, we reach a real pretty street, some quiet part of the city. Dense, warm air—walking through Tonatiuh's breath, as he travels the sky, renewing himself each day. Feeling reincarnated, like the sun god of old.

From the corner, I point to the attic that's my place: windows open, everything open, nothing locked away. The door to the rooftop balcony's open, see my red dress, my dancing dress, hung to dry, waving and twisting. You seen nothing till you see a redhead in a red dress. The building has one of those old cage elevators, with a clock hand and big black buttons. Higher we go, more quiet it gets. Warm and quiet. My place is simple, comfortable—a couch where I lay looking into Untitled No 4, best painting of a sunrise ever. Plain wooden table, bottle of wine, jar of olives. Nothing fancy. Nothing that makes noise. Mocha sits next to me. Feel her warmth. We breathe slowly, as one. We sit still. Together. Breathing.

'Riz.' Far away. 'Riz.' Coming close. 'Riz.' Swerving over my brain.

Godawful, so I close my eyes. But the goodness has gone.

'Riz, I don't have time.'

What there is: a machine counting heartbeats. My life as steady, sterile beeps. Another machine makes gushing sounds. Lot of wires sucked themselves into my body. This room, its walls a toneless grey. Big TV—solid, glossy black oblong. A cupboard and table with bowls and packets. A half-scrunched helium balloon stuck to the ceiling, the shape of a football with 'Get Well Daddy' in crinkled letters.

A chair pulled close to the bed and Salwa Abaid glaring at me. 'You're alive then? Back for more?'

'Have I been dead?'

'Not exactly.'

'I dreamt of heaven.'

'You had 30 mils of morphine. You probably flew there.'

'Am I hurt bad?' My face, I thought. Tried getting my hands up to feel it, but they were plugged with wires.

'You haven't broken anything.' She sounded disappointed. 'Video from the pursuit car shows you bounced off the road like a nerfball, cut between traffic and landed on a mattress dumped in the ditch. The morphine was to sedate you.'

I got the shapes her mouth made. The words happened later. 'So I'm okay, huh?'

'You're under arrest.'

'Mmmm.'

'Theft, dangerous driving, assault.'

'Assault?'

'You took a swing at the paramedics. Someone uploaded it to YouTube. You already got twelve thousand views. It's like a clown punching a sack.'

Now I was awake, pain creeping through fingers and toes, majorly spreading into my legs, my back. Worse than the blondest beating I took off school princesses. 'There's been a mistake.'

Salwa had even-toned, coppery skin, deep, no-messing eyes. Almond-brown hair that slunk and strayed, always needing adjustment. Close up, her mint and lime scent shamed my unwashed exuberance. Every second, pain got worse. The heart monitor upped its rhythm.

'You were busy. Since you disappeared yesterday evening.'

'Disappeared?'

'After dinner. You said you were going to bed. You never got there, it seems.'

For the bajillionth time, I couldn't guess what she wanted me to say.

'I spoke with Rose Ducati.'

'Oh, yes?'

'She was sleeping when I got there. She isn't your

friend, it seems, and hadn't planned to meet you last night.'

'She didn't?'

'Very helpful, Ms. Ducati. Told me she took a call from you. Said you seemed extremely agitated, pretending to be a children's nurse, claiming your Father was blowing off work for a playdate. Why would you call her and say those things?'

Though wretched with pain, I knew to go careful. 'We're here together, so I thought score some family time, y'know.'

'Bollocks. You hate your family. Why see them today?'

'I'm tired. Can this wait?'

'I spoke with your Mother. She left about an hour ago.'

'She came here?'

'To sign the form. If you go brain dead they switch off the machine.'

Mum would switch off the machine. She'd Instagram it.

Salwa maybe mistook my silence for surprise or fascination, dropping her voice a near-sisterly tone. 'Your Mother is talking about having part of your brain removed, to normalise your behaviour. That's where it's got, Riz. She will find a surgeon. Do you think there are none? She will put you in a state of medically induced infancy for the rest of your life. Docile, passive, controlled. That's where it's got. See how easy it is? You had a serious traffic accident. Who knows what damage is done? See how easy it is? You go to hospital. They release you, changed. Head trauma does that. Brain injury has extensive effects. Accidents change people. Who's going to question a caring Mother? I'm the one between you and the knife. Think I'm trying to scare you?'

Sweat pooled under my spine.

'I know this, Riz. In Iraq, under Saddam, this was business as usual.'

'How about Syria?'

Her dark eyes, wide and clear. 'Where were you last night, Riz?'

'Working for you.' Weighty tiredness dragged my limbs. 'I was with him. You know that. Your guys followed us.'

'They lost you when you took the scooter. Quite a stunt.'

'I was working for you. Doing what I said. We went to this warehouse. South of Battersea Park, some industrial site.'

Now those eyes locked with attention.

'These Russians were there. An old guy, a soldier. And a guy with a plastic hand. They had this stuff.'

'What is "stuff", Riz?'

'Boxes and sacks, and The Man and this woman: she said they were taking this stuff to Tehran.'

The chair tipped forward as she leaned onto the bed. Her soft hands gripped my fingers. 'What woman, Riz? Her name?'

My fingers squeezed hers. It's nice to hold hands. 'Felina. Denisa. De… something. Dersima.' Her grip crushed my wrist. 'And the Russians and her, they know you. They spoke like you're a bad person.'

'You think I'm a bad person, Riz?'

'I don't want my brain cut out.' I started to cry.

Kinda troublesome, with the wires and stuff—and I guess not her natural behaviour—but Salwa reached over and hugged me, smelling nice as a fine day in a sweet town. She said words that sounded like '*alfqyri almstrjli skhyf*.'

'I don't understand.'

'Poor silly tomboy.' She brushed back my fringe.

'That woman, who is she?'

'Not your problem.'

'She doesn't like you at all.'

'A wise enemy is better than an ignorant friend. You did well, Riz. We know where they are, thanks to your little adventure. It would be good to know how your neighbour fits with their schemes.'

'He said their interests coincide, something about the global loans guy.' Now I properly felt a snitch.

'Finance and disruption. Why Tehran?'

'She said kebabs. A better kebab.'

First time—possibly ever—Salwa tossed back her head and laughed. Her intractable hair flicked over her neck, showing off cool gold earrings, kinda half-eaten Oreos with Cherokee feathers.

'Is that funny?'

'Yes, Riz. To me, that is funny.'

It was a delicate moment. 'I'm tired, Salwa. Could you please not let them hurt me while I'm asleep?'

'You are under arrest, Riz. No one can do anything to you. Except us.'

She moved to the door, a swing livening her hips.

'Salwa? The Vespa. Say sorry to the owner, please? I did try to take it back.'

'They'll have a new one today. We don't need insurance men clumping around.'

When she'd gone, I lay feeling my bruises and cuts, till morphine took hold and the room faded black. Tried getting back to heaven. But the gates were locked and I wasn't welcome anyway.

There's ways to wake up, some pleasant. Having screaming sharp metal bust through your skin isn't it. I jumped, yanked back by wires invading my body. The sting went harder. My eyes sprung wide. A damn hypodermic the size of a rocket nosing inside my arm. A suspiciously shiny liquid shot through my veins by long, powdery fingers.

I didn't see the blue uniform at first, the name badge nor retro hanging watch. I saw snow-white hair, frosted skin, eyes of bottled lightning.

'Hello! You wake up now.'

Fear kicked an almighty whack. Shot me up and splashed me down in the sweat puddle beneath me. Lilija pinged the needle from my arm and prepped another dose.

'What you doing?'

'Is naloxone. You take much morphine I think.' She did me again, her coke-white fingers plunging the needle with backyard haste.

'Stop.'

She frowned. 'We must hurry. You must be awake.'

'I'm awake.'

'Then get up.'

That's when I noticed the nurse uniform, the watch and hospital badge, neatly printed LILIJA in capital letters jammed so close it looked Arabic. My lungs filled hard and heavy, mad energy busting each vein. Startled, I clawed the air. 'There's a freaking balloon on the ceiling.' Tried grabbing it down, beating at the tubes sucked into my arms.

Lilija got busy detaching wires and pipes, popping off valves, flat-lining sensors that served the machines.

'You know how to do that?'

'Is okay. Back home I am veterinary nurse.' She unhitched me with sure precision.

'Where are my clothes?' I'd been levered into these eye-splitting candy girl pyjamas. Horrendously, someone swapped my underwear for incontinence pants. Just hope a nurse did that, not Mum.

'Oh,' Lilija gave me the full sunshine, 'they don't want you to leave. They take your clothes.'

'Can you check the cupboards please? What's that mean, they don't want me to leave?'

'They arrest you, hotel girl. Keep you here. Your Mother visit. Too sad to have picnic. Your Father is busy. He goes to work as normal.'

'It was just a day at the park. Why does it matter?'

'Some people want your Father not to go to work today. The police, though, they want him to work.'

'How you know this crap?'

145

'The police have meeting last night at hotel. They get food. No one sees the waitress.'

Morphine and naloxone slugged it out under my skull. Blood pressure swinging high to low. Bleary and wide awake the same time. Actual, parasitic bugs burrowed into my skin. Could see my skin moving with them. My tongue couldn't fit the words my mind was saying. 'So you come to spring me from hospital?'

She was rattling cupboards, cranking hinges. 'Of course. You must have picnic.'

Then I lay back and laughed because, what else can you do? This picnic I never wanted had become talismanic, immense. I laughed and the bugs laughed too, doing some ugly-bug mambo.

Meantime, this fluorescent genius got a lockpick from her pocket—for real, worm-head metal—to bust the cupboard doors.

'You got a gun?' I ask casually.

'No,' so matter-of-fact. 'If I need, I can get.' The lock gave a clunk. She loosed a little squeak of success. 'Clothes. I find.'

Scuffed with mud, torn, but they'd do for the great escape. As she brought them over, I read her watch. 'Is that seven this morning?'

'Is right.'

'This morning?'

'They find you at 3am. Now we are late. You dress. I help.'

No, shouts my head, loud and clear. 'Um, could you go outside, please?'

'You are stiff with bruise. Too slow. I help.'

'Please. I'm embarrassed.'

She grins those blinding teeth. 'Is okay. We have same, yes?'

So that was another first.

When she settled my bruises and scars-to-come into my grubby clothes, she arranged my hair with her fingers, parting and smoothing, twisting strands behind each ear. 'There,' she said, artisan. 'You are pretty again. Now, we have test.'

My head tingled. 'Test?'

'Of course. Police guard the door. I tell them I come for routine check.'

'So if we just walk?'

'They get angry. Not good.'

My receptors didn't know which drug to believe. 'So what you suggest?'

'We think outside the square. Side of hospital there is small road where ambulance wait. You know?'

'I don't even know what hospital this is.'

That look, she used it a lot, when she expected better. 'Is no matter. You find road. I get you. Now, behind door. There. And quiet. I talk with police. When I signal with hand so, you run. Is clear?'

'Run?'

'You want more naloxone?'

I took another shot because it seemed life would get busy. Sweating hard, each of my limbs twitching a different way.

She fixed me with that look again, then yanked the door half-open. 'Officer. Is girl. She want to speak with detective.'

Muttering from the hallway.

'No, she say only detective. She remember things about Russians. Tell detective, Russians.'

Even then, that seemed off—when had I told Lilija about the Russians? What the hell was she doing there anyway? Surliness seeped through the door. I could guess the lines: I was told to stay here, don't tell me my job, I'll call her.

'You get her.' Lilija's voice, rising beyond the strictly natural. 'Girl has much damage. We not tell her. She has maybe hours to live.'

Couldn't help the squeak that broke from my lips. It seemed likely someone was lying.

Lilija, fully outside the door, repeated what she just said but more insanely. Then her voice dropped too low to hear. That really got me shaking.

This weird, floaty butterfly swept round the door, did a loop and vanished. Took five seconds to realise it was Lilija's hand. Not knowing the least what to do, I peeked round the door. Lilija had two officers facing her—she made cutting gestures against her head and started tapping her watch.

A blast of fear boiled my guts. I shot into the opposite hallway, taking off like a pack of methed-up prom queens were chasing my arse.

Bruised bones flipped with dope and terror dodged me between angry porters wheeling angry patients. Plain enough I should head for the ground, though every sign only pointed the way to more treatment. I fully embrace paranoia—it's part of the package—yet actually people were talking about me, or at least wondering where I'd sprung from. Fully dressed, I still had 'Patient' tattooed on my head and the fact my clothes were crapped and bloody hardly helped me go unnoticed. It was also the case police wanted me. No wonder a quarrelsome voice was telling my head to trust no one.

'Can I help?' This concerned, Scottish voice I didn't recognise. I possibly growled something hasty.

'Are you okay?' Ah, so the voice was outside of me. A young guy, a nurse or something.

Weighing the evidence, I wasn't okay. By default, the freckle smile kicked in. 'Oh, I'm after the exit. I'm a bit late.'

'Sure.' A friendly, Scottish 'sure'. 'I'll show you the lift.'

Lifts are always suspect, especially with armed men after you. 'No. I mean, thanks. I'll take the stairs. Shift some gut.' I slapped my stomach. It hurt.

'Are you okay?' He looked me over psychiatrically. 'Can I get you something?'

'The stairs.' I mean, I know my eyes get bulgy, I try to curb it. As he gave me directions, he seemed more concerned I'd leave with something unresolved. Which was precisely what I wanted to do.

'Can I get someone for you?'

Dumb bad luck that, just as he said it, two goons with Glock 39s—I'm guessing—come storming around the bend, making more fuss than surely was sanctioned by the occasion. Ripped with focused energy, I grabbed this pleasant Scotsman and threw him across their path. I never thought that would actually work, yet pleasingly they got tangled up and I only just remembered to stop enjoying it and beat for the stairs.

Crash the doors and I'm running, that soon-to-be familiar sound of police boots beating behind me. These guys yelling 'Stop' and 'Wait', trying to net me with menace. One even shouts I'm under arrest, which is to shout at a bolted horse.

Running fast, stairs falling under my feet, body and lungs flayed. Take a breath, glance up—guess what? Really, what? One of these nuts aims his gun down the stairwell at me. The other shouts something and I keep running.

Big fat G painted on the wall makes the greatest invitation. Clatter open the doors, chasing through the E.R.—these sick, sorry people sunk into metal seats, dripping blood and gawking. So I think they're zombies and start to scream, convinced these shifty undead will rise up behind me. Instead, two nutjob policemen bowl through, hastily snugging their weapons away from the cameras.

Shouts go up, flashes of glass and uniforms.

Outside, this ambulance discharges something bad-looking onto a gurney. Got to swerve around it. The paramedics yelling and whatever they're handling looks pretty pissed too. There's metal and sunlight blinding me, a yard with tall glass walls. From behind comes heavy pursuit.

Hit the end of the yard, ambulances line one side of the road. Lurch across, screaming so loud the sound disconnects from me. Lot of paramedics looking baffled and angry. Then it appears from the end of the line. Leaf green with the top down: a little Take-A-Whiz electric two-seater. Lilija slams the brake. 'Girl!'

Just manage to mosh myself into the passenger seat before she cuts away, sudden speed from an engine so scarily quiet, I hear cops swearing to the end of the street. 'This is your car?'

'Of course not. Is horrible car. But easy to hide.'

Seems a ready bet those gun-happy cops'll scorch our tail. I doubled over with pain—or would have, if there'd been room. My bruised bones a mass of fire, lungs so spent I could taste their emptiness. My heart crashing against my ribs—actually thought it would snag and my tombstone would say I died in a go-kart.

'Get head off dashboard.'

'I'm dying.'

'Is cameras everywhere. We must look normal.'

Got the glare off her star-bright hair. Yeah, we looked normal. 'Who are you? Who d'you work for?'

She flicked me this curious look. 'I am Lilija. I work for hotel.'

My busted up phone still caught a signal. Usual missed calls from Mum—you might think she wanted me back. Even Dad bothered to spare a few words. Salwa, too, struggling her rage to some voice that might land kindly. 'The detective. Won't she be angry if I show at the hotel?' I assumed that's where we were going.

'She likes control, yes? She will make that she planned it this way.'

Lilija sailed this battery-powered box along Euston Road and into Great Portland Street. Everything early and busy, stores open, people heading to work, cycling and walking, purpose in every step. Though none with so much as The Man. Where was he, when I got hauled from a ditch?

As a smart looking café rolled by, its heavenly tang enveloped me through the open roof. 'Pastries.'

'Is what?'

'Can we stop for pastries?'

'No.'

'I haven't eaten since dinner. Lilija.'

She pulled up. 'You are troublesome girl. Is not room service.'

'I'll go.'

'You stay.'

'I'll give you money. Soon as I have some.'

She vanished behind the car, looking, I guess, keen as a nurse going about her good works. I jabbed the radio. It came to life with some talk station.

'The arrival of the fund president increases pressure for delegates to reach an agreement. As well as immediate assistance to countries unable to repay their debts, the summit has complex issues to consider around how to maintain liberalised lending markets while preventing funding for terrorist groups. Increasingly, terrorists access funds from legitimate sources through fake transactions and companies, based in jurisdictions where controls are weak. The global loan fund president will call on delegates to agree stronger controls and better information sharing, as a condition of further lending.'

Geekily, I understood that from prying into Dad's

files. Mum liked to talk it too, so neighbours would respect her as an informed participant, not think of her as Dad's hang-around, which she was. That conference was pretty important. Of course Dad should be there when the loan fund guy arrived. He would be, now I was mashed up in hospital.

'S'cuse me, love.' A woman wearing a blue uniform, her cap busted over to resemble a beret, undecided if she should crouch to peer through the window or stretch to see over the top, waved a console thing to draw my attention to a traffic sign. 'No stopping. At any time.'

'At any time?'

'Is this your vehicle?'

'Kinda.'

'You need to move it. You can't stay here.'

'I'm just waiting for someone.'

'At any time,' said with scriptural significance.

This toy car, so crampy, it was pretty easy to slide across to the driver's seat. There was a keypad, lights and switches, a gauge saying the battery fill was healthy. Pressed a button or two and the quiet motor came alive. This woman watching closer than, really, I cared for, I tinkered around the weird controls till the thing rolled forward.

A shrill blast of Russian shot over my head and Lilija was there, in front of the car, holding it still with her hands, one of which also gripped a big paper bag. She yelled something, then yelled it again in English, 'Cut the engine.'

Though slight, she brought mountainous, snowy

anger as she thumped me into the passenger side, dumping the bag on my lap. The bag smelled divine.

Horrified, the parking attendant's voice climbed several notches. 'This your car?'

Lilija tizzed her hair. 'I tell her, she is bad girl. Bad,' straight at my face.

'Is she…' The parking attendant's fingers felt for the word.

'I take care of her.' Lilija slammed the door—which didn't actually make much sound—and manoeuvred us aggressively into traffic.

The bag she threw at me had croissants, a bear claw and plain round buns with curd-looking stuff seeping through.

She caught me dabbing a finger at it. 'Is *vatrushka*.'

'Who?'

'We eat. At home. *Vatrushka*. Is treat,' said somewhat grudgingly.

I got the hint. 'Sorry about back there.'

Shake of the snowy mountain top. 'How you live? How you live being you?'

'She said no stopping. At any time. She looked official.'

The car lunged to a stop. I curled forward, hugging my breakfast. She slapped her palms on the wheel. 'So if someone say: do something, you do it?'

'I thought we already had enough trouble without getting a ticket.'

'So, if someone tell you: push this button, so, launch this bomb. If someone say: this not your country, this my country. If someone tell you: take these people, put them on train, you obey because someone look official?'

This unexpected, unexplored fury starved me of breath. I snuffled.

'So, you cry. You obey and you cry.' She gripped the wheel, rocking the tiny car on its springs. 'You must learn, girl. You make cement your veins. You make steel your heart. You must learn.'

We spun passed Hanover Square, purred through Mayfair. Big office buildings doing who-knows-what, tight arsed-looking bars, stores with no price tags. Kinda place Mum wanted to be. A place The Man could be, because he could be anywhere. And Salwa? What was her place? With her cement veins and steel heart.

Really, I wanted no fuss back at the hotel. We couldn't, of course, just arrive. Lilija parked off Rutland Gate by the big Russian Orthodox church, the little eco-machine blending with the green shadows of leafy streets. She had her hotel uniform stashed under the seat and got changed sitting down. Hopelessly caught with her small, perky development, I looked elsewhere for distraction. She had a humungous tattoo across her back—an eagle, exultant, rising from flames. Stark as blood on snow. Wanted to ask how it found such milk white skin, but we weren't speaking.

The police, more nervy than last time, checked Lilija's hotel ID. They recognised me and started the awkward questions. To stop me talking, Lilija commanded, 'You find Detective Abaid. Girl must see detective.'

'Wait here.'

'We wait inside. I have work.'

Brisking through back corridors, we met the maître d'—maybe Lilija had a device or something to warn him. His look of supreme distaste greeted our escort. 'You have business with my staff and guests?'

This cop was maybe twenty and knew nothing. 'Security, sir,' he said stoutly.

'Of course.' The maître d' smiled. 'One of my trusted wait staff and the daughter of a distinguished guest are bound to raise suspicion.'

'Orders, sir.' The cop turned defensive.

'Indeed.' The maître d' caught Lilija's eye. 'Orders.'

As pain became the new normal, as memory turned from amazement to accusation, bigger problems pitched at my head. 'You know my neighbour? The sharp-dressed guy from the next suite?'

Lilija's face gave nothing.

'Can you tell him Abaid spoke with me? About last night.' Ridiculous phrase.

'I do not know this guest. He does not call room service.'

# 11

8:30am and I'm with a woman who wants my skull sanitised. Her bratty offspring, told the picnic was cancelled because Riz pulled a midnight manoeuvre, thought me being back made the playdate official again. Kid sister mainly thought that. Brother could take it or leave it, the sanguine old fart.

I could barely process what happened with Mum. Reversing out from her big speech of family values was nothing against the satisfaction of knowing I was hospitalised, comatose and prepped for backwoods surgery. My arrival, sweaty and bruised in torn clothes, babbling how I so wanted this family outing, made her Lady Macbeth dicked by soiled Banquo. Believe it, Riz Montgomery 'displaced the mirth, broke the good meeting, with most admired disorder'.

'Your Father's already gone to work.'

'Get him back.' Kid sister's quivering anger should have worried Mum more, if you want my opinion.

'It's difficult, honey.'

'Call Ducati.'

She said that, she said Ducati.

'Tell her. Say Dad come with us. Now skanky's back we have picnic.'

'I think,' brother stroked his bald little chin, 'we agreed last night for Dad to spend time with us.' He wiggled his jaw, the freak. 'I think we agreed that.'

'Honeys,' Mum meant the pair of them, 'can I have a moment, please?'

'Want to go now.' That little girl was psyched.

'You and your brother just go to the other room a moment, okay? Just for a moment. Watch TV. Will you take your sister, please?'

Brother, immune to the little cat's bawling, led her into the other room with overblown promises of what might be on the box.

Mum closed the door, aiming to look concerned and decisive. 'Should you be here?' Her voice almost hushed.

'I didn't break anything. I'm… it's just superficial.'

'The doctors advised you to stay at the hospital for your own good.'

This quiet, reasoning voice bugged the crap out of me. What was she trying to prove? Was she wearing a wire? 'They let me go,' I lied, badly.

She knew it. 'They allowed you?'

'Yes.'

Now she stood close and I'll say for my Mother, she was no way a bad-looking woman. Brittle, harsh under bright light, yet tidy and sleek as any at the school gate. As she spoke, she called me Amelia, hinting at some bond. Her voice so steady I wanted to scream. 'I spoke with the doctors, Amelia. You had a major psychotic episode. You were found at the roadside, violent and delusional. They had to sedate you to get you to hospital. It's online, Amelia. Everyone saw. You hallucinated all manner of things.'

'I didn't hallucinate incontinence pants.'

'It's not working this way. You need medication. We tried it your way and look where we are.'

'Medication? You mean a lobotomy.'

A sorrowful look got heaved my way. 'Don't be silly. No surgeon performs that now.' She folded her arms. 'It's time you got the help you deserve.'

Swishing into this mess, Salwa Abaid didn't look happy either. Beefed up with a couple of plainclothes Nancys, she resembled a heavily-armed Queen of Sheba. Though Mum may not have relished the police trampling into her lounge, decorum forced civility. Abaid and her wingmen declined coffee. 'Mrs. Montgomery, good of you to see us. I had hoped to bring your daughter myself, but she can move fast when she wants to.'

Mum had a razor-keen sense of status. She knew Abaid's role—or the role Abaid affected—and recognised her personal power. Mum's social antenna also discerned something off with this dark, angry woman. 'I thought my daughter was being kept in for observation, detective? Obviously, I'm pleased to see her...' *Mierda*! '...however, I'm surprised she was discharged so early.'

The painful smile that choked Abaid's lips dissolved just as quick. 'I spoke with your daughter this morning. She mentioned a family event today. A picnic, I think you said, Riz?'

Mum did the most blatant eye-roll, voice dripping

with fake indulgence. 'Oh, you call her that? Honestly, she made up this silly nickname for herself. It's a joke. No one uses it. Yes,' she caught Abaid's irritation, 'we had planned a little outing. Of course, with last night's incident…'

'It might do her good.' The detective cut Mum's yakking. 'She had a remarkable escape, all things considered.' Abaid flashed me a look. 'Perhaps family is the best medicine.'

Screaming exploded next door—kid Satan, peeved at something.

'We'll talk later.' A whole desert of grief burned Salwa's voice as she stalked away.

9am and imagine how great it was for Dad to get called at the office and told to come back for a picnic. Mum did the deed, concocting a fanciful tale, how the doctors were satisfied I was okay and the police had no more questions. Apparently, no one would press charges, which was nice. Eavesdropping while the kids sucked TV, Mum reprised her last night's rage at our lack of family cohesion, its effect on discipline, notably the nutjob eldest who now had a heap of Likes from YouTube skate punks. I watched it and, yeah, I did look awesomely an idiot failing to punch paramedics. That I was two feet below them as they tried to haul me up made it extra cheeky. Most comments were pretty abusive, though a twelve year-old boy said I looked kinda cool. While Mum was winning the argument, I went to my suite to get changed.

As the drugs wore thin, I hurt a lot. Taking a shower,

the range and colouration of bruises gave my pain visual expression. Purple and green, mauve and ochre. A big tawny hump, nearly the shape of a heart, across one leg. Its centre stippled red, set in blue. My torso red on maroon, a scheme fitting for Rothko. Poor little hula girl on my hip took a beating, lost in black welts. Got her when I was twelve at a backstairs parlour, on Mum's day out to this seaside town. Female tattooist, obviously, and the humiliation of a lifetime taking off my jeans under her gaze. But I wanted to go home changed in some way Mum wouldn't know. Hula girl was the most that woman could do in twenty minutes. Hurt more than getting thrown off a Vespa.

Clothes had got problematic, my stash eaten up by mud and sweat. My plan to make friends that week meant I packed my coolest stuff. So not thrilled to wear it for family playtime. But Mum would bitch and Dad would glower if I showed up looking wrong and I just wanted a calm time. Plus it was Hyde Park and anyone might see me. So I wore skinny dark blues and Elliott plaid—yeah, it was cool then—hung loose and buttoned tight, my hair scraped into the collar. Through the misty bathroom mirror I looked a bruised, alarming boy. That's okay.

Big worry was next door. I told Salwa too much, that was chokingly clear. And she wouldn't keep my squealing to herself. The thought I did my neighbour harm was immense. I slipped a note under the connecting door, saying we had to speak. Then remembered about paper trails and tried fishing it back with a straightened hanger, which so doesn't work. Then

I thought if something happened to him, I should be loyal, stay implicated, which the note did. What would they do? It was jail or Grover. Then Mum called and down came the red mist.

The hotel catered the picnic—a manly basket for Dad to lug and stowaway packs for us. Mum costumed the kids with designer playtime duds that signal intention to other parents. Truthfully, they were dressed monkeys. Mum was a swish like always, the right buttons strategically undone. Dad chose a yellow vee-neck and slacks, some approximation of Fun Dad so pitiful I had seizures. For a long time I wondered how life would go if the folks got divorced. If a heap of emotional ooze would make things better. Dad's face said we were damn near finding out. He got blackmailed into this nightmare, caught a reprieve when I hit dirt, then discovered that was just fooling. No wonder his fingers kept tying a spectral garrotte.

As a kinda sideways insult—at least, I took it so—Rose Ducati booked us a cab, so we had to sit bunched—actually touching—rather than stroll pleasingly far apart. Watching kid sister bounce on Mum's knee, playing the baby, made me want to hurl her at the heads of surprised passers-by. That kid was abnormal.

Where I'm from, truly, you could die and no one notice. Parks were for solitary walks, with little hollows to hunker and cry. I knew Hyde Park wasn't that, yet felt unprepared for the industrial-scale leisure time going down. On grass scuffed the yellow stubble of old men's heads, folks fired barbecue brunches, cheapskate parents running kids' parties, impinging each other, their rowdy games a horrific brawl waiting to happen. Kid brother was already sizing up their coolers.

Personal trainers with ludicrous hair got super-fit women to bounce around, hench guys pulled sit-ups clutching medicine balls, while little drones took pictures of the a-holes flying them. Dogs chased cyclists, as pallid smog smudged the horizon.

Shirtless guys speckled the grass, oiling and flexing, cooking themselves to order. Kids with must-have trainers sang along to their phones, laughing at nothing. Maybe among the lousy fields, some girls were talking Rothko. I pledged to die of boredom.

Dad, I'm sure, wanted to be at work. Mum wanted to be proved right. I wanted to be drunk on a boat moored off Shanghai. 'Oh,' says Mum, 'there may be a spot over there.'

Dad's phone kept buzzing, of course. Deceit was his angle, he had Ducati call each quarter-hour. He agreed a time with her when he would just have to go back. Each call, he built the tension. 'Really? Have him message me. Check the pack. Sure he knows. Tell them to play it easy.' Efficiently setting boundaries. At the playground he walked round back of the slide, pretending that was more private. I know he did heavy business. No way, though, did he have the stature of the cold voice next door.

The playground was humiliation. 'Wipe the swing for your sister.'

The swing was crusted in guano. 'With what?'

Mum tossed me her wetties.

Not sure how I got the job, I suggested, 'Can't she do it?'

I thought I sounded controlled. But Mum heard different. 'She's a child, she'll get messed. Wipe the swing.'

'It's because she's got boy clothes,' cackled the brat.

I flung a wettie at her. 'Wanna swing?'

Mum's voice caught a hollow tone. 'I have asked you twice to wipe the swing for your sister.'

'Why?' I was dangerously close. 'She likes crap.'

'Hee-hee.' Kid sister rubbed her treasured bottom. 'Crap.'

Mum did that horrid thing, prissing her lips, kissing the finger of silence. More obscene to watch than whatever kid sister said.

Brother inspected the plastic seat. 'Properly speaking, it's lime.'

'No it's not.' I never wanted, and couldn't help, getting tangled with him. 'That's what you have with tequila.'

'You drink tequila?' he asked, a miniature attorney.

'No, of course not.'

'Do you?' Mum zeroed in. 'Drink tequila?'

Dad reappeared from behind the slide, staring at us. So I mopped bird crap, feeling so far from the night before, I wondered what was dreams and what kept me awake.

So they pushed swings and played at being married, four-fifths of the family involved. The swings were filthy, little kid swings—I knew without trying my hips wouldn't fit the chain. Sometimes, girls hit the playground after sunset, to kick high the swings till the chains cracked, to spin the roundabout blitzed on tequila. I hated I was always the first to get sick.

The park was broken with islands of trees and a sick-looking lake, The Serpentine, where okay dads took their daughters boating. Above the woods, dragon kites hopped the breeze, curious, dangerous hunters. At the hazy horizon towers rippled and gleamed, stacked with city girls getting by, paying bills and hitting deadlines, assured and unafraid. Beyond the lake, roped-off grass had boards stuck down to spread the weight of machinery, hauled by the unpadded clatter of squat tractors. For a second—just that second—I wanted to yell: 'The fair's in town!' But no one cared.

Methodically, we enjoyed ourselves, Dad on his phone: giving orders, mailing stuff, managing his workday al fresco. Mum pretending not to notice and the kids running round being dumb.

Whoever at the hotel prepared the picnic had only a tenuous grasp of what humans eat. Among choice moments was brother dissecting a sandwich, scraping gunk off his finger, and telling us it was: 'Pate. Maybe goose.' From nowhere, kid sister invented this freaky fear of cherry tomatoes, bombing them into the trees, yelling they were nasty. Manically fretting the pips from her skin, she bawled, 'This suck.'

'What did you say?' Mum bristled-up.

'This suck.' Kid sister, slapping her fingers to jog off the seeds, looked insane. 'This picnic suck.'

Uncharacteristically rowdy, Dad threw a chicken wing into the grass. 'Whose idea was this?'

Now, that food was nothing to do with me. I'd bring dry-roast peanuts and chocolate Wackios—a fine dessert straight from the pack. 'I didn't want this. What you looking at?'

If bridled is a real thing, Mum bridled. 'Don't be rude.'

'Huh?'

Mum was working I guess, giving Dad his money's worth. 'Apologise to your Father.'

'What?'

I misjudged how crazy she'd got. 'We were up all night worried for you. If we hadn't called the police, they wouldn't have found you. Why steal a moped? Why do that? Your Father made arrangements to be here. Then unmade them, then had to remake them because you discharged yourself against the doctors' advice. You still haven't said sorry for that stupid call to Ms. Ducati. What are you smiling for?'

'I'm not.'

'What's that on your lips then?'

'Lipstick.'

'Why are you wearing lipstick?'

'Because she's got sores.' Brother was drowning ants with pate. 'She has sores round her mouth. That's why she paints it.'

Dad realised he had to take charge, the slow talking tough guy. 'I agree with your Mother. It's time to see Dr. Grover.'

That did it. I was up and into the woods, their shouts

breaking behind me. Not actual woods: a city treescape, trimmed and moderated. Narrow stands of what I didn't know then were birch, anchored by knotty old oaks. I leaned into a smooth-sided silver birch till it gave a little, trading that impulse to skewball into another. Building momentum, trunk-to-trunk, I ricocheted across the wood, bouncing, recoiling with kinetic relations to the smooth bark. Gave my bruises something to hurt for. The shock of stopping hurt worse.

Light busting through from the end of the woods bathed a pile of rocks and, sat up high, a woman. Very cool on the rock, a dark sateen jacket and sari-skirt. Stacked hair made her neck an old painter's notion of beauty. I must have made a lot of noise, pinballing tree-to-tree. Guess she knew it was me.

Sunkissed, desert eyes, from a desert town where the waitress asks: 'Is that all, *señorita*?' slipping loose a hairclip. I wanted to stare till our faces dissolved and I could stop holding my breath and my head stopped hurting. Conscious how stupid I looked, I said, 'Hi.'

The woman whose name I never knew, who I call Mocha, looked down at me—a travelling angel, bringing good to the city. 'Thought I heard you.'

'Huh?' I could think of nothing cool, or otherwise, to say.

'The noise. Thought it was you.'

A smidge of knee escaped the sari-skirt. So wanted to touch it.

'Am I hallucinating you?'

She popped her tongue. 'If I say I'm real, how would

you know it's true?' She had this grandad-looking tin, with a sail-ship picture and queasy old-time writing. 'Want a smoke?'

It seemed disrespectful to get too close, so I stood below and we passed the joint up and down. Her weed smoked spicy and sweet—I've had nothing like it since. What mattered more, that slight dampness to the paper, the little folds made by her lips I got to taste.

She says to me, 'You had a busy night,' so I see her then riding the curves alongside me.

'You mean the YouTube thing?'

'There's always someone I know in hospital. We're risk-takers. They told me a lot of police around the private rooms at UCH last night.'

'The what?'

'UCH. The hospital you were at. A friend waiting for stitches this morning was a little surprised when you screamed through, chased by some overwrought fuzz. You do have an eventful time.'

'It's not really what I planned.'

She laughed and, dumb little fool I am, I thought everything was forgiven. A spike of sunlight struck between trees, setting warmth through her beige skin. 'I heard you're still getting special attention. That Syrian detective who saved your arse at the party. The one you're double-crossing.'

She remembered! I told her something and she remembered! 'I wouldn't say double-crossing.'

'Salwa Abaid.'

I gawked. Did everyone know everyone?

'Her interview technique, hold your head under water while you're plugged to the mains.'

'I… I didn't find that.'

Light struck her hair and neck, her face, those eyes staring at me. 'It's not about you, Riz. The world isn't all about you. These aren't your wars. Go home.' With a single, slim move she slid from the rock, light turning liquid around her. 'Believe it, Riz. You're not from here.'

No, because if I was from here, I'd say I know a place where they mix great tabbouleh. We could eat honey cake, then walk it off at this gallery with the most beautiful, heart-stopping paintings. First you cry, then feel resolved, because someone lived the pain for you. You fall to your knees and rejoice. I'd walk you to this cafe where the waitresses don't rush you when you don't understand. Then I'd show you where I leave my dresses to dry on the roof, where afternoons are quiet and juniper-scented and so very long. The buzzing would stop, the cramps subside and I'd be Riz the right way. If I was from here and you were with me.

She had this way of tilting her head so light spread through her black hair.

'I'm really okay. I'm no trouble.'

'You're not okay, are you? You're a magnet for trouble.'

She took steps towards the edge of the wood and it took me a second to grasp she was moving away. I stumbled behind her.

'There's a party, Riz. When those guys appear from the conference hall with their grubby deal tomorrow, we're having one big party.'

At the edge of the wood, heading into the sunlight. 'I'll come with you. I can help.'

She turned—her mid-Asian features, her hair loose and languid twists, her slender neck, the dark sateen jacket tracking her shape exactly. Her strength and vitality. What did she see? A nervy young female. Ginger, scruffy, bit of a belly. Willing and stupidly eager. She asked, 'Would you follow me to the ends of the earth and do terrible things when we get there?'

'Now. We'll go now.'

'No, Riz. You snitch for everyone, how could I trust you?'

'You can trust me. I want to fight for your cause.'

'I never doubt my allegiances. The question doesn't arise. It doesn't exist. We are right, they are wrong. People like your Father are wrong.'

Didn't she hear me? 'Absolutely.'

'You're a drifter, Riz. You go with the wind. I need soldiers, not guns for hire.'

What was wrong with her? 'I'm totally committed.'

We left the woods, slipped back into regular daytime. 'You don't have ideology, Riz. You chase shiny things. I've only known you a couple of days and look what's happened. I know what hurts, Riz. I get it. That's why I tracked you here today.'

So she had wanted to see me. I never knew till then how you can break up with someone you never got with. I've found—as life goes on—it happens more than you think.

'Goodbye, Riz,' she was saying. 'Hope you get the help you need.'

What's left to lose? 'You're the help I need.'

She shook her head, smiling. 'When the wars are won and the tyrants are dead, who knows?'

I watched her walk into the blinding light. Till the world dissolved in salt water. I went to call her, one last time, but my voice failed. Only a terrified whisper, 'The fair's in town.'

Then my phone, that dumb ringtone it defaulted to even though I reset it. Mum shouting, 'You come here right away.'

I spewed till I was empty as a suicide's weekend.

# 12

When my skin burned so my freckles turned white, I flipped the handle to cold. Water beat hard against me, its impact overwhelming. I washed clean, really clean. Flipped the handle to hot. Like getting smoothed with a knife, the burn kicked through. I flipped hot to cold for maybe an hour. Then air hit my body and I was dirty again.

Got dressed without drying-off, water soaking my clothes. My bruises scalded raw, my stitches tight wire. I forced myself to walk, to push against the corrosion. A robot, aware of the pain in rust, its commands landing hollow on trashed machinery.

I picked up the room phone, listened to the dial tone till it cut dead. Did it twice more. This was my home now, this comfortable suite, to which bored policemen listened while I betrayed everyone.

Mum understood I was tired, sick, a nightmare of weary accidents. That I hadn't been eating well and had morphia cruising my veins and prescription painkillers she tipped down my throat embraced me like barbed wire. So although I was confined to my room, it was really for my own good. A rest cure, time to heal. It got me out of family dinner.

When I told Mum I was headed for an early night, she aimed—unwillingly—at caring. 'Are you due? Have you got everything?'

Maybe there are mums who know when their kid is due. And if I hadn't got everything, as she put it, the hotel shop opened twenty-four-seven. I'd been dealing with it myself for three years and as she hadn't asked how I felt the first time, I didn't care what she thought since.

The usual same-different guy stood watch outside, headset flickering blue and red, the whole of police intelligence patched to his brain. No doubt he'd wonder why I took the stairs, no doubt he'd report it.

The stairs were as shoddy as stairs in grand places always are. Front of house all onyx and chrome, the back stairs raw concrete. A window at each mezzanine gave an inspiring view of the service road and backyard buildings beyond. These windows didn't open.

My immediate problem was Salwa Abaid, who I'd made everyone's problem. I had to know if she'd been to the warehouse and what that meant for my neighbour. He wasn't around and that was a worry. Pressed against a view of grey nothing, I hit her number.

'Is this urgent?' Some commotion behind her, clunks and thuds; maybe stuff getting moved.

'I'm back. You said we'd talk later.'

'Riz, you're not my priority right now. If you're at the hotel, stay there. We've had enough excitement.' She broke off to shout at someone.

'That stuff we said. The warehouse.'

'Riz, you're not my priority.'

'I don't want to cause trouble.'

'Then perhaps you should let your Mother have her way. Riz, I am not going to discuss police operational matters. We will talk when I'm at the hotel. Right now, the grownups are busy.'

So I took ten minutes staring outside, so the guy keeping watch would think I had a long call, which might make me interesting somehow. The buildings across the yards were offices, I guess—part of those millions of work days happening round me. I wanted to belong somewhere—a location, an inbox, tasks to fulfil. A route to independence. Sure, there were other ways—Mocha, The Man, their ways. Right then, being a receptionist or making coffee seemed the grandest freedom.

Dirty air blew dust and grit. Nothing looked sharp or defined. A security guard sat in his hut, watching cameras. Some maintenance guys horsed around. A couple who slid round the side of a building to smoke, huddled up into the wind, talking close like lovers. I scratched at the glass, but they were busy and far away.

Across came the shock of Lilija—who could miss her?—her starlight hair, the orderly swing that made her uniform special. Walking beside her the maître d', hurrying with elegance, explaining with his hands. Two brisk figures, involved beyond my understanding. Lilija was talking fast. Maybe the maître d' spoke Russian. They went quick, heads and hands explaining.

Stodgy and woeful, I lay on the floor of my lounge sucking TV. Hard to avoid seeing Dad in conference reports, either actually, or through the language of promises. Like always, there were problems—big, butch presidents, sensitive as prom queens—splits and disputes over words, the length and strength of commitments. I'm a basic vocabulary woman. I never understood Dad's night work, reshaping words to change nothing.

What killed me was the reporter, saying the city was braced—for breaking news, cities get braced—as the beatnik-hippie-punk-eco-freaks hit town. Not her exact words, the gist. She pitched the usual angles: smashed stores, wrecked cars, lost business for the productive economy, lost credibility for London. Counterpoint with an intense police presence to keep trouble clear of the conference. Especially, to safeguard the loan fund guy, burned in effigy across a swathe of the aspirant world. She assured me, a resident of an eight star doss house, I'd be properly insulated from other opinions.

Honest truth, I don't sympathise with people who go looking for the beating they could get back home. Yeah, it felt queasy those decisions involved Dad and, by association, me. Yeah, if someone gave me the chance, I would have been out there with them. The most righteous of all. For her.

I tried the connecting door, soft, then loud. I wondered where he lived—what kind of place, what town. If his apartment was flash or deliberately drab, and whether he just ignored whoever knocked at his door. I wondered if he even had an apartment—couldn't see him lugging trash, fixing plumbing, watching the game. Calling friends. 'You see that game? What a gyp!' Can't imagine what he'd be, when he wasn't being tough.

Turned the radio loud, some rock DJ playing Jefferson Starship, Black Sabbath, Jethro Tull. Bands I liked from before I was born. Didn't hear the knock, till this sunny voice bellowed, 'Room service.'

She trundled the trolley, making a pantomime of clamping her finger against her lips, before I could say I'd ordered nothing. She flapped her hair vigorously, shooting white sparks up the walls, 'Is Black Sabbath. *Paranoid* very good album, but *Sabotage* better, I think.'

'I kinda like *Sabotage*.'

'I'm sure neighbours enjoy this.' Lilija dropped a stagey wink. 'It bug them.'

By then, I'd given up trying to figure who was and wasn't real. I never liked that distinction anyway.

From under the cloth, she pulled a mixed salad that managed to combine potatoes, olives and strawberries, with dips and bread, and a bottle of Sauvignon Blanc. Someone had my welfare at heart.

'You check order, please.' Into my face, she thrust her phone, showing a draft, unsent message—something barely there with no trace. It said: "Trust me. Don't tell police. Is bad habit."

'Is right, yes?' Lilija hit delete. 'Is so.'

One long, lonely evening—eating salad, drinking wine, watching TV. I forgot how it was to do nothing. I hated it. I watched *The Wizard of Oz* though I hate how it makes me feel. I watched *Breakfast at Tiffany's*. I really hate *Breakfast at Tiffany's*. I hate everything about it. That film is some key lime pie that tastes only of cold. When I read the book, the part with the postcard's lipstick kiss, when the guy finds the cat, I knew Hepburn couldn't be Holly. Just a kid and I knew it.

Way after midnight, watching these Warners gangster pics: 1930s wise guys and fluty blonde dolls. I switched off the TV and lights. Through the slat-blinds, cops paced the street, each measured step ensuring my security. Guess someplace they had family who never got used to when daddy came home. I thought of the guys with me, listening to old movies. Deliberately, I hadn't made a sound, hadn't talked to myself nor sworn at Hepburn. So they just got the TV and my fidget breath.

The room's three-quarter darkness let the shape in the mirror I guess was me become a smoky night sky. But the moon and stars had other girls to shine for. I started to cry, small at first then weeping. The mirror dissolved with hurricane tears. My colours bled like Rothko in the rain.

A hammer hit—a sharp, necessary reminder. As I opened the connecting door, I recalled the surveillance guys would get my tears and what came after. I didn't hit the lights nor fix my face. I didn't need to.

'Why the damn hell you cry so loud?' The lounge behind, lit with table lamps, made the set for an old-time movie. I guess someplace was a whisky glass, the business pages and photographs shot from inside a car. 'You bawled yourself deaf or something? Why you crying?'

'I'm unhappy.'

He stared like I stole his magic beans. At gunslinger speed, he whipped his phone from his pocket, tapped it, showed me an unsent message: "Where were you?" At the same time, he yelled: 'What you got to be unhappy about?'

Took a minute to find my phone, open my message app. "In hosp. Abaid had me." I grizzled full blast, 'I'm grounded. It wasn't my fault.'

'They clip your wings?' He punched the screen: "What you tell her?"

'The picnic went wrong. Mum got mad.' Awkward, confessing to being a grass. I mashed at the screen, trying to keep up the pace: "Warehouse & Russns. That wmn. Had 2 tell her."

'How does a picnic go wrong?' His phone was slap in my face: "You gave them up to Abaid?"

'Crap food. Kids wouldn't stop. Dad didn't want to be there.' What did he expect? He wasn't the one who got threatened. I typed: "Ab save me frm Mum. Dad wnt me gone."

'He ain't the only one. I don't want to hear you shriek all night.' His phone zoomed at my eyes: "You made a mistake. Put it right."

I was losing it, anxiety off the scale, heart banging from my chest. Dirty bugs burrowed everywhere through my body. 'I can't help it. I cry to feel better.' My phone screen slippy with sweat and tears. What did this big man want? "How pt rght?? What cld I do 2 Ab?" I laid him the caps lock: "MUM WILL CUT MY BRAIN."

He stared at the shouty non-message. Backlit, large and solid above me. His eye flicked to the window. 'What else might make you feel better?' Swiftly, his fingers told me: "Enough chat. Creeps see lights on the blinds."

Swallowed hard to get my voice even. 'The fair's in town. I want to go to the fair.' I mauled one last sloppy message: "Sorry. Wht shld I do?"

'Go to the fair.' From his pocket, he got the note I shoved under his door. With a fine-looking pen, he wrote something.

'I can't. I'm grounded.'

'Get ungrounded.' He held up the paper: "Keep feeding Abaid. That's what you do."

I shrugged, dumb.

His impatient hand made a speed up gesture, as he added to the note.

'I been told to stay here. I got enough trouble.'

'Nothing actually keeps you here.' He held up the paper a last time: "You're smart. Work it out." He folded it, ready for burning. 'If you want the fair, go to the fair.'

My heart cut through my ribs. I fell forward, beating his shirt, flapping against the silk till I felt myself lifted back. He held me arm's length, watching my paddling hands with a fascination that wasn't humiliating.

'I can't.' I flapped and went limp. 'I can't.'

'I'll take you to the damn fair. I'll invite you, how about that? We'll go tomorrow. Just stop crying. You always cry that way?'

'Kinda.'

'Well stop.' He let go my arms. They slapped down.

'We'll meet at 10am, okay? The park. We'll meet there.'
He turned back at the door. 'You're a fruitcake.'

Minutes later, I realised he said that stuff about going to the fair out loud.

I got up early, took a fine, scalding shower to unlock my rainbow bruises. My bones hurt, my muscles stiff and surly. I aimed not to show it. Practised walking till the spasms damped down. Wore the same clothes: skinny blues and plaid shirt. Important to hold Mocha's smoke around me, not carelessly toss her memory down the chute. At least I'd have company at the fair, though my wallet got sadly thin. Not sure where my money went. I couldn't ask Mum for more. Keeping me broke kept my wings clipped. But I'm a resourceful fruitcake.

Some new guy standing watch. There were four, maybe five, working shift I guess. Guess someone stood there the whole time. Even night time. Listening to whispered dreams. The lobby buzzed with a kinda administrative excitement. The day the big conference cojones hit town. Keen to cut whatever deal most suit them. Dad probably went to the conference block at 5am or something. Bet there wasn't one slice of bacon left in the place.

I went cautious around the reception girls, on account of their hatred for me. The tightly-knotted mademoiselle with the flicked-up brunette bob actually picked up her perfume spray when she saw me.

'Um, hi. Is Lilija around?' I figured we were close-enough acquainted to tap her for a loan.

'Pardon?' Inflected the French way.

'Lilija. With the hair.' I mimed the hair. 'Weird, awesome eyes.' I stared at her, staring at me. 'Lilija. The waitress.'

'I am sorry,' sweet sing-song. 'The Assistant Housekeeper manages those staff. We do not know where they are.'

'And who manages you?'

I never knew how mortified looked till then. 'The Front Office Manager.' Quickly adding, 'She is very busy. You see?' She flicked gestures round the lobby. 'The conference. Is that all?'

'Is the maître d' here?'

Wilfully, she shifted attention to a laminate guy beside me. He wanted to arrange private lunch for six. I ceased to exist.

Not for the first time, I kicked my arse about not getting a job. I was kinda grownup looking, I could have asked around. But I did wasting time way better. I doubted The Man would sub me all day and I didn't want him to. I annoyed him enough without getting tagged for a leech. And that tipped me into thoughts of Mocha. You bet she wouldn't let anyone pay her bills. Thinking about her was one big ache. Worse than all the bruises. If only she'd seen what I could be, not just what pissed her off.

Unconsciously maybe, I latched to the smell of coffee from the restaurant, nearly colliding with this meaty wall of police checking ID at the door. I had no such thing and no need of it.

'It's okay, she's immediate family.'

Last time I spoke with Abaid I was not her priority.

181

Yet the day before that she hugged me. So I guess we were upsy-downsy, especially then, as she chivvied some Bajan waitress to find me a table.

Salwa sat with me, so caffeinated she had to grip on the table to stop herself fizzing. The bulge of her gun looked larger than usual. 'I'm not angry. Don't think that. What you told us was wholly correct.'

'Um, the warehouse?'

'Was empty. Or rather, full—of sand and building supplies. That's not the issue.' Her wired voice twisted her accent. 'We know they were there. Forensics found particulates.'

'Particulates?' I needed that coffee.

'Military-grade explosives hum with nitrogen dioxide. Maybe they were storing fertiliser. I don't think so. We got hydrogen cyanide too. Speck of that drops you cold in ten. Whoever was there left too quick to clean up.' That seemed to excite her. 'We know they were there. Someone tipped them off. Don't worry,' she fixed on me. 'We know where you were.'

Close up, again I breathed her fresh, healthy scent—cool, scrubbed, even after a million espressos. She gripped my wrist—not my shirt, the skin of my wrist—a very personal way. Her fingers explored my radial bone and ulna, squeezing them, flexing my joints inside my skin. The most weird, intimate feeling, she could move me around without my involvement. 'Am I your priority now?'

'Very much.' Her lips an undodgeable smile.

# 13

Okay, so it was a sweepstake who I was working for. Everyone thought I was just what they needed, except the one person I needed. The Man told me keep feeding Abaid. Abaid told me keep tracking The Man. She gave me folding money to do her good works. Guess she could claim it or something. So, yes, I took her silver.

To celebrate this quality life-choice, I hit the hotel shop for hair gel. Sometimes I slurp my hair right back, scrunched to look real short. I mean, yeah, I could have cut it—that's commitment though.

The hotel shop opened twenty-four-seven. Maybe the guys who watched the halls idled the early hours with the very entitled blonde who, the second I walked in, pulled the most arsey scowl. To be dangerously truthful, I'm hard now, through experience and stuff. Back then if someone looked at me wrong, I felt as if I'd failed. I didn't want to be late for my ten o'clock, so blurted it out. 'You got gel?'

'For problem hair?'

'Um… just to slick back.'

She gleamed, solidly spiteful. 'Guess you need a hard hold. Something thick.'

The shelf she pointed at so low I had to crouch,

which was double humiliation where I was a feast of sorry bones. Burning up in her snotty glare, I did everything to keep pain from my face. A heap of noise from my head told me I looked worse than a dog. My voices are not kind.

Among packs of gel with pictures of black girls, their hair glossy-wet as a highway on crash night, I found one with this gorgeous ginger, tight bob sculpted behind her ears, blood lips, a killer parting.

Shop girl looked at that picture. Looked at me. 'There's no refund.' She tossed the change on the counter for me to chase.

Seeing those coins roll and clatter just did me. With a grand sweep of my arm, I crashed them onto the floor, bar the measliest coin, which I flicked across the counter. 'Try and get something to eat.'

Before I could flee, the bitch grabbed my wrist. Dug her nails deep. Blood bubbled up. 'Listen dogbreath: you could buy the store, get the biggest makeover. You'd still be a scab-mouth paint-job.'

I swung my free hand—she clenched it midair.

'Touch me and you're drinking your meals.' She shoved me so hard, I smacked over a shelf of shampoo. 'Spazzy little bitch.'

Can't lie. I ran upstairs. Couldn't face the lifts, those mirrors frowning at me. At the mezzanine, I looked over the service roads, not able to understand what I'd done. She hurt me, made me a victim—and I was to blame. Rolling with the grownups, I'd forgotten the world saw a weird girl to be bullied for pleasure by promising blondes. That's the natural order and I upset it. The freak who wanted her open highway, the stainless love of someone special. She'd tell everyone what a great move she pulled. I threw the gel down the laundry chute.

Behind the locked door, my arm caught fire, this heavy, biting pain from elbow to wrist. Nail-punctures, four bloody holes leaking untidy fluid. I tore spit-dab plasters and lay on the floor till twenty-past nine, only dragging myself back around with the knowledge of someone to meet who wouldn't forgive a no-show.

I chose a white shirt with a black bra, where that's always classy, black skinnies that took some tight breathing to haul over my womanly hips, cord jacket and my red All Stars for that carnival touch. I scrunched my hair boylike inside my collar, took a lick at some wine red lipstick and went to the fair.

The lift was rank with laminate traffic—though weirdly, everyone stepped aside not to crowd me. If anything, the road was even more closed than usual, the cops more psyched, the sliver of sidewalk more surveyed. I knew they were all talking about me, underground in control rooms, saying things I could hardly believe were true.

Down by Knightsbridge, I saw the maître d' smoking. Not furtive like kids nor rushed like the conference staff. He smoked luxuriously, like he could smoke anyplace, just preferred the alley. He threw me a hat-tip salute, smoke snorkelling round his fingers. When I looked back, he was giving a light to some waitress, cupping around her hands though it wasn't windy. Walking brisk, I watched my back. I was

185

grounded, bruised, Mum mad enough to do anything. To get the cops I knew were tailing me to drag me back, to party with the razor blade.

He never said where to meet so I hung by Hyde Park Corner, with dateless kids and hopeful early prostitutes. You could tell they were prostitutes, though they tried to be girls just hanging around. Alert, nervous, sharp for the money. They moved around each other elaborately, never getting too close. I wondered if they got a coffee break, went to a bar, dropped the mask. Swapped stories, bitched about the trade, checked each other's makeup before hitting the street again. I wonder where they lived and who they loved.

Don't know if he ever dressed different, fully suited though the heat was sticky. The hookers turned to face him, tank fish at feeding time. He stared that scratchy, underwhelmed way I was getting used to. One of them made a move and he cut her cold. She looked beat. He saw me. 'You're looking exotic.'

I was surprised he showed. 'I've had a stressful morning.'

'Who's a special snowflake, then?'

Yeah, it was the park again, but this time I was grownup—or at least, accessory to a grownup. 'I am sorry about the other night.'

'Next time you feel like acting the dick, save it for the home game.'

Okay, that stung. 'I saw Abaid. Feeding her, how you said.'

'I said nothing.' He stared stone at the horizon.

'You said meet here. Said it out loud, you did. Now

186

there's a pair of cops two hundred feet behind us.' I felt smug. I knew this. 'Man and woman. Woman's a butterscotch blonde. Man's Lex Luthor.'

So casual, The Man flicked his phone to his side, stole a shot of the walkway behind him. 'Nice suit he has. So what the detective tell you?'

Strolling, that's the word, beneath the trees, shooting the breeze, under heavy surveillance. 'She said a few things about you.'

'About me?'

'Yeah, you.'

'She said a few things about me?' Not joking, yet a tiny, wilful thaw in his tone.

'Ruthless clown, she said.'

'She said that?'

'She had a lot of coffee. And that other thing. About military-grade explosives. When the birds flew the coop, they left feathers behind.'

'Is that some local language?'

'I was up pretty late watching B movies. That warehouse. The stuff's gone.'

He sat and I sat beside him, and the cops, somewhat peeved, had to walk by. We watched their embarrassed backs as they ambled away, arguing how best to swing it around. 'You wearing a wire?' he said, ordinarily.

'She said I should. But anything stuck to my skin makes me crazy.' Though I still kinda thought they wired me up while I kicked and bit through dreams of falling. A wire, no thicker than a hair. They could hear my thoughts anyway.

'Why you slapping your head?'

'Um, I'm scratching.'

'Yeah, looks it.' He stretched his tall legs. 'When you became Evel Knievel, I told them their cover was blown.'

That was harsh. Unjust, even. 'You took me there, then told them I'd snitch?'

'I had to, in case you did. If their friends knew you squawked to Abaid, they'd take you apart piece by pretty piece. If I didn't shift their arses, you'd be facing a heap more trouble. I wanted them gone.'

'You wanted them gone?'

'Well dah. Why you think I took you there? They wouldn't leave on my say-so. You brought Abaid, she's a credible threat.'

'So I am working for you?'

He slapped his hands against the bench. 'I have been seriously inconvenienced by you. I'm sitting here now, instead of working.'

'This isn't work?'

'Every day with you is a holiday.' He got his pack and flicked me a smoke. 'The woman you might have seen—don't say names—has difficulties not of her making. The others you might have seen are low-grade anthrax fronting as kryptonite. I don't need the distraction.'

As dirty nicotine bit my blood, it seemed to me he was trying to weave some doubt over what I knew. Same as Mum, with her rattling tales of my delusions. 'Who are they? Why they hate Abaid?' Now Mocha, she hated Abaid. I didn't mention that. I didn't want him to know her.

He hissed smoke from his upper lip. 'People you may or may not have seen have a certain view of life. They may hate Abaid from experience. Maybe they hate lots of people.'

'Who are they?'

'It's not a school trip, Riz. I'm not naming the sights.'

'Don't you trust me?'

Those blue eyes froze my veins. 'You hang a lot of luggage off that question.'

What was it, with the water? Was I truly lonesome? I saw the lake and boats, I saw girls getting shown oars and how to steer by people who trusted that they could learn. It looked fun, the water. 'The water looks fun.'

'So long as you don't drink it.'

That guy could row. We travelled way beyond little kids splashing their ditzy circles, beyond guys showing off to chicks—way around the scrubby island. Feeling regal, I trailed my hand over the side. Greasy water gummed my fingers.

'You not worried for piranhas?' He spoke so Bogart, I didn't know if he was fooling.

'Piranhas?' I saw my fingers from underneath, limply inviting to cold-blooded eyes. 'Piranhas?'

'Travel any river in Brazil, you keep your hands to yourself.'

'You been to Brazil?'

'Briefly. Long enough for piranhas.'

My hand was numb and sludge green when I hauled it up. Warm breeze blew across the park, a bright, stinging breeze. 'How about those things Abaid said?'

'About what?'

'You.'

Willows draped the water. A few cresty birds—maybe Chinese ducks—scrabbled, squawking dumbly. He laid his hat on the seat, stood to slip off his jacket. If I did that the boat was sunk for sure. He dipped the oars and we swung about. 'Focus, Riz. Everyone's working the angles.'

'Whatever you say I'm none the wiser.'

He gave me another cigarette. 'How much you hate your folks?'

Those smokes of his, rich and tarry. 'Are these American?'

'I don't take a round trip to a question.'

'You seen *The Birds*?'

'I seen *Vertigo*. How much you hate your folks?'

No one listened when I told them about Mum. No one believed me. Dad didn't count—he was intermittent and not involved with me anyway. 'So, Tippi Hedren meets Rod Taylor. He's after some lovebirds. That's significant I guess. Anyway, they drive to this plush little town and get it on. Then the birds. Something gives with the birds. They watch. They do stuff. They get real mad for no reason. They make this noise.'

'You get your wings clipped?'

I threw my cigarette butt overboard. It began to dissolve. 'I'll row.' The oars were heavy, waterweed dragged them. I pulled till my shoulders clicked. We didn't get anyplace.

He watched me fight the stodgy lake. 'Why Rothko?'

'You were there,' my breath broken with effort.

'He said, "Silence is so accurate". I like that. I like silence. I heard your interference the second I arrived. You mumble the whole time.'

I couldn't get the oars to move the same way—we sliced random arcs and got nowhere. I was sore and pissed I couldn't work a rowboat. 'Do not.'

'And you cry. You always cry.'

An oar slipped loose its rope. I yanked it back, batting a bucketload of pondlife over my jeans. I was sweating. The water was cold.

'Allow me.'

I surrendered and his strength travelled us to shore.

'Shouldn't we, like, take it back to the boat place?'

'They say that? You hear them say that?'

We picked a parched spot of grass where I could dry off. So many people just laying around doing nothing. I wasn't looking for any of them. 'You think there'll be trouble?'

He pulled up a swatch of grass to see it die. 'Yeah, there'll be trouble.'

'Dad never talks about that stuff.'

'He doesn't need to.'

'Why did you want him away from work yesterday?'

'There it is again, noise to signal.'

I'd take a slap off his big, clean hands sooner than have him be mean to me. 'Sorry. I forgot you don't do questions.'

Could hardly see him for the dazzle of sunshine. 'I

was meeting an acquaintance. Someone your Father knows. What the eye doesn't see, that baloney. Your Father is no interest to me. He doesn't have enough to revive me from a light sleep.'

'He can Mardi Gras in Bogotá and come home clean as Heidi.'

'Yeah, my acquaintance said that. He's very incidental.'

'Seeing as you don't do questions, I won't ask again what's your line?'

'Repo.'

Man, I laughed—I could just see him seizing a pregnant chick's car. 'You stay at plush hotels for a repo man.'

'I clip coupons from free magazines.'

So I figured, being on the police payroll, I ought to be getting the inside track regarding his motivations. 'You sure must travel.'

'What?'

'Around. Like, from whoever.'

'What whoever?'

'Whoever you're travelling from. Your girl.'

'My what?'

'Thought you might have a girl.'

'I have places I go.' Sometimes, he seemed nearly amused with me—or at least, not as annoyed. 'And you, Riz? You travel from whoever?'

My clothes were slimy and didn't fit. 'There's no whoever.'

'There's no one.' That wasn't a question. 'Just the end of a fist.'

I hadn't told him nothing, careful to act informed. 'What you saying?'

Now he had me, square in the eye. 'What I'm saying is you're a loner. An outsider. You haven't taken one call, one message, one shout. There's no one.'

'I muted my phone.'

'Don't lie to me, Riz. You don't do that TikTok, Facebook, Instagram, Twitter, that stuff.'

My voice crept small. 'It's the time, y'know, and keeping it fresh.'

'And you're bullied. That's right, isn't it, Riz? Bullied for your looks by girls whose faces scare dogs. And bullied for your issues by girls with shit for brains. Am I close to right?'

A ball of hard air jammed my throat.

'You get bruised for real on the street and burned on some dandy website. That's why you want a taste of the action.'

So what do you say, when someone peels back your skin? 'I'm lonely.'

'Get your phone.'

'What?'

'We've been seen around together. Might as well get a picture.' He was galvanised by the idea. 'Two drifters, off to see the world.'

So we huddled close on the stinking grass. To fit the frame, I let him put his arm around my shoulder— loose, but a tourniquet choking my skin. Neither of us smiled. When I had the shot, he got his phone, opened an app, touched our handsets together.

'What you doing?'

'File transfer. I want to keep this. I'll tell people you're my niece and a riot to be with.'

Two familiar figures came greasing across the grass. 'There's the cops.'

'Well, I hope so. I hate to dress up and get no attention.' He stood and pulled me to my feet, his grip a bear trap. 'Let's catch some sideshow.'

# 14

The carny swinging the entry gate had the ink-smudge tattoos of a stretch in jail. 'Where you going, dude?'

The Man considered this mulletted creature, his pasty skin stained with blood orange bruises. 'We're off to see the wizard, the wonderful wizard of Oz.'

The carny's ratty eyes flipped to me. 'We hear he is a whiz of a wiz.'

Split-second, his gaze shivered between us. Then he yanked the gate with a stupid mock-bow. I made sure and gave him a stern look. He bared his teeth at me.

Before I could flap my yap, The Man bought a roll of tokens and asked what I wanted to ride. Left to myself, I would have run round scarfing spun-sugar. With him, I wanted to hit the fair with hep and nuance. Caffeine breakfast and prescription painkillers blistered my brain. I didn't want to get sick, so I took him bowling.

Cutting school sometimes, I hid at the union hall and bowled with laid-off guys, so I had the smarts of technique over strength. My signature move was to flirt with the gutter then sidelong the pins off a chain reaction. The Man took a power shot, driving a wedge down the centre. He left four open and wasn't happy.

Next frame, I left him half a dozen where a fly buzzed my face. He took them down without pleasure.

From being a loose-and-lazy fairground thing, it became vital to him to get a strike. His jacket and hat hung on a candy pole, resembling those troubling shrines at the clown cemetery, he cranked his arm, determined on a wipe-out.

With a couple of pins left rocking, the stall keeper said something informed-sounding, that the ball got bias. My neighbour didn't take that kindly. 'That the inside track, son? Some dope you got on the level?'

Maybe the fairground guy bust people's heads if they said his game was rigged. He looked ill-at-ease close to The Man. 'Just saying, buddy. It's the ball. It got bias. You got to compensate. Just saying.'

'Show me.'

'I don't leave this counter, buddy. I got the boss up my hole, get me?'

'You don't leave the counter?'

'I don't leave the counter.'

'So what the damn hell you know about bowling?'

Looking to regain the party spirit, I found my favourite stall at the fair. Tell you, *es muy mágico*. Blue smoke from the generator seeped through the canvas, powering vertical blasts of ice-cool air. I floated my fingers over the table, little hurricanes striving to push them apart. That rising breeze froze sweat to my skin. *Chantilly Lace* hummed from the speakers. 'First to seven goals.'

If there's one thing I can truly do, it's air hockey. Light with hunger, sweating a storm, scarcely looking my personal best, at that table, right then, I knew I could compete.

Especially as that guy, for all his acuity and distance, hadn't learned everything. First shot, he laid out the classic beginner's error: he smacked down the puck, forgetting it wasn't a ball, forgetting the jets of air erupting from the table. If you smack the puck too hard it catches air and takes flight. That's a foul. If you're really lucky, it hits someone and starts a fight. That's entertainment. Shooting the puck off the table, that's a real beginner's boner and, boy, he didn't show much grace when he went to get it back. Second time, he struck the thing so louche it hovered to a gentle rest a mile shy of my goal line. I hit a ten-degree diagonal, slid neatly into his goal. I waggled my goalie around. 'You're kinda meant to do this.'

By the time he was three-nil down, his lips got sucked into his face. That guy had smarts, started to copy my moves, gave his duster the uphill flick that's my signature on the air court. Over hit, though, or laid it soft—he tried to fight the jets. He thought strength and cussing ruled the table, amazed every time he clattered the puck somewhere east of the slot machines. 'How you get so good at this waste of time?'

'Practice.'

'Cute. C'mon.'

Walking with him through hotdog air, I checked my phone, that wearisome duty. Usual needling calls from Mum. And one from Dad, his concerned words disinterested and unwilling. They were worried for me. I could smell how much. I messaged kid brother, told him to tell Mum I was fine, that crap. Seemed a muddled compromise. If I cared, I would have called her. If I didn't care, I'd let it be. What I was, was indecisive, a weakness Mum and Dad and Grover could make lethal. It's a wonder I was right at all, with the shit I had going down.

'Practice.' He was burned at getting beat. 'Okay. Let's practice.'

A very illustrated guy stroked air guns a delicate way. Seven foot tall, barrel-wide, his skin big on obscenity, the hands of some creepy surgeon, stroking guns. Baikals, I think, with the narrow snout. Gun guy saw the jacket and tie and fedora, gave a nod, the way nightclub goons nod the big dog through the rope. 'One?'

The Man made a huffy noise. 'Two.'

Like all girls I yearned to have a big gun, I never guessed they sat so awkward. Even those Baikals, which weigh just a couple of kilos. He let me struggle, watching me paw the plasticised grip with the closest he got to amusement. The barrel slipped, thunking against the counter and the carny laughed a kitten-drowning way.

'Allow me.'

I'm really, really not good with being touched, but had to submit to The Man as he flexed my shoulders, laying the stock against my collarbone—his hands near my actual chest—threading my fingers round the trigger blade, warm from the sun.

That voice, low and humid, 'See the cans, those cans

right there? They killed your dog. Now they're laughing at you. You hate them. Go get 'em all.'

So I'm dumb. I thought—this being a theme park world—the guns would shoot laser light and a robot voice call hit or miss. I didn't expect that gun really shot. Not till the butt took a chunk from my shoulder and the pellet drilled wild through the gun shack roof.

The carny grunted. 'Cans still standing.'

My arm on fire, my neck seared by the recoil, tears flooding the rims of my ginger eyes.

And that dirty dog voice, 'Try again.'

The zing died with a soft thunk. My arm felt broken.

The stall guy pulled a big grinning chimp off the shelf, holed and bleeding toxic fibres. 'You shot the monkey.'

Hot, horrid, The Man viced my shoulders. Pushed me down so my heels bit gritty earth. 'Riz.' His voice underground. 'There are guys out there that will kill you. They pack their piece and gift you a one-way ticket. What you do? Wisecrack? Cry, so they think, "Aw shucks, she's just a girl"? Is that what you do?' His fingers dug hard. 'This is not a game. Those cans, they're your Mother.'

Took aim sharp as I could, staring wide to keep from crying. Where his fingers gripped, their pressure remained. Where he spoke, his voice stayed in my head. I squeezed the trigger.

Gravely, a real curator, the stall-keeper picked up the can, showed its raggy, angry hole. 'Good,' he said, not joking.

The Man tapped his finger against the burst metal.

'One day you'll do that every time.' He shouldered the rifle. 'Like this.'

One to six, he scorched every can off the shelf. Then the next row just the same. Everything gone with a clatter of metal. The carny racked up another round and the guy in the suit took them down.

'Cool.' I meant it.

The Man said nothing.

'How you get so good?'

'Practice.'

Dirty-hungry, I recognised the burger cart as unwholesome. Didn't want to faint, though and wake up back in hospital with my brain down the waste disposal. Some pretty little lacy dress laid out for dainty, scrubbed Amelia. At the cart, a radio pumped breaking news: a brawl in Trafalgar Square, right beside Rothko. Families fleeing in terror, screaming kiddies, that crap. Police going hard with the pacification. Elsewhere, Russia denied supplying chemical weapons to Syria, while desert guys trampled babies to be king of the rock. I got a double with blue cheese and chilli, and felt better.

The Man surveyed stalls and tents, looking for things he could win at. I checked for the cops, a little sorry for them. We had the lake, we played a few tents—we did nothing of interest to what I assumed were professionals with careers to fill.

'You hear that?'

I heard chilli dancing flamenco round my guts.

'That kid. With those bozos. Called you a skank.'

With crashing certainty, I knew which bozos he meant. Cutting through the crowd, tatts and piercings that made the carnies look modest, Mocha's army. The kids I got busted. Except in bright light they weren't kids—they were rangy bastards. No brainer why they were there—while the rumble ate up the West End, they slipped from the cops to hide in the dumb crowd. That's what I do.

'He called you a skank. I heard.' The Man seemed to be waiting for something. 'What you gonna do?'

What did he mean 'do'? 'Roll with it, I guess.'

'Roll with crap? You not angry?' He was angry.

'I take bruises. Let's hit the rides.' Again, my arm got the force of it—my arm that smacked the highway, that got flexed by Abaid and cut by some shop-bought blonde. 'Eek eek.'

'Don't make that noise.'

'You keep touching me.'

'I'll touch your head if you don't shut up.' Growling, sleek as an angry bear. 'That cock-face called you a skank and walked away. So what you tell me? You roll with it? That's enough? You think life's got infinite space to be Helen Keller?'

By then he was really burning my wrist, driving his rage into me. A quick flash of tears I couldn't shake.

'Yeah, cry.' He flung my arm up. 'Don't you just cry.'

'What do you think I can do?' I shouted, not to wail.

He poked my actual chest. 'You stand your ground. Call it home, call it love, whatever makes money. You step up.'

'What?'

'You make him sorry.'

'I do what?'

'Or you blame someone else, or cry. You always do.'

In phonytown, where I got kept till then, I took beatings. I never told because no one wanted to know. As I walked towards the warehouse tribe, my head shouted 'No!' so loud, I looked round thinking the voice was outside. Right to the second I hit their airspace, I hadn't a clue what to say. 'Um… hey. Hey.'

Twenty pairs of eyes locked on me. I remember tatts and smoke and tall, dancing shadows. And clean, springy muscles, visible strength crackling through. That tribal sense of being swift and legion. Guess they lived every minute on the edge of a fight. They had ingenuity, one of life's most powerful drugs.

'Cops taking care of you, snaky little bitch.' A cartoon guy with a gnome goatee. 'Looks like shit, smells like shit.'

'I was locked up because of you,' a fried skate-girl said needlessly. 'They wouldn't let us piss. You tell them to do that?'

'Well, no, I didn't.' I already got they were circling. 'I just heard. Well, my friend heard…'

'Your cop-bitch friend?'

'No, um, we heard, you maybe called me a name.'

Now they formed up, I could tell who was the dog. Funky dreads and complex sideburns stained toxic blue, a smooth, lip-hugging tache and sparrow beard. The skinny black tee and tight jeans of the real troublemaker. These massive hubcap earrings, altogether too many teeth. He invaded my space,

202

looking down at me keenly. 'You did a bad thing,' his voice a swamped, judgemental calm. 'You broke up the evening. Delayed our plans. You got people hurt.'

Enough teeth for a bone maze. 'They were going to bust you anyway. I sprung you out. I told her that.'

'Told who?'

Now it mattered, I didn't know her name. 'The girl with nice hair.' My back prickled hot, the mass of them no more than six inches away. Tall, cutting me off from the world. A gang of kids huddled and no one to see I was locked between them. Except the guy who set me up.

Top dog yawned, his big, nasty mouth blasting stale smoke and cheap brew. 'We just had a gutful of your friends down the road. Wherever we go, they know it. And then here's you.'

A sharp jab at my spine. I spun around. Dread-guy palmed my shoulder. I faced him and got spiked in the back again. 'What you talking about? Everyone knows you guys. They had you under surveillance before you arrived.'

'Really?' He palmed me again. 'You know so much about it. Skank.'

He struck this beat from my shoulder bone while someone played tunes on my head. 'Quit it.'

'Or what, skank?'

'Skank.' It went up around me, with all the soiled names I got so used to.

'Ginger pig.' Skate-girl had this skate-girl whine that irresistibly pulled me to her. 'Know your name, then,' and, quite theatrically, she spat in my face.

Punches, front and back, connected through my body. Someone yanked my hair. 'Hey.'

'Skank,' the guy shook his dreads, 'we didn't start this fight.'

I went down quick, bidding up my fists, so someone yelled, 'It's that spacky kid off YouTube. The kid in the ditch,' and somehow that made it worse. So much hurt beat into my ready-bruised body: my wrists got grabbed, someone knuckled my skull—I saw bright, nasty stars. My legs bowled aside, the ground smacked hard up at me. Just this little, distant patch of sky, then faces closed in and I got kicked. Skate-girl bent low, spit pearling her lips. Then one big shout.

'You stopped laughing. Why you stopped laughing?'

This reedy, squeaky voice. 'Who are you, man?'

'I'm the guy spoils everyone's fun.'

The crowd broke. This sudden, dark shape swept the ground. The Man picked up the shank that dreadlocks guy dropped, flew it toward the kid's chest. 'This how you do, big fella? Razor in the eye? Want a taste, huh? Want to lick it?'

Some failed sacrifice, broken yet still breathing, I sprawled as this twenty-foot figure punched chests, smacked skulls, told the crowd this party was through. I watched their captive horror as this sharp-dressed apparition forced the dog to lick the blade he planned to use on me. A casualty at the fair, hot tempers and a stray knife. Common business. I heard planets shift gears.

Seeing his comrade dishonoured, the puffball-goatee tried for alpha status. He came back at The Man. 'You can't hurt us, dude. You can't touch us.'

'Or what? You call your lawyer? Let's make it worth a damn.'

When I was small, I loved milkshakes. One day, I found if you blow down the straw these big, rowdy bubbles blurble up. I liked that sound. I heard that bubbled noise right then. That, and a woman scream. Not a movie scream, not a clean, bright scream. An untidy yowl, punctured with messy breaths. I've heard screams with way more conviction. Her shriek and that bubbled sound: the rising whine of a hose clenched tight against water. Then this real calm voice, my voice, saying, 'Leave him. He's just a kid.'

Then the fair got hold again, the whoops and tumbling bells and carnies shouting how everyone's a winner.

'Yeah,' said The Man, 'You rockstars got no better things to do?'

By the time he sat me up—explaining that folks laid out create needless attention—Mocha's army had retreated, concealed, plain-sight, in the crowd. The Man asked was I badly hurt and how well could I not show it. I told him that was in my skillset.

So he yanked me till my bones fell back in place with a jumbled crunch. Trying to drive my scarecrow limbs, I told him, 'You're the bravest.'

He grunted. 'I should care. You fought them. That's brave.'

Dutifully clutching his tough shoulder, I adopted a

lame-dog hobble to make it seem to the gawkers that I just twisted something. 'I got beaten though.'

'You got scared and didn't stop.'

I was starting to understand that mattered.

Round the edge of the fair, painted stalls gave way to big diesel wagons streaked with mud and roadkill. Power cables and water hoses meshed between them. A constant thunk of generators gave the air a smoky flavour as scuffed-looking kids played jacks with stones. They looked at us like nothing was surprising.

He propped me against a truck wheel. 'You want to throw up?'

'I ain't going to.'

Then he checked me, I mean, like a sports coach checking damage.

'I'm okay.'

'You got kicked bad.'

'No, that's where I hit the road the other night.'

He cuffed my cheek. 'You sure soak it up. C'mon, you earned a drink.'

'Did the cops see that stuff, you reckon?'

He gave his chin a thoughtful tweak. 'The cops following us will now believe you are wholly against those rebel shenanigans. Which is useful.'

Yeah, I got that. 'Working the angles, huh?'

'You're so smart you scare me.'

I breathed the blue-fringed air of carnival's edge. Tasted heat and the highway. *Calles anchas, grandes cielos.* 'What you do to that kid?'

'Explained to him about repo.'

# 15

North of Hyde Park, the streets had edge—more cops than I ever saw, showing guns. At every corner, a knot of skate kids, ash-faced women, guys who looked unslept. Some kids wore latex faces, politicians and pop singers. Surgical scrubs, gas masks, steelworkers' face guards. Industrial, metalled, hard, experienced. Cops videoed kids. Kids videoed cops. A taste everywhere of wanting to get it started.

The Man glared. 'Droogs.'

I got that, and felt cold.

I flowed in his slipstream, how he walked, where no crowd could deflect or delay him. I tried looking full of meaningful bruises, not some girl who got beat at the fair. Each breath, I tasted more tension, each corner more psyched than the last. By Gloucester Square, a squad of cops blocked traffic, asking questions, checking ID. My paceman hung a left into Stanhope Terrace, dived us through prosperous side streets. By then, my chest was killing, my lungs squeezed against soft tissue lesions. My legs hot pillars of pain.

He strode into an alley. Catching air between stiches, I watched how he filled it, wide shoulders scraping tag-heavy bricks. Electric-coloured letters, dissed and smothered. Daggers and words like daggers, fat middle fingers with star-point rings, bone hands holding pirate flags, claims that read kinda hollow. A sunrise landscape of waiting sands that was Rothko in quick-dry. The same ochre that hung priceless in low light. Rothko was around, still, when TAKI 183 and Tracy 168 got into business. Did he see those fades on subway cars? Did he check passing throw-ups and recognise art within the noise? I love to think he picked up a spray can one time, just maybe.

Behind a modest green door, an older chick sat at a counter, actually smoking like smoking inside was okay. Butterfly kisses overfilled the ashtray—guess what she did was smoke and fix up her lips. Her attention went to him. I didn't exist.

'Got a table?'

'Bar or club?' Her voice the most old-time sandpaper. 'Say club. We have a show.' Then she saw me. 'Oh.' Her lips got a pinch. 'Guess it's bar.'

For no clear reason, he laid a note on the counter. She flirted a little with it, before folding it into her hand.

I stumbled behind him down spiral stairs. 'What is this place?'

'Bar.'

A passageway led to a cellar, plain-paste walls streaked yellow from gas-style lamps. Low-rent, square wood tables, hard chairs. Blow-up repros of city streets gave that underground room weird altitude. A few guys talking with guys. A few women old as Mum. I checked my phone.

'We're below the signal.'

A smooth, worried man came over, fetid in a heavy suit, his Errol Flynn lip-hair waxed and twitchy. 'Welcome, sir. You are welcome.'

Those hundred-mile blue eyes glanced off the guy's sweaty forehead. 'Well, it's a pleasure to be here. Two Tom Collins.'

The bar guy's face danced between hospitality and regret. 'Can I ask, Sir? If I may ask? Is your companion of age?'

'What?'

'Is she old enough?'

'She's old enough for Tom Collins.' He crossed his arms. 'Is there more conversation on this?'

When the guy slid away with a promise of drinks, The Man turned those eyes at me. 'You got pain?'

Everything hurt: head, spine, abrasions everyplace. More than ever, I yearned to be brave. Through the wall, this dead-sounding beat rumbled, topped with laughter. 'I got experience with pain.'

He pushed a bowl of pretzels at me. 'You sure are the hoo-ha.'

'People say it's because I'm, like, pubertal.'

'No, this is you for keeps.'

Guess hydrogen peroxide must be a vitamin, the waitress looked so healthy. Frizzed, punky, tall and built, a studded face and suggestions of tatts up her sleeve. A smoky voice that said to enjoy our drinks. The pain shifted.

The Man swapped the glasses. 'They'll have given you sub-strength.'

'Don't you have it now?'

He downed the tall drink and shouted, 'Two more Tom Collins.'

I took a bite—Tom Collins was friendly.

The waitress brought refills. 'Thirsty, honey?'

'Getting hot out there.'

As she slopped her hips to another table, he turned to me, 'Time for you to go back.'

Starkly, I understood that tomorrow they'd take me home. 'They won't care if I never go back.'

'You really think they'll pull you apart?'

'They hate me. It's a prison.'

He held the glass to his lips. 'You ever been in prison?'

'I never asked to dangle on the nipple, know what I mean? People see you have money, nice place to live. They think it's okay.'

'Well, it's a start.'

'I'm unloved and unwanted.' I never said that to anyone who didn't write it on yellow paper. 'You think I'm dumb?' The waitress's arm intervened. As she landed more drinks, I saw a beautiful ink-line of strong, bare legs slipping from her shirt sleeve. 'Is your tattoo Betty Grable?'

'Other arm's Rita Hayworth.'

'I got a stamp. A hula girl.'

'Nice.'

Kinda scratchy, he took a long drink. 'I don't think you're dumb. I think you ain't figured what you're about yet.'

Cold gin slipping down gave the room a frosty-sweet glow. 'Tell Grover.'

'The shrink?'

'He takes kids' heads and breaks them apart. Sends them back ready for school. One more time with Grover and I'll disappear.'

'I don't find disappearing stops me getting things done.'

He so didn't get it. I slapped his arm, my palm making zero-impact on cold-cut linen.

He watched my fingers slip back. 'I'll tell you something and punch your arm so you hear what I'm saying.'

'Huh?'

'What my old man said to me. I'll tell you something and punch your arm so you hear what I'm saying.'

The idea he had family was so grotesque, I giggled. 'What's your Dad like?'

'What's he like?'

'I mean, what's he do?'

'He does nothing. My Mother killed him. She's a fruitcake.'

It was too delightful. 'There's crime in your family? True crime?'

'There's none in yours?'

'Aw, phooey.'

'Some people say pallying up to guys who start wars ain't so healthy. Not me. I love the smell of napalm.'

Guess the plenary had started. Guess the party had too. Through quaking streets, Mocha would lead her heroes in old-school revelry. Maybe the kid who tried to knife me was her special someone. Snuggled tight, between wars. 'Guess your Dad loved your Mum, though?'

He grunted. 'Maybe. I wouldn't play house with her.'

So he had a story, for all his toughness. A story as shabby as anyone's. 'You see her?'

'She disappeared when she busted prison. So what you doing, to stop being lonely?'

His gross trick worked a charm. Through the streets, Mocha, head high, would be yelling at cops about justice. Taking on the whole world, with no need for me beside her. 'I'm okay. Don't worry for me.'

He gestured the waitress—she brought more drinks, treating me a sidelong glance from her cat-eye makeup.

The Man said, 'Fine, you're okay. That's great. Now let me try and explain this a way you might understand. There's you, okay, Riz? You walk down the street. You hear important-sounding boots behind you, boots you just know belong to someone swell. You don't turn around. Why would you? You're young and the boots are behind you. They get closer and there, beside you, there's the most wonderful person. Awesome. Heart-stopping. Whatever words mean something to you. Walking right beside you, their boots hitting ground next to yours. Tad faster than you, but that's okay—you're young. Then they start pulling away. See their head and back, legs and boots, see them, richly ahead. You don't speed up. Why would you? They're just a fraction ahead. And you walk, and they walk, every step, pulling further and further away. Their boots hitting ground you can't even see. Then you speed up, test yourself, how you used to, when you were young. You know what, though? You can't catch them. They're too far ahead and you don't have the push that you used to. Then you feel fear. You can't catch them ever. You let them go. Though you could have kept up, when you were young and they weren't a lifetime away.'

Big, angry heat swirled my body. My head fell weirdly silent. 'That happen to you?'

He tossed me a note. 'Go settle. I'll be outside.'

At the paydesk, the waitress did stuff with receipts and a calculator. Her hair looked overslept and the bar light showed her tawny, solemn cheeks got a brush of acne so cute I wanted to dot-join with my fingers. As Betty and Rita slip-slided from her sleeves, my head got rowdier than ever. Hungry lungs strained for breath, heart beating so hard I felt it through my tongue. 'Huh.'

She turned. I had her attention.

'Pretty neat. Your ink. Really cool. You know Rita, she was the bomb.'

That waitress grinned a ruby tooth. 'You just getting used to it, kid?'

This burning flush through my stomach, like steam from a busted pipe. 'I dig it. Your ink.'

'Come back in a couple of years, yeah? I dig redheads.'

Her finger drew a cold, hard line down my cheek. 'Ohhh.'

'Don't rush it, kid.' She pinched my chin, folding change into my hand, so gentle and strong. 'Live single first. Gathered flowers are dead.'

I didn't want to go, the cab driver didn't want to take me. He said I was drunk, while The Man explained to me that I'd be no help to his business. A lot of noise blowing up nearby.

'You let me come with you before.' Damn, I sounded petulant.

'I told you for why. This is a different affair. Besides,' he cocked an ear to the racket a few streets away. 'We need you indoors before the fireworks start.'

'Listen, mate.' The cab driver waved a meaty arm from his window. 'I got to get back to Chingford. I got five years' finance on this.'

'I'm not going to no hotel.' And indeed, I might have stamped my foot and loosed off unladylike language.

The Man didn't have kids. I knew, by how he talked to me. So when I busted a tantrum he was lost. Fronting guys with guns is easier. 'You want me to walk, I'll walk. You're not my problem.'

'How much booze has she had?' The cab driver didn't have a neck as such—his head swivelled by some mechanism of chunky, reddened skin. 'Should she be drinking at her age?'

That riled me, so I flung more unladylike language. He told me what I could do with myself and drove off.

Then a jangle of breaking glass nearby and a mean-sounding cheer.

'I'll walk,' The Man repeated. 'It's not an empty threat.'

'It's no threat at all.' I really slurred that.

One second, he was caught between keeping me on his leash and getting on with his own damn business.

'Don't hesitate,' I said grandly, 'doesn't suit you.'

'You're one sharp little cat, you know that?' He forced a wedge of cash at me. 'Get a cab. Get to the hotel. Seriously. I don't want you involved.'

'With what?'

'With what's next.'

Battered though my legs were, they got an awful itch to run after him when, as promised, he walked. I felt I sort-of belonged at his side and getting left flat was frankly painful. The other night when he walked, I had that Vespa to deal with. This was daylight, though, and a swank London street. Sure, the ache in my cheekbone called me back to the bar. To the only touch till then that showed actual impression for me. But she said a couple of years and I wanted that in my back pocket. Something to sustain me. A flame in the dark. Sure I'd return, two years to that day, and present myself for approval. A promise I could keep with me, wrapped tight in my warm heart.

Torn between two excitements, my head said follow The Man. Not right up his back, I'm not dumb. Didn't need to get close, he showed so big among nervy shoppers and wussy kidults looking to dodge the action. Supremely drunk, I was bulletproof, tracking him through the jumpy herd while, surely, the cops tracked me.

The Man, he walked a lot. I don't think he wanted anyone controlling his location. To Marble Arch, along Park Lane, every snooty hotel guarded by Turkish guys in choking collars. A smooth left into Upper Grosvenor Street, very much the fat part of town. Mount Street,

Berkeley Square, swish and sterile as a photoshoot. Everywhere had security teams—baseball caps and puffy jackets. No doubt covert persuasion stashed in their pockets.

Drunk, the whole street gleamed shimmery bright, its chrome the ice in a hi-ball. Some blocks away, the party spreading, filling streets with this low-down roar.

Everywhere with chipboard nailed over the windows. Jewellers and yacht shops and swank car dealers stashing their luxury. Man, I was laughing to think a young woman made that happen. A young woman who knew me. Okay, no happy ending, but her delivery was top-notch. Tom Collins got me gleeful. I smiled so hard grownups stepped aside, thinking I carried some joyous contagion.

Cop wagons came speeding through. Not just with the wire mesh, the freakin armoured wagons. The ones they throw you in and a scrap of chopped liver comes out. By then I was getting air horns, fireworks, breaking glass, tourists bolting for safety. Sure enough, Mum called, wanting me back quick-time. I messaged that I was hunkered with a friend and best not to travel. She messaged back that I didn't have friends.

Still tracking The Man, walking tall and fast. Then I lost him. He cut across Regent Street slick as a knife, while I got tangled with a panicking tour party. Once I fought clear, he'd vanished. Only comfort was the cops lost me too.

Never knew till then how so much of rioting is standing around or walking one place to another. What I felt from that crowd, the ache it transmitted, this total sense of trying to find where it's at. Wanting some, being relevant in the seat and domain of the action. Their need to unite and belong to the trouble, wholly alien to me. In my eyes, they were painted glass and I was the only thing moving.

To get clear of the fuss, I went around back of some snoot-looking bar—heavy with bull-necks watching the door—into some dowdy street, dark except for a red brick palace, lit like Chinese Christmas. Its tumbling neon waterfalls cascading around a sign, bright red: 'The Golden Arm Grande Luxe Casino—Roulette and Poker'. And more modestly underneath, 'Members Only'. It looked glitzy and fake and disgusting. So why not?

A black stretch Hummer pulled up and these penguin jackets came galloping to fawn at the doors. Some entourage dudes climbed out, then the real dog—big and blinged and looking a total bastard—unfolded himself and stomped inside, leaving everyone chasing after. Some girls followed too, the usual spackle.

Checking my looks, it seemed pretty plain even a wildly-generous door policy wouldn't stretch to accommodate me. My reflection did not say high roller. Couple more fat-arse cars pulled up, discharging elegant trash. Even the frauds of the entourage looked more convincing than me. Just starting to calculate if I could manage to climb a drainpipe, swing through a window, that shit, when a black van with a stretch chassis showed up, its sides decorated with the likeness of a big red hand with complex fingers and 'Prince Federico's Fearsome Flamenco' in bloodied script. The penguin men directed the driver around the corner. So I hustled to that side street, where the van parked behind the casino. Call me Queen of the Loading Bay.

So there's me: drunk, invincible teenage woman sliding into dirty twilight, among the back shadows of some deluxe asylum for wasters. A half-dozen guys climb from Prince Federico's van, modelling the most appalling shirts with red and yellow ruffles, black trousers so tight their balls squeak. Clumpy, stack-up boots. I'm not dissing the culture—I live for flamenco—just these guys were a whole different wrong. They clumped round back of the van to unload a heap of white chairs, guitars, plastic palm trees and tacky statues of midget bulls.

Oh yeah, and there was the dancer. Riding in back, tall sitting down, rising to imperial height as she stepped to the road, busting this fantastical dress, black, embroidered with green and gold flowers, a black Manila shawl bound tight round her waist, and black Cordobes hat with green and white band. Colours of the Andalusian flag, I know that now. She flicked around a tricky-looking fan, a tool for giving orders. She had dancer's physique, a commanding voice and I'm pretty sure she was trans. I scuttled around behind her back and started unloading the bulls.

'Who are you?' The guy sounded neither Spanish nor friendly.

'Busboy. Boss sent me to give you a hand.'

'You don't look like a busboy.'

'I got here late.'

Now those bulls were souvenir crap. Heavy, hard at

the tail and this sloshing round the midriff that made them awkward to carry. I didn't think just then why that should be. The flamenco dudes faffed with chairs and potted palms, though frankly their calzonas hugged so tight they couldn't carry much.

We lugged this supremely authentic junk into a concrete passage, where some old bloke gave directions, translated by the queen into chops and flicks of her fan. As we lumbered through the back halls of the building, I heard the siren call of slot machines, rinky piano music and the civilised excitement of people burning money. I just knew The Man was there, playing alligator stud with skills he learned in repo.

Up to then, no one spoke to me much. But as they set up, one guy said something about 'this busboy' and things got predictably interesting.

'Busboy?' A young man who had carefully slid himself into a frozen shirt stared at us. 'You had a spillage?'

That troubled the flamenco master. 'Why you say that?'

They looked at each other. With the tiny amount of stealth I possess, I backed away. The casino foot soldier tried again. 'You require one of our busboys? For the show?'

With an almighty clack of her fan, the queen took charge. She wheeled its black ribs, gave a left-hand twirl and jabbed the boleta at me. 'That.' All she needed to say.

Plagued by a moment of clarity, I realised how dissonant I looked, among marbled walls and fake

Persian rugs. Just the other side of the curtain was laughter and the heavenly sound of cash raining from slots. Getting chased through happy punters by agitated tailcoats would do nobody any good. So I shut off the fear and let rip. 'I'm here for the job.'

Casino guy did a pinched little shake of his head, as though a stranger to English.

'Mr. McSweeney at the agency said to roll right in. I got such a work ethic, I start before I'm hired. Shall I go to the kitchen now? I'm so psyched to lay hands on those dishes.'

'Kitchen?'

'This way, huh?' And I'm away through the curtain. Though not before I got burned from the flamenco men, whose eyes said they weren't fooled.

# 16

Stumbling through reasons to look how I looked, with everyone else like a watch ad at Christmas, I bypassed the slots though I itched to drop coins. Those machines are cool; so great when you win, you forget losing. It was no Vegas parlour, with banks of machines and flashing tubes in the ceiling. A London place: grey and playing more swish than it actually was. A waitress gave me a what-the-eff look, but the punters were locked with the rolling sevens and saw nothing as I breezed through the big flowers and pointless chandeliers. The toilets had an oval fountain – fake marble with fake gold trim – which seemed a bizarre and frankly off-putting idea. Beneath its sprightly waters, a shellac of coins and chips gave tribute to the foxy superstition of gambling women. I revelled in their luscious uptalk of chances taken and losses forgiven. It was worth the tip I gave the old crone with the towels to have spent a few minutes among such sharp and shrewdly vacuous females. Acting blonde for the men but each, I knew, was a terrifyingly slick operator. When you live on your looks, you make your paycheques quick-time.

If The Man was in that building I had to find him— casinos have more cameras than a London street. No doubt, guys in tuxes were already checking my moves. From the hallway with its luxuriating wasters, rooms gaped open all sides, except one set of doors at the end that were tight shut. Looking a purposeful elf for the cameras—glad at least I wore a white shirt: maybe I could pass as an oik from the basement—I cruised the doorways till I heard the magic of the rattling ball.

Now, I love roulette. I don't even aim for cash, just love how it plays. You know the number series have names? Right round the wheel, they have names. Twenty-two through twenty-five are the *Grands Voisins du Zéro*. Neat, huh? It's the most complex, brilliant, maddening game. Once you get over the arseholes who play it. Creeping into the roulette room, my heart cutting up rough. Way young, I hadn't played much to then. Just online, amateur fooling. The place had a dozen tables, the dealers a mix of slinked-up Polish girls in cocktail sheaths and bald wheel-masters rocking dinner suits. I spotted the pit boss straight off—a large, graceful, older man, clapping backs, sharing jokes, noticing everything. Don't ask, I knew he saw me.

And that sound, the rush of the ball, slowing, eddying, clunking down, repeated over and over, with the laughs and sighs of players hitting big or coming down. The French instructions, '*Rien ne va plus*,' and everyone stops breathing. Just stuff I grew to love, on the road to being me. The cash The Man gave me made a credible stake and I was no dummy. The house edge on a single number bet in the European game is 2.63%. On the wheel you got one way to win and thirty-six to lose. Which means the house eats you 98% of the spin. So what?

I picked a table with an older guy dealing—to avoid distraction issues—slipping into a seat before the spin closed. Nobody won, so a kind of serene detachment went round the players—hey, we all lost, we sail the same boat. The players were a standard bunch of lounge suits and festive dresses—maybe even some laminate people, seeing the sights. None had the cool burn of the pro nor the fret lines of the big loser. Some sharp looks came my way, but we're all trash nowadays.

I slid a note over the glorious felt. 'Change, please.'

The dealer—a real old maestro—didn't turn a hair, just nudged me the chips. Plain red jobs, consistent with the modest amount I laid. Did a couple of straight up bets and lost both times. Then I laid a quad and got paid eight-to-one, which caused a mild ripple—though my winnings wouldn't have scored a beer in that place. I went 17-and-the-neighbours three times straight, got creamed then shovelled my last chip on a six line with a 16% chance of winning and got paid five-to-one. Best twenty minutes I had all day.

Factually, I got so caught with repetitive wonder, I thought that tap on my shoulder was a bystander wishing me luck. I turned and, foolishly, let out a squeak.

The Russian guy from the warehouse, in a different everyday suit with another horrific tie, knocked his plastic hand against my shoulder. 'Miss Montgomery, I think. Is truly small world. You are here to expose the capitalists at play?'

'I'm just playing the wheel.'

He glanced beyond the table, at the pit boss. 'Your playing brings much attention. Perhaps we move to the lounge.'

'Er, not really.'

'I hear the lounge is *prevoskhodnyy*.'

'Ner?'

'For once, I am disappointed to be proved right Miss Montgomery. Perhaps you would explain why you bring the police to my door?'

So we went to the lounge. I mean, I could have pulled the 'this man's bothering me' crap, but if he got slung so would I, and at least he stood me a vodkatini. Basically, the lounge was full of everyone who busted their wedge, the action big on talk, short on chips. He held his glass with his plastic hand, which was bizarrely beguiling. He had a trunkful of Muscovite charm and he hated me.

'To move so much product at pace is costly and awkward, you understand. An unexpected drain on scarce resources. It makes our clients nervous.'

I was dealing with a lot of vermouth—like being force-fed coriander—so maybe I struggled to notice his toxic tone.

'You think this is not so serious?' He put down his glass, meaningfully.

'I think they're shorting the measures.'

'The Syrian detective, you know who she is? You know who we are?'

I tried not to get drawn into the ghastly pattern of

his tie. 'I'm new to this line of business. It's a bit of a misunderstanding.'

'Oh no, no, no.' He picked up his drink. 'Is no misunderstanding. Is fifty million dollars of product transported unexpectedly because some *glupaya devchonka* believes what is told by a liar.' He grinned. He looked awful. 'Perfectly explained, yes? Your associate, who is *ublyudok*, very much so, he tell us you and Salwa are house on fire. That's the expression, yes? I hear she is mummy to you.'

'I wouldn't say that.'

'You shut up now. Now your friend is involved, our clients feel the desert wind, you say, in their crack. Our staff are nervous.' He leaned across the fancy table, spitting angry breath. 'We come here because this conference is both opportunity and distraction. Money men are here, police protect them, business gets done. We do not buy this product sale or return—we need customers, yes? Customers who feel safe from misguided attentions of the jolly British police. Now you, you bring Abaid, you bring fear. Fear is expensive.' Just as he seemed fit to bite me the lights went down. 'Is what?' Side-tracked by guitar commotion from onstage.

Prince Federico's boys, churning those strings with quick menace. Not the greatest guitarists, but forthright, they tickled and plucked and jammed so the dancers got moving. I say dancers, but the spruce, tight-jacketed guy mainly strode about, clacking his palms as though rounding up truculent sheep. Where the action was was the woman. She struck a pose, then began winding her fingers through smoothly sinuous shapes over her head. Looking unwholesomely fine and savage as music cranked hard around her. She traced her hips with splayed fingers, made come-get-me gestures—the kind you'd think twice about latching onto—then danced, wholly feline, down front of the stage, making extraordinary percussion with her heels. Flicking her skirt, doing astonishing things with her wrists, while the unwashed guitarists chuntered around, slinging rhythms beneath her feet like rose petals.

Even the Russian stopped giving me grief, an appalled fascination settling around his knife-edge cheeks. The crowd clapped along, the risk of jollity rising, especially when some delusional second-lifers got chumping around, their moves misbegotten in any field of flamenco.

The band played another dance, the crowd totally clapping off-time and I started to feel through my watery guts something horribly amiss with the whole caboodle. Calculating how fast I could sprint to the exit when, with a mighty '*Olé*', they reached a crescendo, the woman's arms shooting the chandeliers. As the crowd went nuts, the woman gracefully stretched her hands towards them, expressive fingers shooting 'Pow' and 'Pow'.

Down went the guitars with a jarring clatter. The crew grabbed the bull statues, tipped up their heads, did something around the tail. Something with propulsion. From the cannon-like neck of each tacky bull came a wicked explosion of thick, greasy red paint that sprayed maybe twenty feet over the crowd, from the deceptively fulsome reservoir of each bull's belly. Folks at the front tried surging back to avoid the sludgy gloop, slipping and rocketing headlong, upsetting tables and spilling drinks as everyone tried vainly to dodge a drenching.

Running low on bull juice, the guys grabbed the plastic palms, ripped the heads and split the trunks, whipping out sawn-off shotguns stashed in the hollow insides. The imperious flamenco queen declared, 'Your capitalism has failed you. You are its sacrifice.'

Then the fire alarm screamed in, sprinklers erupting. Raining hard as shots sang over a chorus of breaking glass. Right then, the strongest claw I ever felt bit my shoulder, dragging me backwards through the screams like baggage. I'm a stocky little piece, but that plastic hand had the grip of a backhoe loader.

We busted outside and, before I knew, I was flung headlong at the backseat of a car, the Russian pretty much sitting on me. I tried struggling and he slapped me, actually slapped my face. 'What's that for?'

'Starters.'

The moustache from the warehouse was driving and, passenger side, some long-haired heavy, tapping his nails on the dashboard.

'Where you taking me?'

'I think the English phrase is mystery tour.'

'Did you know that stuff was going to happen?'

The Russian dude shrugged. 'We know there is trouble. Is always trouble when money comes to town. We plan for that trouble.' He gave me an icy look. 'You are different trouble.'

Things got wretched outside, kids making hay on

that vibe of low-cal rebellion. Flares lit the sky, while smoke softened the rooftops. Thought I heard an industrial buzz saw, and sirens all round, but no sense of them arriving. Streets deserted, the driver adept at dodging lumps of concrete flung in the road.

The guy with his nibbled ears, his fat-smelling cologne, thumped my arm to get my attention. 'The French call it nostalgia for mud. Take the primitive, make it romantic. Take the early days of your tribe and make them the law. We have clients do that. These children,' he waved at the glowing night, 'they wish to go back before capitalism, is so? Just as some of my friends wish for before *perestroika*. When we were properly respected.'

So I thought, get him talking, be constructive, perhaps keep some of my limbs. 'You're in business, though, right?'

'The *krasnaya golova*, she starts to get it.' He repeated in Russian and got no reaction, the guys upfront alert for mud-lovers. 'Yes, girl, this is business. Fifty million dollars' business.'

'You selling that stuff to the Middle East?'

'Maybe. Maybe we sell it here.' He tapped the driver's shoulder and we sped up—heading from the city, from sirens and fires, heading where road signs said The West.

'You can leave me here. Honestly, I'm more of an inconvenience.'

'You?' He laughed and slapped me again.

So I went to the fair and got trapped at the circus.

Someplace west of London—Burnham, leafy and discreet—a big house of angry Russians and high explosives. I knew that, because the guy in the suit told me. A big TV played the riots live and direct—the breaking glass and random kids liberating trainers and headphones. Clueless police jogging about, busting all the wrong skulls. Pretty much only me watching. My hosts more busy with phones and maps and shouting and drinking vodka. Plus, they wouldn't speak English, so I only had TV—which is how I learned the final plenary of the conference had been delayed till tomorrow, to give the Prime Minister chance to tell the streets how cross she was. The peak of impotent power.

I had to sit still and shut up, and my phone out of juice so Mum couldn't call demanding I come right home. Slowly, I realised I was a hostage. 'Am I a hostage?' Had to say it a couple more times before anyone noticed.

My kidnapper held up a finger, finished what he was saying into his phone, then sleekly motored over. 'We prefer you think you are helping international relations. Your associate, who I do not see here to help you, told us that you might get this most awkward detective to do her business elsewhere. Only fair, I think, seeing as you led her to us.'

I had quite a headache by then. Listening to Russian is up there with jackhammers. Odd, maybe, I didn't feel so afraid. After the casino, I'd gone kinda numb. They were just people who wanted some game. 'What you want me to do?'

He shook his head with the special glee of the

smooth boy getting tough. 'Not you, Miss Montgomery. What you do makes work for everyone. We think of you more as our gambling chip.'

'I really don't understand.'

'Miss Montgomery. We do complex business with nervous people. We want to make money. We don't want to pay. We go to Heathrow, we leave—all civil. While we have you, we are not targets.' He glanced at the TV. 'Your police, they put up a bad show. This will keep them busy, I think. So we take you and we leave, all is nice. You may even enjoy it.'

'What?'

A beaming grin busted his lips. 'Damascus. So bracing, this time of year.'

'I'd really rather not.'

The grin continued. 'Indeed. But, Miss Montgomery, you sit there and I stand here.'

At which point, the grisly old solider from the warehouse arrived, stamping into the room, making like he still had young bones. He saw me and slung a firing range of words, smacking his hands against whatever made noise. This nasty old man, with tatts and bad breath, barked in my face, 'We put you in crate. Send you wooosh.' He flung up his hands, treating me to his armpits. 'They drop you as bomb, with desert crazies, ha? You like that, ha? With crazies?'

'I'm already getting some practice.'

He didn't get it, but went off ranting till the young guy tamed him with vodka.

'Can I go to the bathroom?'

No reaction.

'Do I go to the bathroom or pee where I sit?'

At that, I got the full tour of the stinking veteran's eight-ball teeth—you know, two yellow, two brown, two green... 'You sit in pee,' he tells me. 'You play in pee.'

Right from the go, they called me Salwa's pet. So I thought, why not shake a paw. 'You guys think you're smart. Once Abaid knows you don't treat me well, there'll be no freakin Damascus.'

The grin flipped around the young man's face. 'Really? You game us?'

'Abaid won't trust you, will she? She'll want to see I'm okay before letting you through. And what about Dersima? If she doesn't get what she paid for, I don't guess she's so forgiving. So that's two wars you started. Can I go to the bathroom?' Factually, I no longer cared. I had it with that day.

From flushing water and men coming back, adjusting their zips, I knew there was a toilet down the hall. My spiffy host assured me I didn't want to go where the men go—a shake of the head, a moue of the lips, 'Not nice.' Better I go with him, upstairs.

Really, I needed to pee—and though I didn't want the house tour, arguing for which toilet to use didn't strike me as smart. Now, that house was one swanky place, mostly unused. The Russians and their business occupied the ground floor, some first floor doorways opened onto unmade beds. We went up to the second floor, the quiet carpet killing our steps, oil portraits of inbred chancers getting our man nostalgic. 'Here, such houses are usual, yes? In Russia, big houses are gone—they are government institutes, or burnt down, or lost.'

'Houses get lost?'

'In Russia, things get lost. Or trillionaires take them. Maybe with this work, I will be a trillionaire.'

Couldn't hear a thing, night outside dead quiet. Thirty miles away, London was burning. In the drab countryside, people slugged wine and watched gameshows. 'I think I can find my own way back. I mean, it's only downstairs, right?'

'Miss Montgomery. Riz, isn't it?' That made him smile. 'You are a prisoner. You will not find your own way anyplace. Please.' He indicated the toilet door. 'Use the bathroom. I wait.'

'There's really no need.'

'There is every need. You play poker? You are ace in the hole.'

That toilet hadn't been used for a while. Paper felt dusty when I wadded it into the bowl to soak any sound. Mum would have ripped those fittings right out. She disliked any bathroom more than a couple years old. The bath was panelled behind seedy slats. Mum hated that, which is why we had some freestanding job I was frankly scared to use.

Focusing hard, I tried the window. It was jammed fast and two floors up and too small for me anyway. These guys weren't beginners. No one would come to my rescue, so I had to get smart. Nothing laying around would do for a weapon, unless I could drag a water pipe off the wall. I washed my hands and made peace, best I could, with the mirror. Bruised and tired, learning what it costs to stand your ground.

As promised, he was waiting outside. He looked at my face a thoughtful way. 'I should not have hit you there. I am sorry for that. It is being tough, you see? Showing off to tough guys.'

We were standing awkwardly, in an empty hall, in a luxury house those guys kept for business. The evening cool, though we were both pattered with sweat. 'Miss Montgomery, I appreciate you are very young.'

'I'm new adult.'

'Indeed. When we sell our merchandise, there may be chance of a small vacation.'

'In Damascus?'

'In Tel Aviv.'

'Isn't that…?'

'We are mobile people.' Moisture from his real hand streaked his plastic fingers.

'How you get that?'

He held up the jolly pink limb. 'Carelessness. I have learned. I hope it does not distress you. Tel Aviv has many fine places. Quiet places. Perhaps, Riz, we might vacation there?'

'What?'

'I admire you. You are tough. Really something.'

'I'm a few years off.'

'No. You are a woman.'

At least it was his real hand that reached towards my face.

Wrong, so many ways—what he did, what I did. I had to let him touch the bruise he gave me. It was sort-of his and, touching it, he stayed soft and concerned. His sweaty fingers stung. I didn't show it. My voice rang false to me, burdened with wrong. 'There are things you should know about me.'

'We have time.'

'I see things that aren't there. In the sides of my eyes, in shadows, I see things.' I stood close to him. Something horribly resembling trust lit his eyes. 'I hear voices. The whole time. They shout and quarrel at me. They say do this, do that. They make me forget stuff I ought to know. They tease me and let me get blamed. With what I see, what I hear, I fill gaps in reality. I busy-up those spaces. I have bugs burrowing through my skin. I have echoes in my head.'

From some sense of honour, maybe, as I moved, he stepped back. I took another step, he edged backwards a little more.

'That's not the worst about me, though. What you need to know. What you most need to know. I'm reckless. Impulsive. I switch just like that.' I jabbed my elbow under his chin. He stumbled, startled—with both hands I pushed him, full force, backwards. I kicked his balls. I pushed him back. He tripped and fell downstairs.

There was a scream and rolling thuds as he fell. Then one big crash and he didn't make noise anymore. Soon as I pushed him, I ran down the hall, into some room with furniture shrouded in blankets like an old movie. Ran to the window, heaved up the sash, night air stung my face.

Didn't know what happened to him or who might be

coming for me. I heaved up the sash—didn't think, just ducked outside, my All Stars gripping the tiny ledge. Maybe thirty feet above ground, but the ground was dark anyway. Something rustling—ivy, twined through wooden slats pinned to the wall. Was I scared? I should have been. Should have been dropping my guts. But the look on his face when I knocked him down. That did for fear.

The wooden frame was shallow, loose—felt it give beneath me. Trying to move before each hold collapsed. That ivy was old, tough as wire, its complex veins directing me as they probed and snagged my skin. The feel of it nauseating—smooth and sharp, glossy and wanting to choke me. Up close, it smelled of wickedness, of a poisonous, bad girl. I could have died hanging there and by morning be gone. Nothing left, just a new shoot of ivy.

As I climbed through its grip, getting hold, feeling it tear, sliding down, my thoughts were with him. All he wanted was time with me. I mean, he couldn't have been more wrong about me. That's so not the point. No one I met that week cared a damn for consequences. But I do.

I fell the last few feet, picked myself from hard, damp ground. Got the usual noise—TV, guys talking at phones. Then a shout, a commotion of chairs kicked down, running and slamming doors. Then Russian, loud and deadly. I started across what I guess was the lawn. More shouting and I moved faster. Then running, as gunshots sang over my head.

Shooting through the dark, though their aim was

drunk and careless, any second a lucky bullet could chew my spine. Shatter my neck. Burst my lungs. Silence my head forever. I ran and they shot at me, some animal they could kill and it didn't matter. In a humdrum English village, this weird eruption of some distant war. I threw myself at trees that scratched and mauled me. Battling thorns that gathered to hold me for target practice. Those men shooting, shouting orders, sounding beyond angry.

Stomping the bushes, I lunged and tumbled into some snarky pinch across my chest. Jarred with shock, I lashed at it, realised it was wire. The boundary fence, razored along its edge. Trees grew right up to it, dipping rangy branches across the wire. I'm not so athletic nor good at sports, but in woods thick with bullets I channelled the lithe and titless girls I saw ride the pommel horse. Jumped and grabbed—fourth attempt, got enough to claw a low-slung branch that bucked at my chumpish weight. Flashlights sliced the trees—men shouting, not caring who heard, wanting only my head mounted over the mantelshelf. I scrabbled along the branch and—with stupidly terrified lack of sense—jumped at the fence, bounced off the top wire and met the ground in all the wrong places.

Adrenaline kicked big. I ran like a solid chocolate Olympic medal was waiting for me, dropping to an embankment on some patch of green. Gunfire came clean through the trees. Maybe the locals were used to night hunting.

Down the road, a sweet cottagy pub. There'd be a phone, I could call the police, they'd arrest me and I'd be okay. Quick as I could where I picked up a limp, I jogged towards the festive lights, the blackboard promise of local ales in friendly surroundings.

What stopped me—a jet plane roar from the end of the street, a crystal flash that burned everything white: the headlights of a black Ferrari 458 moving at warp factor 10. I dived for cover, laying waste some garden gnomes.

# 17

'You have not been bitten by a poisonous spider.'

Easy for her to say. I slapped my legs. 'I'm stinging.'

'You fell into a load of crap.' She changed up a gear—she had seven to choose from—and the countryside liquefied. A radio crackled, she grabbed it up, driving one-handed. 'MP Aurora Code 12 Copy.'

More crackle.

'Target retrieved. Go to Ops 1. Deploy PT17. Copy.'

More crackle.

'My pleasure, gentlemen. The playground is open.'

'Um, is this your car?'

Salwa made a huffy noise. 'No. Obviously.'

By then, spider venom was leaking into my joints. 'I might only have minutes to live.'

'*Kol Khara.*'

'What?'

'It means do you have any more questions?'

Didn't sound as if it meant that. 'Only the obvious.'

'How we found you? Check your trainers.'

'You bugged my Stars?'

'Star. Right foot. GPS surveillance device.'

Tried getting my leg up to see. 'So you heard those guys?'

'I heard your feet.'

Up ahead, closing fast, a carnival of red and blue lights, a blistering wave of justice. Cop cars and chunky urban tanks. Blazing through the country night, headed behind us. Tried turning to watch, but the car was flirting around the hundreds and g-force snapped me down. 'Are they going for the Russians?'

'They'll find plenty of evidence. They'll do considerable damage.'

'They'll kill those guys?'

'You mean the guys who tried to kill you?' She changed up again and we left the ground.

That poison ran close to the seedy back door of my heart. 'Um, I got a confession.'

'Riz, I'm sure whatever happened was traumatic. Even for such a robust civilian. You won't get charged, whatever.' She couldn't have sounded less sincere if she'd been whistling the Macarena.

'I killed someone.' The poison hit. Weirdly, I didn't die.

We left the lanes, hit the motorway, streaming towards the big lights. Lot of countryside, black and dead-looking.

'You must have heard. The man I pushed downstairs.'

She slapped the horn at a trucker. He swerved his rig, blasting a long, angry note. 'They held you prisoner. You escaped. It would be the highlight of your story. If you were allowed to tell it. Which you're not.'

'But he's dead.'

'He will be by now.' She flung a razor glare. 'You

should break this habit of thinking such things are your problem.'

It's a cliche, I don't like to do it, that sick-puppy, mentalist, pressing-my-head-with-my-hands thing. Right then, I scragged my temples, the drumbeat of blame busting my skull. 'What's happening? Death everywhere. Those people killed at the casino.'

That bored, pissy sigh. 'They were not killed. Those morons were firing percussion caps to cause panic. They streamed it on YouTube. A distraction. Now the world's talking about the "London massacre". Made us look like fools.'

That riled me. 'Still, such things aren't your problem.'

Traffic building, she had to brake. 'Soon nor will you be. Weren't you meant to be tracking your neighbour?'

'I lost him.'

'Hours ago.'

'Sorry, I got kidnapped. I'll try to be less selfish.'

By then we were scraping the suburbs, screaming down Western Avenue, through Northolt, Park Royal. Miles of streets, seeming far removed from the disaster playing through the police radio. That chopped-up, code-heavy jargon, said the West End caught it bad. West End and City. Helicopter reports maybe a million people ruling the street. Maybe half protesting the conference, driven by maybe ten, twenty thousand hardcore. The organised—Mocha's army. The rest, poor kids and chancers, people needing a fight, crooks filling orders for phones and consoles. The casino wasn't the only deal—there'd been other showstoppers to sucker the police to all the wrong locations. Tourists slung off

Tower Bridge, smoke bombs on the London Eye, some ludicrous hoo-ha about fake anthrax. Distraction. While the hard cops, the ones who enjoyed it, were tied up protecting the global fund tsar, and the presidents, and the man I called Dad.

'What's that mean—I'm not allowed to tell it?'

She kept her eyes on the road and six hundred horsepower in motion.

'Where we going Salwa?'

'Getting worried Riz? Are you a problem I should deal with?'

'Just asked.'

'Do you think the things you have heard about me are lies?'

'I really don't know. Can we go to the hotel, please?'

'No Riz.'

At least she let me charge my phone from the dashboard. I made a thing of deleting the messages unread.

My geography not so great, but we were getting into town—the engine held angrily down around eighty, the smoky view masted with tower blocks, intersected by slicks of darkness. Nearly no traffic. Heavy sense of the hard and awful.

Without warning, she hit the West Cross Route, heading for Shepherds Bush. That took us slam into hometown streets—she had to cut back to fifty-five, fifty, down around forty—too slow for that car and that woman. A right and a left, and there we were—a dismal little road, hardly lit from a couple of greasy streetlights. We rolled up beside flats that were maybe pretty neat when Rothko was a kid. Now they just occupied dead-end space, huddled and sad. The engine left an empty echo. She unhitched the radio, muted it, slipped it in her pocket.

'Stay,' she told me.

'Where you going?'

'The answer's stay.'

From the passenger side of a million's worth of sports car, I watched her cocky swagger to the door of the flats. She worked the keypad and went inside, the door dead-slamming behind her. I got out, woozy with stopping the ride. Slipped off my right trainer under a streetlamp and digged at the star. Something about the size of a nano SIM carefully folded into Chuck Taylor's stitching. Pretty unsporting, how she let me get kidnapped and shot at before doing the cavalry thing.

A solid-built ginger cat strolled by, looking pleased with itself. It stopped so I could fuss its neck and I pressed the bug into its collar. As it scaled a fence and sauntered away, I wondered were cops still tracking that little blip onscreen. See 'em, later that night, yelling my name up a tree.

The door to the flats had bars and wasn't friendly to inquisitive fingers. Had to call someone up. Tried a few numbers till this old-sounding article answered—he seemed pretty scared, I guess with it all going down. I took absolute years off my voice, smiling to sound harmless. 'Oh Hi, oh Hello. It's my cat, he got into the hallway. Could you just let me through to rescue him? Please.'

'Your cat?'

'He followed some lady. She smelled nice to him.'

'Make sure you shut the door tight when you go.'

'Oh, God bless you.'

The hallway tasted of bleach and dust. 'Mr. Styx. Here. Come on Mr. Styx. Who's a sausage then? Yes, you are. Yes, you are.' I opened the door again, slammed it, then started upstairs. A balcony ribbed each floor, circling the building. Accustomed by then to the chase, I moved with quick purpose, tracking each balcony, feeling the air, moving up to the next floor. TV movies and comedy shows—a little something to numb the panic—though a loud TV at one window played rolling news. There were deaths, maybe half a dozen, someone caught in a crush, a knifing during some personal war, beneath the wheels of a police truck. Fighting and looting in unrelated places. Who knows what that meant—how is anywhere unrelated? Meantime, the conference building, that area, locked down, cops hanging tough and, among those they served, resolve undiminished. The finale would play first thing. Order prevails.

Continued up, listening at windows and doors. Music and babies—a fight: a woman shouting, that shrill, tight way women have. Shouting, 'Why me? Why this?' Man shouting back, 'You always do this. You always do this.' Gathered flowers are dead.

Top floor balcony opened to a dark, hazy sky. Around the turn of the block, a boy, my age maybe, his legs dangling over the wall, hands gripping the ledge, staring six floors down at the road. Hair cut a little jagged, black leather jacket that didn't look intentionally scuffed. Very still, sitting there.

'Hey.' My husky whisper at one with the dense air.

He turned—fine cheeks, dark eyes. Good looking, maybe. His tee-shirt clung tight—looked stewed, like old clothes washed too many times. Guess he saw a bruised, grubby redhead, steep canyons under her eyes.

'Hey.' I leaned next to him. 'You see a woman up here? Tall, light suit. Wild dark hair. She up here?'

Not once did that boy blink. He stared and stared. His arms tensed, he swung around sideways and dropped off the ledge onto the balcony, smooth and sure like he did it a million times. For a boy, he had lovely hands—slim, at ease doing nothing. I followed him, not even trying to think what to say. Didn't matter. The night was burning.

He pushed open a door to a hallway that looked like it got painted by stoners. Few toys rocked around. Smell of coriander and cabbage. Smell of damp washing. Nothing looked like it was ever new, or complete, or different. Little girl's voice started up, singing some TV ad, mashing the words. Talking to herself, how little kids do. The boy was behind me. I didn't turn. I wanted to look tough, be tough. I wanted to be something self-sufficient that arrived with the night.

At the end of the hall, yellow light spilled round a door. Didn't pause or peek by the hinges. Too tired and shot-at for that. Just went in. These intricate pictures across the walls, fretted mosaic, blue and white with Arab script—don't know then what it said. Portraits, too, men in suits and uniforms, heavy moustaches, crisp hair. Men looking stern and strong. A picture of a woman wearing a green headscarf, grinning, giving a peace sign, black paper scrunched around the frame.

Three women there. The little girl, barking orders at her dolls. A thin, dark woman, baggy shirt and jeans hanging off her. Salwa Abaid, unfolding a fist of money into the woman's hand. They looked at me, a tableau of wariness and hazard.

I turned and I was in the boy's eyes, dark as the space between stars.

Along Holland Park Avenue to Notting Hill, down into Kensington, with police helicopters—six of them—hovering over the glowing heat of London. Salwa cursing traffic, the huge engine spitting mad each touch of the brake.

Just to provoke her, I said, 'Lot of trouble tonight.'

'Really? I'm sure your Father talks about it.'

'Actually he doesn't. What do you think?'

'Think.' She threw the word at the windscreen.

'About this, the protests.'

'Not my business.'

'Would it be your business back home?'

'We know how to get things done.'

The seats and doors were peach-coloured leather. I stroked its stippled edge, wondering how anything mattered. 'If you had to, would you kill me?'

We went south over Battersea Bridge, crossing the long reflections of burning buildings. She hadn't switched her radio back on—guess we were off grid. 'If it was necessary.' She checked her hair. 'I'd put a bullet through the base of your neck. You'd never feel it.'

'Who was that woman?'

'Don't get adolescent.'

'You gave her money.'

'She's someone's widow.'

'Why give her money?'

She steered the sleek car onto a concrete road between railway sidings.

'You make a promise? It plays on your mind?'

She brought us to a scrapyard. Parked in a pool of darkness behind the huge crane. 'Change of plan.'

Don't know what she had, maybe a Heckler & Koch USP—something harsh and expensive. She showed it me. Under watery light from the scrapyard gantries, she placed its cold snout against my neck. Took the catch off, could have ended it there. My chin held high and death at the end of her finger.

'I don't need a reason,' she told me. 'I don't need anything.'

'I'm told you're a torturer.' I never felt so calm.

'You have good information.' She slid the catch and holstered the gun. 'I also stopped your Mother cutting your brain.'

We walked up by the railway arches—some just empty space, some filled with plastic sheets mounted on struts as basic bivouacs. Smell of shit and heavy weather. She helped me step over a slick of stinking oil. We briefly held hands. It's nice to hold hands. As we got near the road, the arches became businesses—a tyre store, a motor repair shop; one sold fetish gear.

Surprisingly swish-looking cars parked nearby. Surprisingly, she cut into the bushes, dragging me behind her, up into residential streets that backed onto the railway.

Now she opened her radio, said a word or two, and we headed into the neighbouring street, to a white van totally conspicuous at the end of the road. Salwa knocked the side—a sharp, one-two knock. The door slid open. Inside was the most equipment—radios and monitors, night vision goggles, protective masks—and three large men, too important for riot duty. They didn't seem happy. With the van door shut, it was way too close to be friendly.

Salwa got updates, then explained what this poor, battered teenage girl was getting put through next.

'Ms. Montgomery is known to the target. Her presence will be unexpected and a distraction.'

'I'm what?'

'There is some risk.' Those black hole eyes, on me again. 'However, you are proven resilient.'

'Salwa, I want to lie down.'

'It's an opportunity,' one of the big lunks heaved himself over, 'to do something great you can never tell no one about.'

'Remember that.' Again, Salwa's tungsten grip explored my arm. 'You can't say anything about any of this.'

The three men kept busy spying on stuff. 'You guys know what happened to those Russians in that house?'

They looked at each other. They looked at me.

Salwa squeezed my shoulder. 'Time to go.'

# 18

These railway arches, with jarringly impressive limousines waiting outside, these arches were a nightclub. I mean, you couldn't see that. I was told and then found out. Behind the plain grey door and unpromising-looking security men was a happening venue I had to get access to, where I'd be an unexpected distraction. I did try the conversation about exactly how I'd get access. But apparently I was a natural for subterfugenous behaviour and if I played nice I possibly wouldn't get arrested or shot or lobotomised. I didn't exactly feel empowered.

Most obviously, I couldn't walk up to the doormen and say 'Howdy'. My default move—check round the back—less attractive than usual, where the only way round the back was through railway arches filled with homeless people, a quite understandably wary and temperamental population. Now, I'm no princess, but that arch was dark and I didn't want to stomp anyone's head, nor stand in several shades of unpleasantness. Rustling plastic and generally increased breathing said I got noticed.

'Watch it.'

'Sorry.'

'What? Is it the pigs?'

'You the pigs?'

Couldn't see where the voice came from. It was butthole dark. 'Hello? Sorry, I'm trying to get through.'

'Get through?'

'To the other side.'

'Other side?'

'I'm trying to walk through to what's over there.'

'You the pigs?'

Factually, I wasn't. Just their *chica recado*. Factually also I couldn't move—these folks had come up from the shadows. Somehow, they could see better than me.

'What are you?'

I tried addressing the face, though light was near-subliminal. 'I'm Riz. That's what I am.'

Someone shone a phone at my face. The sudden whiteness stung. A murmur went round. 'You been beaten up?'

'It's been a long day.'

A louder voice echoed across the plastic and canvas. 'What do you want to do?'

I don't switch off—my brain churns full time. I'm better suited to lies than truth. But it had been a long, not wholly successful day. Thought again about that poor man, down the end of the staircase. 'I want to get into that club down there without paying. I'm looking for the quiet way.'

They weren't fans of the nightclub. 'It's not the noise,' one said. 'It's the vibrations.'

The voice moved closer, with the soft-footed assurance of someone nocturnal. A young man, made old by the street, stained by lack of choices. Wholly unwanted, Mocha's voice screamed into my head, demanding I admit who was to blame. Yeah, I know. I get it.

'There's a way.'

Muttering got louder. 'How you know she's not the pigs?'

'Look at her.' The young man held the phone to my face.

Don't ask what they saw, but some were convinced.

'She swear she's not the pigs.'

'I just want to go dancing.' Actually, it sounded the last thing I wanted. 'I swear, I am not in any way the police.' Yeah, so that was the edit.

'Stay close.'

Minefield-walking, dark so thick it tangled like cobwebs, we crept around the far side of the railway arch. As we reached the air, a train went past, throwing down oblongs of light. In clattering freeze-frame, I saw the scar, from his cheek down his neck. Looked as if he'd been cut and folded. Whistled under my teeth.

'Gets interest,' he said.

'What happened?'

'Picking flowers in the wrong man's garden. I'm Trey.'

'You mean, like in *Power Rangers*?'

'You're too young to know that.'

'I'm a student of culture. Plus, my sister has a cartoon habit.'

'Mine does crack, wanna swap?'

First smile I had in hours. Though my little, snorting

laugh dropped flat against hard night. 'I'm Riz anyway. That's me.'

'And you want to dance without paying?'

Didn't quite dig how he said that. So quiet and sure—made me wonder. I'd committed, though, to this fraction of some bigger thing.

Round back of the railway arches, a dirt road, scrubby trees, dark, maybe derelict warehouse blocks. Across stones and busted tarmac, behind the autoshop and fetish house, feeling the bassline from the club, my fingertips tingling to party. 'What you think of the riots?' I asked, ready with prepack words to sound vaguely on message.

'Bad for business,' he said. 'Bad for people. If the streets are burning, where do you find a bed? There's people I know lost a lot from this. When you live day to day, you rely on routine kindness. This crap screws you.'

Relief to meet someone sane. 'Weekend rebels.' Surprised at the venom in my voice.

'Yeah.' Trey nodded. 'And you go dancing.'

Back of the club, these serious fire doors totally wired to every alarm for miles. A metal heartbeat shaking the air, constant, fast-pumping beats, scrabbled with train-track clatter. Kicking hard so I couldn't tell train from bass or my raggy heart. Towering noise through the walls, creeping over sullen wasteland.

Enchanted with it, I missed Trey slipping down into a gulley, some night animal at home with the tin-can landscape. 'Where you going?'

'Keep up.'

'Yeah everyone says that.'

He was going down the tail of a little embankment, through a hole ripped in a wire fence, onto a concrete platform, where dark shapes gathered—old robots who'd gone there to die. I'm no wuss, yet that stifled, broken equipment got me nervy. No way to see where I was, no sound but the bass. Tried reminding myself that, with the lights out, it's less dangerous.

Trey cranked at something beneath the embankment. A waist-high door set into the earth. Don't know it was locked or jammed—either way, took time to unhitch it. As he opened the door, wood scraped concrete a loud, sickly way. I stood gawking, not getting the deal, till he said, 'Through there.'

'It's a hole in the ground.'

'Correct.'

'You want me to get in a hole in the ground?'

'You don't want to pay the door charge.'

He explained that from the railway days—when that wasteland was freight yards—cellars and storage hatches ran hundreds of feet every side. Bricked-up and mostly collapsed, but some could be navigated. There were stairs, he said, down to a passage that led to a trapdoor beneath the stockroom of the club. He knew because his crew went there, stealing booze and nachos. That's why they didn't want me squawking about it.

'Okay.' I found that hard to believe.

'There's no light and no air, so keep crawling.'

'Crawling?'

'The roof's like that.' He made a small-size gesture.

'When you feel wood above your head, that's the trapdoor.'

Mmm, how to put it? 'How do I know I won't find a load of bones from girls you've tricked?'

Now he laughed—a warm little chuckle. 'Trust me, Riz. Only bones you'll find are rats.'

'What?'

He put his shoulder to the door. 'Of course, this is valuable information. We don't want it taken for granted.'

From my casino win—which happened in another time, in a galaxy far, far away—I pushed notes through his fingers, palming one back for keeps. 'Seriously,' tried making eye contact, much as I could with pitch blackness, 'you're not fooling me, are you? You won't stick a knife in my spine?'

My roulette winnings vanished into his pocket. 'None of us knows the future, Riz. Be more suicides if we did.'

I tasted vomit when the door shut behind me. Total dark. *Oscuridad total.* Crouched, pretty much crawling, nothing to see, my mind focused on the stale closeness of the roof, uneven sharpness of the floor, my bruises and pain, the sound of my heart, and wars inside my head. Down there, among buried silence, bastard voices ruling my brain, shouting for this and that. Getting called a retard bitch and worse for getting involved, for being there, for everything done and not done the whole of my jackass life. Most people—even the worst-treated kid—can get headspace somewhere private, to work their guilt with a single, solid mind. Not me. I got the chorus from hell and every one of those voices is mine. The unmedicated life. You ain't lived till you tried it.

That twenty-four hours I got tailed by police, kicked at the fair, kidnapped by Russians, climbed thirty feet down a wall, shot at by maniacs, jumped a razor fence, and rode at Mach 1 with a psycho. And it fell away, vaporised, closed up with the hateful, gut-churning horror of total, vivid dark. Darkness so sheer I saw colours, my neurons popping. Nearly no oxygen down there. I understood I could die and if, for instance, I was shot or slung from a car and there was a body to scoop away, that was one thing. But dying there, in a ready-made casket—who'd know? Only a guy with a whole-body scar who charged me rent to be there. I wanted to spew, I wanted to pee. I couldn't do either and that made it worse. Kept crawling, what else to do?

Yeah, did I mention rats? When I touched something smooth and hard, ivory-feeling, and understood he wasn't joking about bones. Screw it, if a rat can't find the exit, doesn't that say something to the average, sensible human? I heard them, scuffling and seeking and thought: should I scream or does that make it worse? If I scream, will one pop down my throat? I started to wuff and huff like a bear when it's feeling lonesome, one hand dragging my carcass, the other scraping the roof. Tapping the mouldy old concrete, calling down my private saints to lead me to escape. Nearly screamed when my knuckles hit wood.

Ground vanished—I freaked for a second, then a grain of common sense led my fingers to feel how the floor bowed into a dip. Course it did. It was worn away. The night arch people would crouch there to push up the hatch. I did the same, squaring myself in the dented earth, shouldering the trapdoor to heaven. By then, the bass was intense, shaking the concrete, taking my stomach to my ankles. Those rats, man, they must be ravers.

I pitched my womanly strength at the wood. Jack nothing. Okay, so it was stiff—maybe damp and warped. You wouldn't want a trapdoor springing open every half-second. Pushed again, trying to jack-knife my back, my hair muddied-up against the wood. No dice.

I traced the flap with my fingers, trying to pinpoint the block, the jam—to remember which way I came, if I had to crawl back, which I wouldn't, y'know, but what if. I mean, if it was locked I could just go back, right? I could find and open that outside door. Right?

Lot of noise down there. This ratchy, rasping breath, my hammering heart, and wiseguys hooting it up through my cranial passage. Telling me I should die, shrivel you bitch. Bugs running thick through my skin. My fingers drummed the wood, I couldn't stop them. Some force down there with me, some physical thing that functioned better than I could. My bones unlocking, falling slack. I could taste the dark. The bolts and plates and components that make the dark. Interested in me, the dark. It's always been interested in me.

The DJ must have finished his set—this huge crescendo of beats then the crowd goes nuts. A lull, just a minute, till the next DJ fired up. I heard footsteps, a voice sounding angry. Impatience tingled through the wood into my fingers. That's when I realised they were standing on the trapdoor. I couldn't open the freakin thing because someone was standing on it. Sheer heart attack.

So what to do? Trey said it was a stockroom, there'd be people coming and going. Hopefully not staying long. This brutal hardcore broke out, a righteous two-twenty beats a minute. The crowd jumped and I heard nothing but hands slapping air. As we say back in England, it was a proper rave up.

I had this neat little comedy vision of raising the hatch with a squad of tooled-up maniacs staring at me. Pretty much the norm for the day. All I could do was wait, no one stays in a stockroom forever. Didn't want to listen too long anyway because of the drop dead beat. That thing where the DJ busts a tune and people's hearts stop beating. The drop dead beat. It's a thing.

Cramp setting in, first rat that scuffed my hand—its fur slicking my fingers—stunned me, a million volts. I clunked them sideways. Riled, they started squeaking. I'd so had enough, just so being taken for granted. Felt another one mooch against my leg. 'When I can move,' my whisper stained the dark, 'I'll bite your bloody head off.'

The stockroom was dark when I flipped the hatch. As I hauled from the hole, the lights came on. A minor freakage, till I realised they were motion-activated.

Kinda charming that whatever bad boys I was chasing cared about utility costs.

Who was I chasing? Detective Abaid said I was known to the target. I was to eyeball the target and give her a yell. Top secret and I didn't care. These grownups reeked of the playground.

For sure, it was a stockroom. Crates of beer and boxes of crisps. Stuff people steal. So of course the door was locked. So I cracked a beer and wasted more of my life. Y'know, the parts of the story they don't show in action movies.

My somewhat imperfect plan was wait till someone came by, hide behind the door and, when I got chance, slip away. If necessary, I'd clonk their skull with a bottle. Harsh, but life's not fair.

A busy club and a busy night, wasn't long till the kids wanted more gummy rings. A jangle of keys and I dived for the door. Lucky for me, the man who grooved in was caught up on a call—his boyfriend I think, by the nature of his demands. Shouting so loud—from habit I guess—made it easy to slide from the room.

One way led to the bar, which fed the dancefloor. The other way, the passage ended at what should be a fire exit, though factually looked no exit at all. That's the way I went.

I remembered, from outside, the club ran across three arches. I assumed the dancefloor stretched most the way through—what if it didn't? As expected, end of the passage was a locked door. *Mierda.* I sprinted back to the stockroom, Mr. Loverman still bellowing good times. With the most acute sense of my wayward limbs,

I carefully wriggled his key chain from the lock and jogged back down, expecting bruises any second. Some nervy false starts and a whole lot of sweat till I got the right key to the door. Pushed through and shut it, soft as snow. Call me Artful.

Could still hear the beats, not so much. In fact, not nearly so much as I expected. When I'd been underground, under concrete and earth, I heard the crowd go bananas. Yet I step through a door and the sound cuts dead. Interesting. The door and walls were steel-cased, panelled with spooky honeycomb shapes. Like the guy said: it's not the noise, it's the vibrations. Every surface I tapped sounded dead. And the lights, which glared this horrid chrome yellow, were bolted shut with wire. Did I mention the corridors also seemed extensive, for the back rooms of a nightclub.

Don't let me sound flip, I'm not saying I solved it right then. I'm not saying I wasn't scared. Right side of the door, I might just be a punter gone AWOL. In that sterile, sound-deadened space I was an intruder. I already had plenty experience of the problems that could bring.

What told me I'd gone through the looking glass? Well, there was a lift. An elevator. Add two and two: an arch beneath a railway. So where's an elevator go? Only down. Maybe those neighbourhood cellars Trey mentioned weren't so empty.

I understood coolly, precisely, that if I went down that lift and there were people where it landed, then likely they'd kill me. I might be eating my last five minutes right then. I also understood if I didn't go down that lift, if I slid through the club and into the night, Salwa would find me and kill me. When she took off the catch and put her gun against my neck, there was no shyness, no awkward remorse. Die head on or die looking over my shoulder. My world or the flat world. I opened the lift.

# 19

Everything I've said to now is totally secret. This part, though, is super-secret. Not for what happened or who was involved—it doesn't make me feel well.

Time and a lot of miles maybe skewed my perception, but when that lift door opened, what I recall is vast. Bigger than the warehouse I went with The Man, flooded with the light of a thousand stars—LED lamps, fifty feet up, underground. Metal shelving, tables and workbenches with—I guessed—lathes and cutters and milling machines. Drills to make your brain tingle. Little cubbyhole rooms with charts and plans and fat-face screens. Signs, actual factory signs, to warn about hazard and spillage. Cylindrical treats even I understood as combat weaponry.

Got quite a look at the place, as the guys who were waiting outside the lift marched me across the floor, down a tunnel, and into an office. A desk and chairs, a sofa, TV screens, a map of the Middle East damn-near life-size. Three colour flag in the corner and handsome Dersima, rocking combat duds, with a look that says I'm vexed and not wholly surprised. 'Miss Montgomery. You have gained battle scars. Perhaps also more courage than is good for you.' She signalled the guards to leave, just the tiniest move of her hand. 'You will have coffee, I think?' She poured a slice from the jug. 'I have no cream or sugar.'

'Is this place for real?'

She frowned. 'Our strength is not make believe.'

'No, I mean, am I hallucinating this?'

'Does the coffee burn?'

'I could easily hallucinate that.'

'If this place is not real, Miss Montgomery, neither am I.' She pulled a tight smile, then we were down to business. 'When we met, you were with someone I trust. Someone I've known a long time. That's why you're not dead yet.'

'I'm what?'

'I presume he has some use for you. However.' She moved close. I tasted hot sand and hair-trigger decisions. 'Since then, Miss Montgomery.'

'Riz, I am.'

'Riz. Since then, we had to move our merchandise, alerted by that same acquaintance. Since then, I hear the Moscow dealers met some heavy weather.' Her accent made it sound the worst.

'They kidnapped me. I didn't know she bugged my Stars.'

'You think Abaid would let you run loose?'

'She was kind to me in the hospital.'

'When you told her where to find me.'

The day was looping and I was sick. Hellfire coffee struggled the breezeblocks in my head. 'You going to say she kills and tortures and that?'

Dersima poured more liquid tar. 'She does. So do I. The Russians were incidental. You say ironic?'

'What you mean, so do you?'

'Are you bugged now?'

'With what?'

'What's in your pocket?'

'Just this.'

Dersima got some kind of scanner, ran it over my phone. 'She is getting slow. Or she thinks you are tamed.' A wise look lit her glorious lines. 'Why don't you ask her to join us?'

'Are you the target? She said I'm known to the target.'

'I would bet a hundred of her M-302s that she doesn't know I'm here. Call her. You'll see how my people deal with a mad dog.'

Call Salwa? She was too hot-blooded to think I could trick her that way. This Dersima, whoever she was, had enough for an army down there. Salwa had been kind to me. Though she did set me up to get people killed. But really, there'd been enough sadness. 'I don't think it's working. With these metal walls.'

'We have relay transmitters down here. Shall I see if it's working?'

Her face—wise and ruggedly of the present, hair greying, eyes of the fox that knows every yard—made it hard to stop the upset. 'It's okay. I got it.'

Did I fake or call for real? Split-second choice, in a day of heavy decisions. Can't say how much I had enough of weaponry and grownups. I only went there for Rothko. I had hoped someone nice would say Hello.

When my finger clicked the button, I was past caring. Call Salwa, why not? I was driftwood anyway. 'Salwa. I don't feel well. I'm coming back. I'm outside the place. Well, outside. The waste ground. It's quieter. Don't bother, I'll come back. Really, there's no one here you want to speak to.'

First, I didn't recognise the noise or where it came from. When I understood it was Dersima, laughing with her mouth closed, I felt more scared than if she'd been raging. 'You are, what? Fifteen, sixteen?'

'Thereabouts.'

'You are playing Salwa Abaid. You tell her don't come, you think she won't come? Girl, now she is certain there is something here to envy.'

Must have shook my head—I heard its noise.

'Abaid envies those who have something to live for. Her only company is her enemies. That devil—she is sad and lonely. Now,' Dersima looked at me, not unkindly. 'You understand I have to do something about you? You appear and you bring trouble.'

'You gonna crate me up and drop me as a bomb? What about my friend, your friend? You think he'd like that?'

'You put too much faith in him. And yourself.'

A knock at the door, she tilted her head, this tough guy came in, this mad-tough looking guy, who she made knock and wait. That's what she was. The ice of her flesh still there in my hand. They spoke this language. While he talked, the big man looked at me exactly how every harsh persuader looked at me the whole day.

Again, that tiny gesture and the guy left, giving evils from his dark eyes.

Dersima leaned back against the table, hands winged a girlish way. 'The dance is over.'

'Does that mean something?'

'Upstairs,' indicated with her tilted chin. 'Abaid stopped the party.'

'She does that.'

'She is looking for you and the "no one she wants to speak to".'

Swear, she actually mimicked my voice. Why couldn't she be my Mother? There was much to like and respect, including her underground stash of artillery rockets. 'If she's looking for me, she won't stop looking.'

'You told her you would go back.'

I got where this was headed. 'Her command van's just two streets away.'

'You are vexatiously fortunate. And helpful. Two streets? My guards will find it.'

'I didn't mean...'

Her hands shaped her athletic hips. 'So I must turn you loose? Is that what you tell me? You know neither I nor my American friends can afford for this to be found.' She zoned into me. 'You have a conscience, Riz. A dangerous gift and a terrible burden. What you see, all this, is to make people free. To break the chains of centuries past. My people, we are the future. Abaid is why there must be a future. This.' Her fingers sealed my lips, her skin so cold. 'This tells nothing of this place. Nothing. If you betray me, your eyes and tongue will lay in the palm of your hand. Wherever you are, I have only to whistle.'

When her soldierly stride reached the door, when she yelled her khaki-suited women to come on over, my heart took a harsher knock than with Abaid or the Russians. Dersima was fighting real wars. She didn't want to be in some underground hole in London. She wanted to be toe to toe with death. She wasn't on salary, she didn't take a percentage. No surprise when she said, 'My guards will beat you, understand? It is trivial punishment for your devotion to Abaid.'

I nodded. She was right. The women viced my arms, I didn't complain. They'd leave me alive—after that, nothing matters. As they dragged me off for a disciplined kicking, Dersima said, 'When you see Salwa, say: if the café in Al-Hasakah is still there, the coffee is on the house.'

Her coldness so sharp I could taste it, right through the neon hallway. When her guards punched me to the ground, when I got kicked square in the spine, that freeze I kept from Dersima's flesh meant I barely felt it.

Things got lively out front. Salwa Abaid stopped parties like no one else. Despite the whole town being one big riot, she found a squad of meatheads up for jacking the scene with regular gusto. Disgruntled kids stood around the sleazy light of the fetish shack, making wah-wah noises into their phones and vaping. Some guys who looked like DJs—y'know, self-important guys—took selfies with cops, pulling faces. Aching right through and keen not to go back to hospital, I sank deep in railway shadows, waiting my chance to limp to the street.

Some delay getting wagons to scoop up the punters. Even Abaid's formidable traction was subject to the logistics of cleansing more upscale neighbourhoods. Some kids slid away—no one chased them. Singing broke out, the scene depressingly folksy.

Thinking to move when up shot new rumpus. The archway people, draggled and pissed, stumbled into what, for them, must be brutal light. Next to the homely club kids, with their party tits and Ibiza tees and appalling trousers, the homeless crew were some serious snotty army. Like neighbours the world over, they were angry about the noise.

The most bizarre ruck I saw all day between mollied-up herberts, who thought the whole world was some ironic pose, and weary folks who lived in a sodding tunnel. I mean, even I got the wrongness of that and I'm drunk. So, there's elbows and wads of saliva, the cops wake up, and the air turns real brittle.

Can't say how hurt I got through that long day running my face into fists. To then, fear and adrenaline soothed me. But waiting to catch a break, while another dumb war broke out, every slap and kick I took was singing. I'm no victim. I don't beg kindness from anyone on this Earth. Just I was alone with my pain right then. That ain't a hot place to be. Might even have turned myself in, for the clubby comfort of a ride downtown. Except I froze, disbelieving what I saw.

Guess Abaid wondered why she bothered, when no one could match her anger. Not the salaried thugs she rode with, nor the skulls she busted—none had her way of meaning it all every second. She shoved and kicked through the crowd, foisting a woman ahead of her who clearly just encountered Salwa the hard way. A woman who was the prize. And what does she see, this righteous detective driving her prey? She sees a gang of milquetoasts shaking their dancefloor culture at a restive bunch of survivors. That's what Abaid saw. Me, I saw she arrested Rose Ducati.

Sour, not easy to like, with her billowy top and jeans that looked older than some of these kids. Her office hair clipped back, giving mean prominence to her forehead. Her bready cheeks distorted by anger and Abaid's knuckles. This woman who'd been at Mum's house, prepped Dad a bajillion times, piloting him through every crucial yawn-fest. Rosie—getting what I had: Abaid's fist up her spine. My jaw so wide, spit streaked my shirt. What was she even doing there? Nothing about her said dancing.

Instantly, the mood changed. Everyone looked at Abaid. Everyone looked at Ducati. Abaid yelling to get things done, get wagons, process the scum. She called them scum to their faces, five hundred people or more. Shouts went up. Sticks were drawn. I pressed so hard to the wall every knot of the bricks bit my spine. Sliding by luxury cars. Pumping my aching legs. Leaving a ruckus of screaming and threats and, beneath it, enough firepower to blow the town sky-high.

# 20

Eerie, sick lights, south of the surly river. Battersea Park Road, I think it was. Cars jammed every junction, riding convoy from club to club, the after party of riots. Demolition is such a social thing. Beautiful black girls in slash-down dresses, locs brushing their backs, constant glint of phones on gold and sequins, laughing, hollering, moving with grace that left me more breathless than every punch I took. Girls who didn't rate Dad's power play nor Mocha's white-kid rebellion. Girls who wanted it all while they were young.

Nodding to the bassline, I let heat and equipment flow round me. Fly girls, four to a jeep, driving stood up and dancing. A fight upstairs on a bus: guys trading punches, parading by in slow motion.

A little girl—seven or eight—running at me, fully the superhero: white leotard, long red cape, a belt of cake tin ribbon, enormous blue wellingtons slapping the pavement. She screeched to a stop ahead of me, 'Trick or treat.'

'Like, it's not Halloween.'

'There's bonfires.'

'The city's burning.'

She screwed up her face. 'You got red eyes.'

I had nothing back at her. 'I dig your boots.'

'Got money?'

'For what?'

In the glitter of neon meeting chrome wheels, I could see ice and diamonds in her grey eyes. 'You smell. Got money?'

'No.'

'Shit then, aren't you?' She ran off, her wingtip arms punching the legs of bad boys.

A siren squalled—they'd know what to do with me now. But I wasn't snitching just to have someone to talk to. The whole day, cops and crooks and, somewhere, sweet Mocha. She scarred me. Not the scars that skin grows to hide. Something happened inside my head, inside my stomach. A sense that everything I feared was gone from me now. Wanting to live and not make arrangements. An exceptional feeling, moving while the world stood still. Whatever went down in those early hours wasn't my problem. Nothing was my problem. Voices bitched and sneered. But they were me, I owned them. Give me the power to flex on these infidels.

Sure I was hungry. I totally neglected the principles of good nutrition. Luckily, there were the broad-striped lights of 7-Eleven. 7-Eleven will save my soul.

Scary bright aisles stocked with the people whose work is to trawl convenience stores at night. Clubbers and lovers hustling late-hours tequila; security guards jonesing on coffee and doughnuts; young mums who forgot to buy formula again; old men hauling filthy bags with nowhere, literally nowhere, to go.

I had one note left and aimed to save it, in case a bar

was still serving. I'm not greedy. *No me gustan.* I'd rather count stars in the sky than rocks on the wrist. Could have gone for a bottle of sierra velvet, pack of high tars, treats from the snack aisle. But I was hungry. Among the cereal range, where no one else was, I found what, suddenly, I knew I wanted for hours. A box of honey Wackios, ten percent extra free. Though not free, as it cost more than it used to. Though, factually, it was wholly free. I was taking it for a ride.

With no suspense, no alarm, no nothing, I walked to the tills. Just one open—a woman, twenty-two or so I guess, short bleach hair, bored looking, screwing her tired, short-sighted eyes at her phone. The uniform—which can look cute—was gamey on her. A sense she got it from someone else's laundry. Fully brick-hard and clearly of the sisterhood. Someone who, once, I would have been nervous around.

I strolled down the lane. Held high the box. 'Just this, okay?'

She glanced, eyes long and straight like an anime villain.

'Just this.'

She raised her hand to take it.

Casually, I switched the box out of reach.

'Got to scan it.' Sharp as lovely splinters.

'Why?'

She spread her hands against the counter, phone still bipping and bopping under her palm. 'You been in shops, yeah? You been shopping? I scan it. Get the price. Yeah?'

I stared, not blinking till my eyes burned. Raised my

head so our mouths were level. I moved in slow and kissed her. I could. So I did. Gold star for ginger. She tasted of powder. Startled, her lips held the shape of mine as I came back to ground. 'Blondie, I want Wackios. I don't want to pay.' I swung through the doors, the alarm screaming behind me.

Next move was uptown, find the hotel, find whoever was waiting for me. Saw a bus and damn near jumped its shadow. The driver's reaction suggested he saw something dredged from mud, still writhing.

When I stared like a fool, he said, 'Contactless,' tapping the scanner with a rank thumb.

Sure he was big and meaty, with stubble from night driving. But I got shot at by uglier men. I pressed my voice in the bullet glass. 'I'm going to sit down and eat my dinner.'

Went upstairs, streets fading behind me. Flopped at the back and busted the box with my fist. Stuffed a big handful between my teeth. Dirt-dry wheat and honey. Eating Wackios, on the bus with skeezers and weirdos. I chewed the rim off that extra ten percent.

A smooth brother across the way, finishing a call to his baby doll, flashed his diamond dental-ware as I pummelled another fistful of carbohydrate down my gullet. 'Hungry, sister?'

'Mwwaammm mmwammm'

He chuckled, took a picture, Instagrammed it. 'Man, I'm glad I didn't do what shit you did.'

'You a mind-reader?'

He chuckled again. He liked doing that. 'Can read yours, sister.'

'What time is it? And day?'

That sent him to sitcom heaven. It was twenty-past three, a time of day I never thought so hectic.

'Eight hours ago I left a casino.'

'Say what?'

'It got messy, riots and stuff. Did that all happen?'

'Check the view.'

We came around by Vauxhall Bridge, the MI6 building twinkling like a huge slot machine, its yard rammed with police and army trucks. I got a sugar rush building by then, so couldn't be sure, but felt certain I saw Salwa Abaid stride across the concrete, wearing a fresh-pressed suit, her angry back catching salutes. Thought I saw her approach some sombre types hanging around a black Hummer, the Stars and Stripes planted each side of the hood. I must have been tripping. I mean, those wars are all local, right?

As the bus took the bridge, I got a clear shot downriver. Too soon for morning, the air ripe and ruddy. Rothko's Number 14 scrawled across a hazy sky. Smoke stood motionless, marble grey, the columns of some ancient ruin. Helicopters hung, five or six, Salwa's magic carpet. Across town the lights were out, buildings no more than tight silhouettes. Fires broke the dark.

The young man got up, we fist-bumped and he vanished into shady Pimlico. Few hundred yards more, the bus stopped, its lights flashed on and off. Over the speaker, the driver sounded a hundred miles distant. No way to Victoria. The road was closed. Police incident. The police were the incident. I had a gutful of processed sugar by then and folded the half-empty box under the arm of a comatose gent. That's how I roll—hashtag Good Samaritan.

With the streets around Victoria Station barricaded by police, I trusted my feet to find a way past ornate hotels and shopping malls, along Belgrave Road— bright as noon and empty—through side streets, back to Knightsbridge. Squalling sirens everyplace—maybe screams, or perhaps that was me. People hiding among the trees of Eaton Square, doing no good business. Coming around some quiet corner, I got heavy breath behind me. Wrapped in that total insulation I felt since leaving the club, separate, numb and powerful, intrigued at excited lungs striving for my spine. Then my voice, 'One step, I bite your head off.' Surprised how old I sounded, how hard. The noise hesitated and stopped.

Jubilant detritus through Belgravia. Bricks, bottles, litter bins, street signs ripped and slung. Soulless and pointless as any art wank installation. For badness, just that, I yelled the names of everyone I hated. Switched into Brompton Road, the big store where I called Ducati broken open and trashed. All those suburban twinklets bundling through the rubble, running off with fistfuls of 28 double-A bras.

Guessing the front approach might be a tad spicy, I took the long way round to the service yard. Police orders were to protect the global conference. This district, all its classy shops, was sacrificed to that.

Needless to say, as I stepped from the dark, heavily-armed police jumped me. Shouted at me to hit the dirt, which I did not do. So they tried pushing me to the ground, which I answered with punches and—as I went down—'Miss Montgomery!' the maître d' brisked over, looking like he was having a ball. 'Miss Montgomery, really.' This stylish arrangements supremo elbowed those gun-toting dicks out the way. 'I'm so glad to have seen you. Your parents were trying to call you right up until they went to bed.'

'What time they go to bed?'

'About ten o'clock. I understand your Father has a large day.'

The polyethylene suits still wanted to can me. But the maître d' had balls of steel. 'Miss Montgomery is immediate family of vital staff. She got lost and has had an appalling time, I am sure. Look at her. Clearly, she has met with misfortune. Did anyone come to find you?'

I gave him solid eye contact. 'Not to my knowledge, sir.'

He swung around on the bewildered cops. 'I shall mention that to the Commissioner when she dines here this Sunday.' He shepherded me inside, enveloped with his cologne.

Through the lobby, stacked with equipment and men in sports jackets, the maître d' steered me to the desk. 'I must apologise,' with blinding sincerity, 'for this disruption. Sadly, not everything is within my control. You seem to have taken a bruising, Miss Montgomery. Are you hurt?'

'Just surface.'

He glanced at the surly men. Laid a graceful,

protective arm on my shoulder. 'You may feel more comfortable in your room.'

Yeah, if I could open the window, squat on the ledge and holler my lungs off.

'There was something else.' He nudged the tired receptionist who maybe should have been home hours ago. Gamely fighting fatigue, she fixed him a bleary smile. 'When you arrived, we forgot your welcome pack. Most unfortunate. Even here, glitches happen. One moment.'

Chiselled guys with guns bracketed the door, and beyond, an ultra-vista of cops and serious hardware. The lights of the slab building opposite burned with all-night resolve. Fake Dad was up there, calling secret phones in secret offices, trying to track what happened to Rose Ducati. My dainty nose found the maître d' nearby.

'Now you're back, please stay inside. For your comfort and convenience.' He passed me a bag with Welcome Valued Guest printed one side and Made In China the other. Inside, tequila, lime juice and Cointreau. 'You may feel more relaxed in your room. It is very late.'

I said that's where I'm going. I lied. I went to the hotel shop. There was the blonde, so bright and glossed and over it all, whistling to some annoying non-music from her phone. I stopped. She stopped.

'I was here this morning.' My voice pleasingly snotty.

A cute little smile dabbled her lips. 'Oh yeah. The scrape-job. The bruises suit you. They hide your face.'

'You know,' the weight of every minute of every day was on me, 'you should watch your mouth.'

Her laugh showed a dangerous gang of teeth. 'You can talk. What is that round your mouth? Herpes?'

'Why don't I pop your eyeballs and sling them up your crack, so you can see what a slut you are.'

'Because,' she leaned close, 'you don't have the balls. You're a freak. Everyone says. The ginger pig's a spazzy little freak.'

Didn't think about it, not really. Fuelled with immediate, practical hate, my hand balled, my arm drove hard, landing my fist between her nose and lips. Felt a trickle of wet from her nose, the kiss of her lips on contact, before she reeled, screeching, hands to her face, festive redness oozing between her fingers.

Scooting for the door, I grabbed a lipstick. 'I paid for this.'

Pretty shaken, not paying attention, stunned when a lightning bolt shoved me sideways into the laundry room. By the dim glow of machine controls, Lilija shone white as Easter.

'You have been where?'

'Everywhere.'

'I have been to club. Six hours' banging beats.' She seemed pretty angry. 'You were told go to club. Abaid send you. So why were you not there?'

'I kinda was.'

'No.' Lilija was mad, her voice the roughest growl. 'I was there when police arrive. When Abaid start playing tough guy. I had to leave in disguise.'

Looking how she did? 'What you do?'

'I take some girl's glitter wig.' She scratched her scalp. 'She not clean, I think. This is not funny.'

'Lilija, I had a rough day.'

'You are dead girl if not for me. So listen.'

Her inner light swamped me, that angry glow chafing my lungs. Desperate to rest my eyes, I stared at a notice taped to one of the big machines. It was busted. Some vandal slung hair gel down the chute. In that place. At those rates.

'You know what happen at club? Abaid got your Father's office girl.'

'Ducati? Yeah, I saw.'

'So you were there?'

'I said I was.'

'Listen.' She took hold of my arms and shook me. 'You were meant to be at that club. Abaid was to find us—you, me and this woman. We get her away from Abaid.'

Heavy, nauseous tiredness fogged my limbs. To that point, I had believed what everyone wanted made no sense. I hadn't seen the godawful truth. 'We were meant to spring Ducati?'

Lilija's hands dropped from my sides. She stared, her lips trying shapes, looking for language I'd understand. 'The dealers are dead, yes? Abaid has this Ducati. How you think this woman behave under water?'

'What?'

'Head under water, wires bzzzz bzzzz. How will your Father's assistant manage that? Abaid has no use for you now. Did she say you could tell the whole world of this? Will she take that risk?' Lilija's fingers pressed my head, squeezing my temporal bone. 'Will she let you go with this business here in your skull? Or will she help you forget?' Her nails cut circles into my skin.

'So all of it was about Ducati?'

Lilija gave a nasty laugh. 'No one sees the waitress.'

Dizzy, too much oxygen, or not enough. 'So if I ask: who you are really?'

'Go to bed. Before you break more things you don't understand.'

Pretty much morning by then. Kept the lights off—the city bathed the gentle grey of smoky dawn. What a fine suite in a fine hotel. What an occasion to brag to friends, those scrapes who connected one time. Going shopping, seeing the sights. Selfies with Big Ben, the Tower, the London Eye. Hitting museums, buying posters, a tote from the Tate, a phone case with a Tube map. Because I went to London and did the right things.

I would never go back to school. I knew, watching the fires die. If I survived, if I escaped, I'd never go back. I met people. Now they're dead. When you say that, when it's out there, you can't sit still while a teacher makes fun of crap you don't know, that no one cares about anyway. Call me old-fashioned, school never taught me how to dodge love or bullets.

My phone so dead it would take a defibrillator to charge it, so I tore a strip from the welcome bag and wrote: 'MARGARITA TIME' with a wet finger, then slapped the big guy's door.

Reliably, wonderfully, sharp-dressed and grownup. I showed him the welcome pack.

'Great. I always do margaritas at five in the morning.'

'We talking now?'

In his pocket he had one of those buggy SIM things. 'Ripped it from that picture frame. No one listens anyhow. Too busy playing patriot games.'

While he mixed cocktails, I kicked off my Converse and stretched on his bed. 'You won't believe what happened to me.'

'Bad day at the office, dear?'

I propped up to take the glass and he pinched my chin, tweaking my face to the light. 'I did try to tell you. You been in a bare-knuckle fight?'

I gave him my would-be-mean squint.

'You look different. You're starting to get some character.' He cocked his hip against the window sill. 'What's the news, kid?'

'I'm never going back to school.'

'Me neither.'

So we drank our breakfast and I told him about it—though I guess he knew some already. I got a bit stuck with the Russian guy, with pushing him downstairs. But The Man just said, 'He was lying to you anyhow.'

'He fell. There was this crash. He didn't make noise.'

'Don't second-guess yourself, kid. It was him or you.'

'That's a cliché.'

'No. A fact.'

Then I got hung up about Abaid and the Mad Max convoy going to finish the Russians.

'Two things.' He mixed me another drink. 'Second thing: they weren't freedom fighters or guns for Jesus. They were businessmen, shipping dangerous goods to dangerous people. Those jobs don't come with insurance.'

'What's the first thing?'

'Abaid. You call her Salwa. Don't get too close. She's one of them holes in space that nothing escapes from.'

He had more advice: when you go down a wall, jump, don't climb: means less time as a target. Don't crawl in some underground hole because a guy says so. When I told him where the tunnel led, that stuff with Dersima, he stared so long I felt my skin crackle.

'Did she tell you to say nothing about her set up? So why you telling me?'

Why? Because he was my neighbour. 'I figured, like, you know her.'

'Someone tells you: say nothing, say nothing. Simple arithmetic, kid. Your life's worth more than a ten cent story.'

Guess I didn't learn that lesson.

'If you're in the market for sorry, feel sorry for your Father's bug.'

'Ducati?'

'She believed the hype more than she wanted the money. Guess that makes you smarter than her.'

He hit the radio, morning news filling the background. The death and destruction that happened while I was busy.

Laying back, the sticky glass against my chest,

staring at the over-smooth ceiling, the over-perfect detail of the room. 'Am I a bad person?'

He jimmied the window so we could smoke. 'I don't know what that question means. People aren't good or bad. They're moving or stopped.'

'I mean, that stuff I did. This fighting.'

'Don't get your halo wet, kid. We live with high anxiety. Why people take beach holidays. Not me. I'm having a swell time.'

Not often I feel something that I can't say. Yeah, I was sorry for everyone, yeah, I love victims. But I was having a swell time too, for all the kicks and beatings. There was Mum ready to pack me away, to make me a woman who—one day—might take up a modest, responsible role in the world. Just a few little scars and a glazed expression.

'Hear this?' He pointed at the radio. 'A squad of these jokers got tied up three hours over the west side, tracking a suspect up and down walls like Spiderman or something. Turns out someone stuck a bug on a cat.'

That got me onto both elbows. 'What happened to the cat?'

'It's flying first class to Gitmo.' He spun a cigarette at me. 'What you think happens to cats?'

# 21

Sometimes, it is my fault. When he slung me out so he could work, I should have showered and changed and packed—I mean, it was already 7:30. My mistake was, I laid my head among pillows, let my spine meld with the mattress and, next thing, this awful hammering hit the hallway door. Had to stagger around for a while before I could even see the door. The second I took off the bolts, I got knocked arse over as Mum barged me aside.

Her canine snout read the air. 'You filthy little drunk.'

So pointless to argue or cuss or say anything. Wave upon wave of abuse rolled across me, while I swayed, looking an idiot.

'Dr. Grover called. You're enrolled tomorrow. He has a secure space.'

Though the Mescalero Apache were stomping my skull, stone cold fear cut through, the way a knife clears a crowd. Wherever my episodes took me that week, I knew Grover was real. Dread overtook my face.

'You better look humble. Your Father's had a lot of embarrassment thanks to you. And this business with Ducati—you're part of that, I'm sure. The hotel told me the maids are repulsed at this sty.' She sneered around. 'And did you think the cameras were off when you assaulted that shop girl? Why do that? You broke her nose. She's bringing charges. Do you realise what that means? The police want answers from you. It's your Father's name, you know that? Look at you. A barroom slut. Lipstick half over your face. And black lingerie. Where did you even get that? You're disgusting.'

What I thought—while she ranted about my deformed, offensive body—was what a damn shame I never saw Rothko again. Truly, I meant to be at that show every day, take the catalogue and a pencil, sit cross-legged and spill wonder in the margins. That week could have been so different.

Next thing she was shaking my shoulders, demanding I say or do whatever, her skin a sheen of excitement, her eyes sparkling hate. 'I told Dr. Grover.' She kept saying that. 'He's made arrangements for you.'

'Excuse me.' Drop-dead cool, The Man knocked at the open door after we both turned around. 'I don't mean to intrude Ma'am, Miss, only my Mother's next door and she's fragile—know what I'm saying? Yesterday's brouhaha shook her up. I'm obliged if you could celebrate some other way. Sorry to intrude.' Then he bellowed down the hall: 'Hey big guy, how ya doin?'

With her stylish, deliberate walk she crossed the room and shut the door. Walking slowly back, beating time with neat, glossy steps. 'See what you do? Cut and bruised, stinking drunk. Don't you wash your hair? Don't you think everyone can see that black brassiere? Your Father will walk this road today with the Prime

283

Minister, the foreign leaders, the global loan fund president. The world will be watching. Don't you think people know who you are? I hear talk about you the whole time. What do you think this does to him, to me, to your brother and sister?'

'I don't have a brother or sister. That man is not my Father.'

My Mother is a beautiful woman: china-skinned, dark, nothing like me. She can wear a black dress and heels, she can wear anything. Since I acknowledge her beauty, I owe her nothing.

'You little shit.' More surprising to hear her swear than get slapped. She was always such a lady. Stood close to press her voice into my head, she looked flawless. 'There were pressures that shaped my choice. I couldn't bear to hinder my husband's chances. If things had been different, I would have solved the problem right then. I would have had that procedure and flushed you down the drain.'

I hear voices, the whole time. Heard a voice tell me: whatever it costs, stand your ground. Sure was the prettiest sound, that crack as I slapped her cheek.

She jolted, a sliver of spit shooting onto the rug. 'We're through,' low and cold. 'The family continues. We're through.'

Don't ask how much of life I spend under boiling water. I'm a meticulous woman. I scrubbed my body, washed my hair, dried it smooth and tidy. Did my makeup real careful—totally girl-next-door at Sunday brunch. I patched the parts that wouldn't stop bleeding and dressed-down utterly straight. A black tee, respectable chinos—every trace of last night shaken and slapped from my jacket.

I called Mum, pushing myself to sound pleasant. Got the itinerary—when the conference closing statement would be made, when her husband would be through with side-meetings, when we'd be ready to go. When the car would take me to Grover. I closed by saying, 'Thank you,' leaning hard into the words, hearing the nanosecond pause before she cut off. Stood at the window, curious how relieved I felt. It was an important day.

Before I went to make nice with the siblings, I took a hard look in the mirror. The young woman I saw, her hair didn't fall right, it stuck to her steepish forehead with makeup and sweat. Her lips an unfamiliar pink, irregular from poorly-disguised sores. Freckles and acne blended under blusher. A nose that would have been okay, on a face less fleshy. Cute little ears. Her eyes this weird peach-ginger, threaded black and too much blood in their orbit. This young woman, she didn't look good or bad, or smart or dumb, or anything. Not yet a missing person ad on a station billboard, nor a faded wanted poster along some lonely road.

The kids were watching cartoons. That old show where robots transform to ninjas and stuff. Everyone shouted wisecracks. A nerdy guy with an underground lair built the coolest weapons. Baddies got beat and came back for more. We watched six of these things on the bounce. Inbetween ads for toys and sugar, this cool-looking chick with real nice hair showed pictures that kids sent her. Kinda nice that kids still drew pictures and sent them to TV shows. She had this heap of pictures and really rattled through, her wide smile saying how funky they were. She did a good job of seeming to like them and, maybe, she did.

After twenty-five seconds she'd say, 'That's all we have time for just now. But keep sending your pictures and stay locked. Coming up, more cartoons.' There was always, like, the next picture she never got round to. You could see it on top of the pile, the colours and stuff, and I thought: some kid knows their picture never got shown. Do they tell their friends, 'My picture was so nearly on TV'?

At the ad break, brother said I looked different. 'Different.' He seemed to think saying it twice explained it.

'Different?'

'Clean.'

'I shower. What do you do?'

'Mum said you were stinking and showing your body. She called Dad to tell him that.'

Five years younger than me, but you have to count double with boys, because of their slow brain development.

'Is she going away?' Sister drooled at some doggy doll that you fed and it pooped itself.

'She's going on a program.' Brother sure was knowledgeable. 'Mum said.'

Just exactly the way that people in comas get talked about over their heads.

'Am I having her room?' Baby sister was a sharp little cat. Truly avaricious, she learned early how to mobilise cute.

'I'll have it,' brother assured her. 'I'll junk those lame pictures.'

The family suite was two floors up from mine, level with the roof of the conference building. I saw cops with body armour showing off real big guns, while other cops took pictures of the city. Count ten helicopters slung across the sky. Their rotors churned the dead-calm air. I changed channel to rolling news.

'Hey,' sister shrieked.

'Quit it.'

'We were watching that.' Brother was sure the affronted old gent. 'Mum set the channel.'

'Hey.' Sister bounced her rosy arse.

'I want to check the news.'

'Why?' brother asked, the forty-plus dwarf. 'Are you on it?'

'Don't you care what's going on?'

'No.'

'Tell skanky change back to the toons or I'll mess myself.' Sister glowed with anticipation.

The news channel fronted a black-guy-Asian-chick combo to deal the juice of riots and recriminations. The pricetag and the deaths. Six deaths. That detail stuck. Six lives cancelled, six unknowns gone primetime. Pictures of the fatalities. A young woman in a dark sateen jacket and sari-skirt. Caught looking over her shoulder, her piled hair falling loose, her lips parted.

Before they shot her in the back. So I'm a cold bitch nowadays.

The Commissioner, her heavy epaulettes gleaming, angry her officers came under fire, her people—tough, honest, family types—broken, blinded and maimed. Her sharp eyes told the camera justice would be certain. The Prime Minister said the conference would close as scheduled: no change of plan, no diversions. Not in England.

Way down the alligator's back, is a point his jaws can't reach. Alligators—any crocodilians—are built to tear what's ahead of them. Their heads can't grip down their backs. You can catch on the alligator's back, beyond where his jaws can get you. If he flips around, you're wasted. You got to hold far enough down his back. He's got real fine duds, Mr. Alligator. *Un amigo elegante.* These boots of mine came right from that place on his back.

So I left the kids gawking at ninjas, while cops gawked at them. I packed my things and messed up the bed—my stained archaeology of life on easy street.

The door was unlocked. Guess The Man knew I'd come by. His shiny briefcase on the couch, he stood by the window, his foot rested up on the sill. Music on the radio. Serious music.

'What's that?'

'Handel. "How silently, how slyly." From Julius Caesar. I like it. Going someplace?'

'We leave at the wrap-up. Cops are escorting us home.'

'I been escorted by cops. To make sure I left. Coffee's fresh.' He watched me slug two shots of tar. 'I don't want to speak out of turn, but your Mother seems somewhat shrill.'

'You should see her on a bad day.'

'I'd rather you on a bad day.'

'Soon, there'll be no bad days.'

His dirty growl, 'The guy who promised that sure got elected.'

I lit one of his Mexican cigarettes. Felt dizzy. The radio continued this insistent string and horn sound, building a taste of menace and betrayal. 'What's your favourite character in an old movie? Mine's Katharine in *The African Queen*.'

'Because she's crazy and won't quit?'

'What's yours?'

'Old movie?'

'Old, old movie.'

'Caan in *Rollerball*.'

'Jon-a-than Jon-a-than'

'You got it.'

Standing behind his elbow, I got a lateral view of the conference hub and steep diagonal onto the road beneath. 'Because you only do things that benefit you?'

'And I thought I was such a nice guy.'

'Why did you take that picture of us?'

'No one would believe it otherwise.'

'Believe what?'

'Who made this happen.'

I puzzled at that, smoke filling me up. 'Better go. Mum's waiting.'

'I don't guess too eagerly.'

I swung around, the room's luxury dead to me. 'I spoil her happy family.'

He chuckled, tipping smoke through his teeth. 'She thinks the others will get less dumb?'

'You know how it is. Some dogs take too much teaching.'

That's when he walked towards me, pointing at the wall. 'What's that in the mirror?'

'Some crazy girl.'

'That's a beautiful woman. Not tomorrow. Not someday. Now. Who cares if Mum's jealous? Who cares Daddy finds it awkward?'

'He's not my Dad. Mum was… y'know, that thing.'

'That must have been a slow night.'

'You don't care one bit, do you?'

'If you work at it, neither will you.'

'Look, I got to go.'

'You got to do something for me.'

If handsome wears four-button cuffs, he was handsome. I really couldn't tell. My phone was harvesting missed calls. Police wanted me right now, about some shop girl. Mum would fetch me. Any deviance from the itinerary went straight to Grover. 'They're going to tube my brain.'

His arms the strongest I ever felt, like to hug or to crush made no difference. He smelled of cologne and cigarettes. Wiped my tears with a silk handkerchief, careful not to mess my makeup. 'You got to do something for me.' His dark coffee whisper embraced the inside of my head. 'That guy down the hall. The big guy. I don't want him there when I leave.'

My guts rumbled. 'What you want me to do?'

'Make noise. Fuss him out the corridor. Seven minutes, that's all I need.'

You may ask why I did what he wanted. Guess if you do, it means no one made you coffee. No one told you that you make sense. No one stood beside you in awe of Rothko. What choice did I have? He was my neighbour.

'Hey Rizzola.' A riverboat gambler, he flicked a silver dollar from his pocket. I caught it. 'If you ever have trouble, real trouble, find the coldest game in town. Show them this and someone will help you.'

So there was the guy, tight suit and chewing a wad of gum, smelling harsh of nicotine, tapping his earpiece.

I propelled myself up. 'Hey, mister.'

His face churned with evident displeasure.

'You hear that, huh? You hear it?'

They got trained to look at me that way.

'Down there, huh? Comes from down there.'

'What does?' Voice dragged unwilling from his chest.

I scrunched my palms to my head. 'The noise, dude. That noise. You hear? Down there.'

He sidelonged the hallway. 'What down there?'

'The storeroom, yeah? Where the maids keep linen.'

'Kid, I'm busy. Piss off.'

'The storeroom. Someone's there, dude. I heard shuffling and spying around.'

'On linen?'

'On the place across the street. What you see, from the window of that storeroom.'

Man, his teeth made a full snooker set.

'Come see,' I tugged his sleeve.

He slapped my fingers. 'Look, this is my station.' Tap, tap at his headset. 'Any second, Code Red, yeah? I got to keep watch.'

'While someone in linen watches the view. Just ignore me, dude.'

'In the store?'

I gave him the full tiger-eyes. 'You want to be the guy who didn't check the storeroom?'

Kinda weird—he looked up and down the hall, like someone was watching him. But he moved pretty spry for a big guy, the busy way of excess baggage. 'Who's got the key?'

'It's not locked.'

'How you know that?'

I hit a hard whisper. 'I was just getting extra pillows. I'm asthmatic, okay? Watch it. There's shelves and stuff for cover.'

Filtered through racks of laundered linen, milky calm light made the room inconveniently peaceful.

'I hear nothing,' he said, the dumb cop.

I gestured at piles of sheets. 'The window, dude. Code Red.'

His heavyset tiptoe got halfway through the room. He sprinted the rest. What sped him up wasn't noise among folded pillow slips. It was noise outside. That one, two, three loud noises. And the screams that followed.

Starkly, I understood it could go very bad for me. I'd love to say I had a plan, a cool plan. I didn't, just ran, tipping down shelves behind me. Fast glance in my neighbour's open door. He left everything tidy, the radio still playing. Back along the hall came shouts and ruckus. I ran.

Pitched into the concrete passage. The fire stairs flew up to meet me, noise rising at every floor. My legs doubling over themselves. Cannonballed off the stairs, straight into Salwa's spine.

That woman, so wary so wired, she got my commotion bowling downstairs—turned, as I leapt, flailing, from five steps up. Smacked against her and skittered back, the both of us alerted by a solid thunk from the ground. Her silky black Heckler & Koch—I'd knocked it from her hand.

Noise going off, sirens, my lungs burning up. One split second, one atom of life. We both jumped. I was one atom faster. Pulling back upright, the gun snug in my hand. What The Man told me: Focus, Riz. Didn't mess up—I aimed one-handed, the barrel that sniffed my neck pointed at her chest.

She started, then let her hands fall limp.

'Stay back.' I had to shout something. 'Keep right there.'

Salwa Abaid, what a cocktail smile. Her teeth shone from the utility light. 'Even you can't miss from there.'

'Stay back.'

'Do it, Riz. Take a shot. No one will hear. Not with what you just caused.' She put her head to one side, hair licking her shoulder. 'Or are you scared you'll screw up? Because you have to kill me, don't you? To avoid something worse. Do it, Riz. Show me what the great Tom Eliot taught you.'

Already, I took too long. She knew it. I should have splintered her kneecaps, winged her or something. Her friendly smile, her warm eyes—why would she need a gun?

'Tell you, Riz.' She stepped forward. I let her. 'I'm selfish. Sure you noticed. I'm selfish and that limits how dangerous I can be. In war, self-preservation is a target on your back.'

'You gonna tell me you still hurt for that girl in the freezer?'

'Unavoidable rules. I was scared I'd get caught. Scared for years.'

Said so intense, I flinched.

'Selfish, scared for me. You, Riz, are not selfish.'

Focused hard to keep the gun on her chest. 'No, don't turn it. It's not about me.'

Another step. 'You've seen things, Riz. A new world and you want some. Do it, take a shot. You'll be welcome from here to Basrah. That's my world, Riz. Could be yours if you want. You're smart and tough. There are always opportunities for talented recruits. But you're no use to me if you can't pull that trigger.'

'Really,' a voice from the arctic. 'You should pull trigger by now.'

Salwa stiffened at Lilija's gun, exploring intricate folds of hair that caped the detective's neck.

'You are told go home. You are told go to bed.' Lilija shone, with her gun against Salwa's head. 'You create much work for people. Listen? You hear?'

From outside, a squall of sirens and shouts, a bludgeon of helicopter rotors beating the city. A taste of panic, of blind retribution. 'I didn't do that.'

'You are too modest.' Salwa smiled, asked Lilija, 'Surely we are on the same side?'

'I think not.' Lilija's gun jabbed her.

'You as well?' Salwa winked at me. 'What an interesting day.'

Now, if I had a gun at my chest and another smooching my neck, I hope I could be even half the swell Abaid was. So neat and languidly still, her smooth self-sufficiency an easy match for the angry ice-woman whose firearm was, frankly, the real threat.

Lilija burrowed her piece against the detective's brain stem. 'We waste time. Where is Ducati?'

That name, among this deceit and clamour, was a scrap of Kansas slung on the Yellow Brick Road. How could anything matter that involved Ducati? 'Yeah, what is this with her?'

'Oh?' Lilija's chilly scorn. 'Girl ask questions now?'

Salwa managed to look impatient—no mean feat just then. 'Why do you think this person got you from hospital? Why take such trouble?'

I had wondered, but morphine plays tricks. 'I dunno. I was scared.'

Salwa jerked a finger behind her. 'She did her nurse act so you'd be at that family picnic.'

'What?'

'So your Stepfather would be at the picnic. So she and your neighbour could get Ducati.'

'Ducati is ours.' Lilija glared. 'She arranged conference access for those men you got killed.'

'And my neighbour?'

Now I heard it again, Salwa's laugh. 'He has his own agenda. You can hear it right now.'

'We waste time.' Lilija hissed. 'Give me gun.'

'No, I need it.'

'Good girl.' Salwa beamed.

'Then you go. Go now.' Lilija gripped the trigger. 'Or I will need two bullets.'

'Don't worry, Riz.' Salwa smiled. 'We'll meet again.'

I turned and ran, shouting for breath, making noise to cover that blunt, final sound.

Smacked through the doors into the basement car park, just enough sense to pocket the gun before I got snapped looking more suspect than ever. Blurred activity on the ramp rising into the street. Silver soft tops and lean-burn cop cars chasing and screeching. Ambulance pulling away from the conference building, police motorcycles flanked around it.

Everything looked a whole lot of trouble for someone.

I took a lungful of gas and kept running.

Lightning Source UK Ltd.
Milton Keynes UK
UKHW041547260722
406402UK00004B/1229

9 781788 649360